EDITED
BY
MARY
HIGGINS
CLARK

# MURDER

## ON THE AISLE

1987
MYSTERY
WRITERS
OF
AMERICA
ANTHOLOGY

SIMON
AND
SCHUSTER
NEW
YORK

This book is a work of fiction. Names, characters, places, and incidents either are the product of the author's imagination or are used fictitiously. Any resemblance to actual events or locales or persons, living or dead, is entirely coincidental.

Published by Simon and Schuster
A Division of Simon & Schuster, Inc.
Simon & Schuster Building
Rockefeller Center
1230 Avenue of the Americas
New York, N.Y. 10020
SIMON AND SCHUSTER is a registered trademark of Simon & Schuster, Inc.
Designed by Karolina Harris
Manufactured in the United States of America


Library of Congress Cataloging in Publication data

Murder on the aisle.

1. Detective and mystery stories, American.
I. Clark, Mary Higgins. II. Mystery Writers of America.
PS648.D4M88    1987      813'.0872'08      87-4975

ISBN 0-671-63466-6

Grateful acknowledgment is made by Mystery Writers of America and Simon and Schuster for permission to include the following:

"New York, New York" by Thomas Adcock. Copyright © 1986 by Thomas Adcock. First published in *Ellery Queen's Mystery Magazine*, 1986. Reprinted by permission of the author.

"Revival in Eastport" by Jon L. Breen. Copyright © 1979 by Jon L. Breen. First published in *Ellery Queen's Mystery Magazine*.

"Gee Whiz, My Lovely" by Betty Buchanan. Copyright © 1978 by Betty Buchanan. First published in *Ellery Queen's Mystery Magazine*. Reprinted by permission of the author.

"The Moment of Decision" by Stanley Ellin. Copyright © 1956 by Stanley Ellin, copyright renewed © 1984 by Stanley Ellin. First published in *Ellery Queen's Mystery Magazine*, 1956.

"It Was Bad Enough" by Ron Goulart. Copyright © 1983 Ron Goulart. First published in *Ellery Queen's Mystery Magazine*, 1983. Reprinted by permission of the author.

"Death of a Princess" by Joyce Harrington. Copyright © 1975 by Joyce Harrington. First published in *Ellery Queen's Mystery Magazine*.

"Captain Leopold Goes to the Dogs" by Edward D. Hoch. Copyright © 1980 by Edward D. Hoch. First published in *Ellery Queen's Mystery Magazine*. Reprinted by permission of the author.

*(continued at back of book)*

In memory of Stanley Ellin, a magnificent short-story writer and wonderful friend of the Mystery Writers of America.

# CONTENTS

Introduction by Mary Higgins Clark   ix

Revival in Eastport by Jon L. Breen   1

The Moment of Decision by Stanley Ellin   9

It Was Bad Enough by Ron Goulart   33

Death of a Princess by Joyce Harrington   48

A Slip of the Lip by Lawrence Treat   54

Snookered by Gerald Tomlinson   61

The Last Escape by Henry Slesar   71

New York, New York by Thomas Adcock   84

A Break in the Film by John F. Suter   100

Captain Leopold Goes to the Dogs by Edward D. Hoch   114

The Waste Pile at Apple Bow by Joan Richter   135

Saturday's Shadow by William F. Nolan   152

The Double Death of Nell Quigley by J. F. Peirce   172

The Enjoyment of an Artist by Gordon Bennett
  writing as Isak Romun   187

Gee Whiz, My Lovely by Betty Buchanan   201

About the Contributors   209

# INTRODUCTION

"Anthology" comes from the two Greek words, *anthos* meaning flower, and *legein*, to gather. Literally, a gathering of flowers.

With *Murder on the Aisle* we believe we have gathered the finest flowers from the field of short stories having to do with the world of entertainment. We invite you, the reader, to become the audience; we place you not only in an aisle seat but also in a seat in the bleachers, a box seat at the races, a seat in a movie house.

When you were a child, were you fascinated by magic shows? You have two chances here to watch a magician perform. "The Last Escape," by Henry Slesar, is a particularly chilling magical experience. Stanley Ellin's "Moment of Decision" shows how even a great magician ought to be more neighborly.

Is football on your mind? Then "Snookered" will become your special treat. Gerald Tomlinson has created a new breed of coach and a team the sportswriters can't ignore.

Ever wonder what happens when an actor's dream of glory remains just that—a dream that turns bitter and jealous? Thomas Adcock's "New York, New York" is a gripping tale of a failed career.

Is music your thing? Then you'll follow with pleasure the tale of a murderer betrayed by his musical training. That's "A Slip of the Lip," by Lawrence Treat.

It's long been a truism that the funniest comedians may be the most tragic real-life figures; and what could be more tragic than when you're finally making a comeback, learning your ex-wife's tell-all book is about to be filmed? You may be driven to desperation. Ron Goulart's "It Was Bad Enough" explores that situation.

What effect does a review really have on an actor's career? Jon L. Breen's "Revival in Eastport" invites you into the critic's corner. Read this story and you'll understand why a favorable review can be a life-threatening experience.

Have you ever tried to stave off death? The protagonist of Joyce Harrington's "Death of a Princess" made the valiant effort. You'll remember the irony of the last sentence long after you've finished reading the story.

Ever placed a bet at the dog races? Ever seen anyone murdered there? When "Captain Leopold Goes to the Dogs"—that's Ed Hoch's story— the Captain doesn't get the chance to take his winnings home.

Are you old enough to remember, or maybe did your folks tell you about, the ritual of going to the hometown movie theater on a Saturday afternoon? Not everyone went just to see the double feature. John F. Suter's "A Break in the Film" proves that not all the excitement and intrigue and romance is happening on the silver screen.

On the other hand, some moviegoers become obsessed. The only world they know is the world created by the characters they see on the screen—shadowy people, more real than the people in their own lives. "Saturday's Shadow," by William F. Nolan, explores the dark side of the compulsive movie buff.

J. F. Peirce takes us back in time to solve "The Double Death of Nell Quigley," the lady of the evening who offered her favors to one too many suitors. The constable gets some highly skilled help in solving this case.

Joan Richter invites you to cover a top television news story in "The Waste Pile at Apple Bow." You'll walk the scarred earth near a coal-mining disaster with an intrepid reporter and a young woman whose family had been among the victims.

Isak Romun invites you to explore a frightening hoax in his "The Enjoyment of an Artist." A famed pianist cannot complete his concert because his piano explodes on stage, and the search for truth begins.

A bouncy private investigator who is working on a case in Hollywood is invited by a "gorgeous nut" to find an elusive figure named Harvey. The twist ending of Betty Buchanan's "Gee Whiz, My Lovely" takes place in a nightclub.

In all, a potpourri of tales about people in the spotlight. So settle back to enjoy. The starter's gun has fired. The curtain's going up. Happy reading!

M.H.C.

# JON L. BREEN

# REVIVAL IN EASTPORT

From the Eastport *Sun*, July 17, 1927:

> Millard Judson, drama critic of this newspaper, narrowly escaped death Saturday night when he was shot at outside the Sun Building. Police report no progress in discovering the assailant's identity.
>
> Though Mr. Judson is inclined to laugh off the incident as "the work of some drunk and disgruntled playwright," the *Sun* has offered a $200 reward for information leading to the gunman's capture.

In the otherwise empty city room, Millard Judson pounded the keys of his typewriter. It was a few moments before midnight. The deadline for his piece was not until midmorning, so, as various members of his family were constantly pointing out to him, there was no earthly reason for him to be working so late into the night. But though deadlines had changed over the years, Millard Judson had not. In 55 years as the Eastport *Sun*'s drama critic, he had formed an opening-night routine he could not bring himself to break. So he was up late for a man of 78. Surely doing the piece now was better for his health than lying at home in bed unable to sleep because the review wasn't written. Why not get it over now, with his memory still fresh?

What he was writing about the Broadway-bound new play, *Heated Encounters*, could only be described as a tepid notice, the due of a so-so play. When he got to the paragraph about Ernest Spivey, though, he beamed as he typed. Writing nasty things was easier, but writing nice things always gave him more pleasure. It was good to be able to write a tribute to an old pro even older than Judson.

"Ernest Spivey, in the role of the nonfoxy grandfather, is an utter delight. Though moving more slowly around the stage than in past years, the octogenarian thespian has lost none of his mastery of character development and comic timing, nor the ability to dominate every scene he is in through the sheer force of his still-potent vitality and energy. And his voice, familiar to generations of radio listeners and film and TV viewers, as well as those fortunate enough to have seen him on the stage, resonates with a power and command unattainable by the younger members of the cast who seem incapable of reaching the back row. Since his first appearance in this city some 35 years ago, Spivey has given us a range of portrayals that stay fresh in the memory."

"That's wrong!" cracked a voice from behind Millard. He jumped, startled, and turned around in his chair to find Ernest Spivey looking down at him. Passing quickly from anger at this severe test of his aging heart to delight at seeing the old actor, Millard rose from his chair.

"Mr. Spivey! It's good to see you. But what a surprise."

They shook hands. When they had first met many years before, they had been about the same height, but Millard Judson was now somewhat stooped.

"The watchman told me you'd be burning the midnight oil."

"Old habits die hard. You certainly approached very quietly."

"I don't know that I did," Spivey replied. "Also," he added, looking at Millard's copy, "I didn't think my young colleagues were quite so muted in their delivery."

"I know what you're hinting at. My daughter is always after me to get a hearing aid, but I can still hear just fine. Besides, if theater can reach only the keenest ears, it is failing, in my view. Anyway, sit down. What can I do for you? And what's wrong?"

"Wrong?"

"Yes, when you came up and made me jump half a foot, you said quite distinctly, 'That's wrong.' So what's wrong?"

"Where you say I first played this city thirty-five years ago. It was longer. I played here in July 1927 as a matter of fact, in a play called *Molly's Treasure Chest.*"

Millard wrinkled his brow. "I'm kind of famous around here for my memory, but I can't remember that one."

Ernest Spivey removed a yellowed newspaper clipping from his wallet. "Maybe this will refresh your memory."

Millard sighed ruefully as he squinted at the clipping. "Whenever possible I try to avoid reading my early scribbling. But I'll make an exception."

Millard didn't know whether to laugh or blush. The clipping read in part:

> The performance of E. W. Spivey is almost beyond words. This tall skinny youth has no presence, no idea of how to move on stage, no rudimentary notion of how to put a line across. Clumsy, graceless, and occasionally inaudible, he is obviously suited for any kind of endeavor but acting.

Millard looked up, shaking his head. "I don't know what to say. I'd never write anything this damning about anyone now. It's simply cruel, and I'm sure you could *never* have been this bad. If you had been, surely I would remember. I guess all I can do at this late date is apologize."

"I must confess, I was very angry and upset when I first read that. It did seem cruel, needlessly so. I'm afraid it affected me so much I almost did something drastic."

Something drastic? That phrase and the significance of the date, July 1927, hit Millard simultaneously, and he felt a sudden wave of fear. "You mean *you* were the one who—?"

"Shot at you? Yes." Spivey's voice sounded cold. Suddenly, on this warm summer night, the air in the city room felt chilly.

Millard didn't know what to say next. Could it be that after 50 years Spivey had returned to finish the job? Could a man hold a grudge about a bad notice for that long?

Spivey laughed. A mad laugh or just a theatrical one? "When I returned in 1942, I was a rather well-known actor and got a somewhat better notice from you, as I seem to have done tonight. Somehow I didn't keep a clipping of that one, though. Just this one. Do you know why?"

"No. Why?"

"Had it not been for your review in July 1927, I would not be where I am today. I would not have become a successful, even famous, actor, if you'll forgive my lack of modesty. I know this to be true. My whole career in the theater I owe to your review. Would you like to hear the story?"

Relieved and breathing more easily, Millard said, "Yes, of course. I'm fascinated."

"I was a small-town boy. Little town in Iowa, maybe ten thousand people then and not much bigger now. My father was not the richest man in town, but we were comfortably off, and he always expected me to join and eventually take over the family hardware business when I was through school. As sons will, I had different ideas. Acting still had a very bad reputation in those days, and my whole family was dead set against my entering the profession. But it was what I wanted to do, so I left home to go after it.

"I tried New York first and like so many before and since, was disillusioned there. Finally I managed to start getting various stints with touring companies, and I saw a lot of the country over those next few years. It was a fine time for theater. There was no commercial radio to speak of, no television, and motion pictures were still dealing in dumb-show. As you well remember, of course.

"My parts gradually increased in size, from supernumerary to bit player to secondary leads, but I was attracting no particular notice, and after a while it began to seem like a treadmill to me.

"Playing my hometown on a one-night stand, I spent a little time with my family. They were semi-reconciled now to my chosen career. At least, my father didn't disown me and assured me that anytime I changed my mind I could come back and enter the hardware business. That same evening I saw my old girlfriend. Helen was her name. Lovely girl. I realized that night that I still loved her, and she loved me.

"We talked about my acting. I wasn't getting anywhere, I told her. I might even throw it all over and go into the hardware business, I said. And then, impulsively, I asked her to marry me and she said yes. But we agreed to keep it a secret until the current tour ended and I left the company and returned home.

"Just two weeks later our troupe hit this city. And your review appeared.

"Getting reviewed was nothing new, of course, but getting my short-comings so strongly underlined was. I had become used to not being mentioned at all in reviews at worst and being damned with faint praise at best. But your notice—well, I probably deserved every bit of it. But at the time it infuriated me. I wanted revenge. I wanted to challenge you to a duel. But all I did finally was take one shot at you."

"I always wondered who did that," Millard said. "I never knew. It was a damned terrifying experience and one I'll never forget. I remember at the time telling one of my colleagues here it must be a playwright who was drunk, but I never thought it had anything to do with my reviewing. I thought it was some kind of mistake, a gun that went off by accident or somebody shooting at somebody else. When nothing further happened, I was sure it had all been just a mistake. The newspaper offered a reward, you know, and a lot of people tried to collect it with some of the nuttiest stories you ever heard. After a while we all just forgot about it. Even me, for the most part. I'd remember it late at night sometimes, but it never made me change my working hours. As you can see."

"Yes. You'll forgive me after all these years?"

"Yes, sure, it's a long time ago. But I have one question. Did you mean to hit me? Or was it just to scare me?"

"I don't think I really meant to kill you. But I was drunk and might easily have killed you by accident. I was a hot-blooded, irresponsible youth."

"But you got over it. I'm pleased you did."

"Yes, I directed my energies elsewhere. Back into acting. I determined I could not go out on a note like that, return home with my tail between my legs. I had to prove I was an actor. Would you say that I did?"

"In spades, yes."

"I wrote to Helen, asked her to join me, but it appeared she wouldn't leave home, more to the point, wouldn't be the wife of an actor. It hurt like hell, but I rationalized that a wife who would stand in the way of her husband's true calling was not worth having anyway. For some years I gave all my energies to the actor's art, and gradually, it seems, I improved. Some might say you made a small contribution to American theatrical history there, Mr. Judson."

"I did?"

"Of course. Haven't I made it clear? If you hadn't written that review, my acting career would have ended and I would have returned to the mundane life of a small-town hardware merchant."

"Well, it's most handsome of you to give me the credit, but—"

"The credit is yours, all yours. Yes, it's been a long run for me in the theater. And on the radio and the screen and the little box. I've made and lost a couple of fortunes, married and divorced four wives, fathered seven legitimate children now scattered to the four winds, most of them drunk and miserable, some parents to my grandchildren who are on drugs and miserable. I am still working because I need the money and don't know what else to do with my time anyway."

"Doesn't the appreciation of audiences give you satisfaction?"

"Oh, yes. Approximately the same quality and duration of satisfaction—if not quite the same intensity—that those drugs give my grandchildren.

"I recently returned to my hometown, Mr. Judson. My parents and even my younger brothers are dead now. The family business remains and apparently prospers, though no longer in the family. I would never have guessed what pain it would give me to see that. I feel great nostalgia for my brief experience as a boy in the hardware business, and I often think I would have been happier had I stayed."

"But think of all the pleasure you have given so many—"

"You imply that the hardware business is not important, Mr. Judson. It is in a basic sense far more important to ordinary people than the theatrical entertainment you and I have devoted our careers to. Also, I think I owed myself something. I deserved my pleasures too, and my happiness ought to have been more important to me than the fleeting pleasures of this amorphous mass we call the audience.

"Helen is still alive, and I gathered my courage to visit her. She is seventy-six, married almost fifty years, and I think reasonably content. As happy as she would have been with me? I don't know. She is still beautiful and I still love her, but it is too late to find out what our life together would have been like.

"It is too late for so many things, Mr. Judson. Somehow it has become 1977, and I am a very old, very unhappy man who will never be a hardware dealer in a small Iowa town. Not ever. And I will never be young and I will never be married to Helen. In so many things I made a start and then turned the wrong way. So much of what I have attempted in life, I have left unfinished."

Though his alarm had left him, Millard Judson was no closer to knowing what to say. Though the actor's talent was undiminished, the old man was miserable, pitiful, and surely a shade unbalanced. What could be said or done to comfort him?

"Mr. Spivey, perhaps you would join me for a drink. I can finish this thing later, and there is a bar around the corner that—"

"I don't drink anymore. Acting is the only vice I have left. There is one other thing I must tell you about my visit to Helen. It's funny, really, in a way. It seems that *she* has a grandson. Fred Barstow is his name; fine young man. And it seems that he too has aspirations as an actor."

"The name is familiar."

"It should be."

"How does she feel about her grandson's chosen profession?"

"Rather proud, I think. Now she thinks a good deal more of actors than I do, which is quite an irony. She showed me a clipping of a review he got recently when passing through Eastport."

"Oh, yes. I think I remember."

"Indeed! You should!"

Millard backed up in his swivel chair and glanced at the nearest exit. The old man seemed angry suddenly, not merely unhappy. And there was a hint of madness in his eye.

Fred Barstow, Fred Barstow. Millard flipped through his mental card file, then remembered.

"Of course. He played here three weeks ago in a revival of *The Country Girl*. Very promising young man."

The old actor rose menacingly from his chair. Watching him warily, Millard rose at the same time.

"Oh, yes," said Ernest Spivey, "a very promising young man. And you have tried to destroy him as you did me."

"Destroy him? But Mr. Spivey, I remember what I wrote. I gave him a good notice—a very good notice."

"That's just it. He has no talent, that boy; I know him. But because of the encouragement of people like you, he will try to pursue a career in the theater and be crushed, the way everyone who pursues a career in the theater will be crushed, talented or not."

Spivey's voice boomed through the city room. Millard trembled convulsively. Would the watchman hear?

"So much I have left undone!" Spivey cried. And then he drew the pistol. "It's the same one."

Millard turned for the door.

"The same one I used in 1927."

Millard tried to run.

"Do you think it will still fire?"

From the Eastport *Sun*, October 24, 1977:

Millard Judson, drama critic of the *Sun* since 1922, collapsed and died Saturday night in the *Sun* offices. Veteran character actor Ernest Spivey was with Judson when he was stricken. Death was the result of an apparent heart attack.

# STANLEY ELLIN

# THE MOMENT OF DECISION

Hugh Lozier was the exception to the rule that people who are completely sure of themselves cannot be likable. We have all met the sure ones, of course—those controlled but penetrating voices which cut through all others in a discussion, those hard forefingers jabbing home opinions on your chest, those living Final Words on all issues—and I imagine we all share the same amalgam of dislike and envy of them. Dislike because no one likes to be shouted down or prodded in the chest, and envy because everyone wishes he himself were so rich in self-assurance that he could do the shouting down and the prodding.

For myself, since my work took me regularly to certain places in this atomic world where the only state was confusion and the only steady employment that of splitting political hairs, I found absolute judgments harder and harder to come by. Hugh once observed of this that it was a good thing my superiors in the Department were not cut from the same cloth, because God knows what would happen to the country then. I didn't relish that, but—and there was my curse again—I had to grant him his right to say it.

Despite this, and despite the fact that Hugh was my brother-in-law—a curious relationship when you come to think of it—I liked him immensely, just as everyone else did who knew him. He was a big, good-looking man, with clear blue eyes in a ruddy face, and with a quick, outgoing nature eager to appreciate whatever you had to offer. He was overwhelmingly generous, and his generosity was of that rare and excellent kind which makes you feel as if you are doing the donor a favor by accepting it.

I wouldn't say he had any great sense of humor; but plain good humor can sometimes be an adequate substitute for that, and in Hugh's case it was. His stormy side was largely reserved for those times when he thought you might have needed his help in something, and failed to call on him for it. Which meant that ten minutes after Hugh had met you and liked you, you were expected to ask him for anything he might be able to offer. A month or so after he married my sister Elizabeth she mentioned to him my avid interest in a fine Copley he had hanging in his gallery at Hilltop, and I can still vividly recall my horror when it suddenly arrived, heavily crated and with his gift card attached, at my barren room-and-a-half. It took considerable effort, but I finally managed to return it to him by forgoing the argument that the picture was undoubtedly worth more than the entire building in which I lived and by complaining that it simply didn't show to advantage on my wall. I think he suspected I was lying, but being Hugh, he would never dream of charging me with that in so many words.

Of course, Hilltop and the two hundred years of Lozier tradition that went into it did much to shape Hugh this way. The first Loziers had carved the estate from the heights overlooking the river, had worked hard and flourished exceedingly; in successive generations had invested their income so wisely that money and position eventually erected a towering wall between Hilltop and the world outside. Truth to tell, Hugh was very much a man of the eighteenth century who somehow found himself in the twentieth, and simply made the best of it.

Hilltop itself was almost a replica of the celebrated, but long untenanted, Dane house nearby, and was striking enough to open anybody's eyes at a glance. The house was weathered stone, graceful despite its bulk, and the vast lawns reaching to the river's edge were tended with such fanatical devotion over the years that they had become carpets of purest green which magically changed luster under any breeze. Gardens ranged from the other side of the house down to the groves which half-hid the stables and outbuildings, and past the far side of the groves ran the narrow road which led to town. The road was a courtesy road, each estate holder along it maintaining his share, and I think it safe to say that for all the crushed rock he laid in it, Hugh made less use of it by far than any of his neighbors.

Hugh's life was bound up in Hilltop; he could be made to leave it only by dire necessity; and if you did meet him away from it, you were made acutely aware that he was counting off the minutes until he could return. And if you weren't wary, you would more than likely find yourself going along with him when he did return, and totally unable to tear yourself away from the place while the precious weeks rolled by. I know. I believe I spent more time at Hilltop than at my own apartment after my sister brought Hugh into the family.

At one time I wondered how Elizabeth took to this marriage, considering that before she met Hugh she had been as restless and flighty as she was pretty. When I put the question to her directly, she said, "It's wonderful, darling. Just as wonderful as I knew it would be when I first met him."

It turned out that their first meeting had taken place at an art exhibition, a showing of some ultramodern stuff, and she had been intently studying one of the more bewildering creations on display when she became aware of this tall, good-looking man staring at her. And, as she put it, she had been about to set him properly in his place when he said abruptly, "Are you admiring that?"

This was so unlike what she had expected that she was taken completely aback. "I don't know," she said weakly. "Am I supposed to?"

"No," said the stranger, "it's damned nonsense. Come along now, and I'll show you something that isn't a waste of time."

"And," Elizabeth said to me, "I came along like a pup at his heels, while he marched up and down and told me what was good and what was bad, and in a good loud voice, too, so that we collected quite a crowd along the way. Can you picture it, darling?"

"Yes," I said, "I can." By now I had shared similar occasions with Hugh, and learned at first hand that nothing could dent his cast-iron assurance.

"Well," Elizabeth went on, "I must admit that at first I was a little put off, but then I began to see that he knew exactly what he was talking about, and that he was terribly sincere. Not a bit self-conscious about anything, but just eager for me to understand things the way he did. It's the same way with everything. Everybody else in the world is always fumbling and bumbling over deciding anything—what to order for dinner, or how to manage his job, or whom to vote for—but Hugh always *knows*. It's *not* knowing that makes for all those nerves and complexes and things you hear about—isn't that so? Well, I'll take Hugh, thank you, and leave everyone else to the psychiatrists."

So there it was. An Eden with flawless lawns and no awful nerves and complexes, and not even the glimmer of a serpent in the offing. That is, not a glimmer until the day Raymond made his entrance on the scene.

We were out on the terrace that day, Hugh and Elizabeth and I, slowly being melted into a sort of liquid torpor by the August sunshine, and all of us too far gone to make even a pretense at talk. I lay there with a linen cap over my face, listening to the summer noises around me and being perfectly happy.

There was the low steady hiss of the breeze through the aspens nearby, the plash and drip of oars on the river below, and now and then the melancholy *tink-tunk* of a sheep bell from one of the flock on the lawn. The flock was a fancy of Hugh's. He swore that nothing was better for a lawn than a few sheep grazing on it, and every summer five or six fat and sleepy ewes were turned out on the grass to serve this purpose and to add a pleasantly pastoral note.

My first warning of something amiss came from the sheep—from the sudden sound of their bells clanging wildly and then a baa-ing which suggested an assault by a whole pack of wolves. I heard Hugh say, "Damn!" loudly and angrily, and I opened my eyes to see something more incongruous than wolves. It was a large black poodle in a full

glory of a clownish haircut, a bright red collar, and an ecstasy of high
spirits as he chased the frightened sheep around the lawn. It was clear
the poodle had no intention of hurting them—he probably found
them the most wonderful playmates imaginable—but it was just as clear
that the panicky ewes didn't understand this, and would very likely end
up in the river before the fun was over.

In the bare second it took me to see all this, Hugh had already leaped
the low terrace wall and was among the sheep, herding them away from
the water's edge, and shouting commands at the dog, which had different ideas.

"Down, boy!" he yelled. "Down!" And then as he would to one of his
own hounds he sternly commanded, "Heel!"

He would have done better, I thought, to pick up a stick or stone and
make a threatening gesture, since the poodle paid no attention whatever
to Hugh's words. Instead, continuing to bark happily, the poodle made
for the sheep again, this time with Hugh in futile pursuit. An instant
later, the dog was frozen into immobility by a voice from among the
aspens near the edge of the lawn.

"*Assis!*" the voice called breathlessly. "*Assieds-toi!*"

Then the man appeared—a small, dapper figure trotting across the
grass. Hugh stood waiting, his face darkening as we watched.

Elizabeth squeezed my arm. "Let's get down there," she whispered.
"Hugh doesn't like being made a fool of."

We got there in time to hear Hugh open his big guns. "Any man," he
was saying, "who doesn't know how to train an animal to its place
shouldn't own one."

The man's face was all polite attention. It was a good face, thin and
intelligent, and webbed with tiny lines at the corners of the eyes. There
was also something behind those eyes that couldn't quite be masked. A
gentle mockery. A glint of wry perception turned on the world like a
camera lens. It was nothing anyone like Hugh would have noticed, but
it was there all the same, and I found myself warming to it on the spot.

There was also something tantalizingly familiar about the new-
comer's face, his high forehead, and his thinning gray hair; but much as
I dug into my memory during Hugh's long and solemn lecture, I
couldn't come up with an answer. The lecture ended with a few

remarks on the best methods of dog training, and by then it was clear
that Hugh was working himself into a mood of forgiveness.

"As long as there's no harm done," he said, and paused.

The man nodded soberly. "Still, to get off on the wrong foot with
one's new neighbors . . . "

Hugh looked startled. "Neighbors?" he said almost rudely. "You
mean that you live around here?"

The man waved toward the aspens. "On the other side of those
woods."

"The *Dane* house?" The Dane house was almost as sacred to Hugh as
Hilltop, and he had once explained to me that if he were ever offered a
chance to buy the place he would snap it up. His tone now was not so
much wounded as incredulous. "I don't believe it!" he exclaimed.

"Oh, yes," the man assured him, "the Dane house. I performed
there at a party many years ago, and always hoped that someday I might
own it."

It was the word "performed" that gave me my clue—that and the
accent barely perceptible under the precise English. He had been born
and raised in Marseille—that would explain the accent—and long
before my time he had already become a legend.

"You're Raymond, aren't you?" I said. "Charles Raymond."

"I prefer Raymond alone." He smiled in deprecation of his own small
vanity. "And I am flattered that you recognize me."

I don't believe he really was. Raymond the Magician, Raymond the
Great, would, if anything, expect to be recognized wherever he went.
As the master of sleight of hand who had paled Thurston's star, as the
escape artist who had almost outshone Houdini, Raymond would not
be inclined to underestimate himself.

He had started with the standard box of tricks which makes up the
repertoire of most professional magicians; he had gone far beyond that
to those feats of escape which, I suppose, are known to us all by now.
The lead casket sealed under a foot of lake ice, the welded-steel strait-
jackets, the vaults of the Bank of England, the exquisite suicide knot
which noosed throat and doubled legs together so that the motion of a
leg draws the noose tighter around the throat—all these Raymond had

escaped from. And then at the pinnacle of fame he had dropped from sight and his name had become relegated to the past.

When I asked him why, he shrugged.

"A man works for money or for the love of his work. If he has all the wealth he needs and has no more love for his work, why go on?"

"But to give up a great career . . ." I protested.

"It was enough to know that the house was waiting here."

"You mean," Elizabeth said, "that you never intended to live any-place but here?"

"Never—not once in all these years." He laid a finger along his nose and winked broadly at us. "Of course, I made no secret of this to the Dane estate, and when the time came for them to sell I was the first and only one approached."

"You don't give up an idea easily," Hugh said in an edged voice.

Raymond laughed. "Idea? It became an obsession, really. Over the years I traveled to many parts of the world, but no matter how fine the place, I knew it could not be as fine as that house on the edge of the woods there, with the river at its feet and the hills beyond. Someday, I would tell myself, when my travels are done I will come here, and, like Candide, cultivate my garden."

He ran his hand abstractedly over the poodle's head and looked around with an air of great satisfaction. "And now," he said, "here I am."

Here he was indeed, and it quickly became clear that his arrival was working a change on Hilltop. Or, since Hilltop was so completely a reflection of Hugh, it was clear that a change was being worked on Hugh. He became irritable and restless, and more aggressively sure of himself than ever. The warmth and good nature were still there—they were as much part of him as his arrogance—but he now had to work a little harder at them. He reminded me of a man who is bothered by a speck in the eye, but can't find it, and must get along with it as best he can.

Raymond, of course, was the speck, and I got the impression at times that he rather enjoyed the role. It would have been easy enough for him to stay close to his own house and cultivate his garden, or paste up his album, or whatever retired performers do, but he evidently found that impossible. He had a way of drifting over to Hilltop at odd times—just as Hugh was led to find his way to the Dane house and spend long and troublesome sessions there.

Both of them must have known that they were so badly suited to each other that the easy and logical solution would have been to stay apart. But they had the affinity of negative and positive forces, and when they were in a room together the crackling of the antagonistic current between them was so strong you could almost see it in the air.

Any subject became a point of contention for them, and they would duel over it bitterly: Hugh armored and weaponed with his massive assurance, Raymond flicking away with a rapier, trying to find a chink in the armor. I think that what annoyed Raymond most was the discovery that there was no chink in Hugh's armor. As someone with an obvious passion for searching out all sides to all questions, and for going deep into motives and causes, Raymond was continually being outraged by Hugh's single-minded way of laying down the law.

He didn't hesitate to let Hugh know that. "You are positively medieval," he said. "And of all things men should have learned since that time, the biggest is that there are no easy answers, no solutions one can give with a snap of the fingers. I can only hope for you that someday you may be faced with the perfect dilemma, the unanswerable question. You would find that a revelation. You would learn more in that minute than you dream possible."

And Hugh did not make matters any better when he coldly answered, "And *I* say that for any man with a brain and the courage to use it there is no such thing as a perfect dilemma."

It may be that this was the sort of episode which led to the trouble that followed, or it may be that Raymond acted out of the most innocent and esthetic motives possible. But whatever the motives, the results were inevitable and dangerous.

They grew from the project Raymond outlined for us in great detail one afternoon. Now that he was living in the Dane house he had discovered that it was too big, too overwhelming. "Like a museum," he explained. "I find myself wandering through it like a lost soul through endless galleries."

The grounds also needed landscaping. The ancient trees were handsome, but as Raymond put it, there were just too many of them. "Literally," he said, "I cannot see the river for the trees; and I am one devoted to the sight of running water."

Altogether there would be drastic changes. Two wings of the house would come down, the trees would be cleared away to make a broad aisle to the water, the whole place would be enlivened. It would no longer be a museum, but the perfect home he had envisioned over the years.

At the start of this recitation, Hugh was slouched comfortably in his chair. Then as Raymond drew the vivid picture of what was to be, Hugh sat up straighter and straighter until he was as rigid as a trooper in the saddle. His lips compressed. His face became blood-red. His hands clenched and unclenched in a slow deadly rhythm. Only a miracle was restraining him from an open outburst, and it was not the kind of miracle to last. I saw from Elizabeth's expression that she understood this too, but was as helpless as I to do anything about it. And when Raymond, after painting the last glowing strokes of his description, said complacently, "Well, now, what do you think?" there was no holding Hugh.

He leaned forward with deliberation and said, "Do you really want to know what I think?"

"Now, Hugh," Elizabeth said in alarm. "Please, Hugh—"

He brushed that aside.

"Do you really want to know?"

Raymond frowned. "Of course."

"Then I'll tell you," Hugh said. He took a deep breath. "I think that nobody but a damned iconoclast could even conceive the atrocity you're proposing. I think you're the kind of person who takes pleasure in smashing apart anything that's stamped with tradition or stability. You'd kick the props from under the whole world if you could!"

"I beg your pardon," Raymond said. He was very pale and angry. "But I think you are confusing change with destruction. Surely you must comprehend that I do not intend to destroy anything, but only wish to make some necessary changes."

"Necessary?" Hugh gibed. "Rooting up a fine stand of trees that's been there for centuries? Ripping apart a house that's as solid as a rock? I call it wanton destruction."

"I'm afraid I do not understand. To refresh a scene, to reshape it—"

"I have no intention of arguing," Hugh cut in. "I'm telling you straight out that you don't have the right to tamper with that property!"

They were on their feet now, facing each other truculently, and the only thing that kept me from being really frightened was the conviction that Hugh would not become violent and that Raymond was far too levelheaded to lose his temper. Then the threatening moment was magically past. Raymond's lips suddenly quirked in amusement, and he studied Hugh with courteous interest.

"I see," he said. "I was quite stupid not to have understood at once. This property which, I remarked, was a little too much like a museum is to remain that way, and I am to be its custodian. A caretaker of the past, one might say, a curator of its relics."

He shook his head smilingly. "But I am afraid I am not quite suited to that role. I lift my hat to the past, it is true, but I prefer to court the present. For that reason I will go ahead with my plans, and hope they do not make an obstacle to our friendship."

I remember thinking, when I left next day for the city and a long, hot week at my desk, that Raymond had carried off the affair very nicely, and thank God, it had gone no further. So I was completely unprepared for Elizabeth's call at the end of the week.

It was awful, she said. It was the business of Hugh and Raymond and the Dane house, but worse than ever. She was counting on my coming down to Hilltop the next day; there couldn't be any question about that. She had planned a way of clearing up the whole thing, but I simply had to be there to back her up. After all, I was one of the few people Hugh would listen to, and she was depending on me.

"Depending on me for what?" I said. I didn't like the sound of it. "And as for Hugh's listening to me, Elizabeth, isn't that stretching it a good deal? I can't see him wanting my advice on his personal affairs."

"If you're going to be touchy about it—"

"I'm *not* touchy about it," I retorted. "I just don't like getting mixed up in this thing. Hugh's quite capable of taking care of himself."

"Maybe too capable."

"And what does that mean?"

"Oh, I can't explain now," she wailed. "I'll tell you everything tomorrow. And darling, if you have any brotherly feelings, you'll be here on the morning train. Believe me, it's serious."

I arrived on the morning train in a bad state. My imagination is one of the overactive kind that can build a cosmic disaster out of very little material, and by the time I arrived at the house I was prepared for almost anything.

But on the surface, at least, all was serene. Hugh greeted me warmly, Elizabeth was her cheerful self, and we had an amiable lunch and a long talk which never came near the subject of Raymond or the Dane house. I said nothing about Elizabeth's phone call, but thought of it with a steadily growing sense of outrage until I was alone with her.

"Now," I said, "I'd like an explanation of all this mystery. The Lord knows what I expected to find out here, but it certainly wasn't anything I've seen so far. And I'd like some accounting for the bad time you've given me since that call."

"All right," she said grimly, "and that's what you'll get. Come along."

She led the way on a long walk through the gardens and past the stables and outbuildings. Near the private road which lay beyond the last grove of trees she suddenly said, "When the car drove you up to the house, didn't you notice anything strange about this road?"

"No, I didn't."

"I suppose not. The driveway to the house turns off too far away from here. But now you'll have a chance to see for yourself."

I did see for myself. A chair was set squarely in the middle of the road and on the chair sat a stout man placidly reading a magazine. I recognized the man at once: he was one of Hugh's stable hands, and he had the patient look of someone who has been sitting for a long time and expects to sit a good deal longer. It took me only a second to realize what he was there for, but Elizabeth wasn't leaving anything to my deductive powers. When we walked over to him the man stood up and grinned at us.

"William," Elizabeth said, "would you mind telling my brother what instructions Mr. Lozier gave you?"

"Sure," the man said cheerfully. "Mr. Lozier told us there was always supposed to be one of us sitting right here, and any truck we saw that might be carrying construction stuff or suchlike for the Dane house was to be stopped and turned back. All we had to do is tell them it's private property and they were trespassing. If they laid a finger on us we just call in the police. That's the whole thing."

"Have you turned back any trucks?" Elizabeth asked for my benefit. The man looked surprised. "Why, you know that, Mrs. Lozier," he said. "There was a couple of them the first day we were out here, and that was all. There wasn't any fuss, either," he explained to me. "None of those drivers wants to monkey with trespass."

When we were away from the road again, I clapped my hand to my forehead. "It's incredible!" I said. "Hugh must know he can't get away with this. That road is the only one to the Dane place, and it's been in public use so long that it isn't private anymore!"

Elizabeth nodded. "And that's exactly what Raymond told Hugh a few days back. He came over here in a fury, and they had quite an argument about it. And when Raymond said something about hauling Hugh off to court, Hugh answered that he'd be glad to spend the rest of his life in litigation over this business. But that wasn't the worst of it. The last thing Raymond said was that Hugh ought to know that force only invites force, and ever since then I've been expecting a war to break out here any minute. Don't you see? That man blocking the road is a constant provocation, and it scares me."

I could understand that. And the more I considered the matter, the more dangerous it looked.

"But I have a plan," Elizabeth said eagerly, "and that's why I wanted you here. I'm having a dinner party tonight—a very small, informal dinner party. It's to be a sort of peace conference. You'll be there, and Dr. Wynant—Hugh likes you both a great deal—and," she hesitated, "Raymond."

"No!" I said. "You mean he's actually coming?"

"I went over to see him yesterday and we had a long talk. I explained everything to him—about neighbors being able to sit down and come to an understanding, and about brotherly love and—oh, it must have sounded dreadfully inspirational and sticky; but it worked. He said he would be there."

I had a foreboding. "Does Hugh know about this?"

"About the dinner? Yes."

"I mean, about Raymond's being there."

"No, he doesn't." And then when she saw me looking hard at her she burst out defiantly with "Well, *something* had to be done, and I did it, that's all! Isn't it better than just sitting and waiting for God knows what?"

Until we were all seated around the dining-room table that evening, I might have conceded the point. Hugh had been visibly shocked by Raymond's arrival, but then, apart from a sidelong glance at Elizabeth which had volumes written in it, he managed to conceal his feelings well enough. He had made the introductions gracefully, kept up his end of the conversation, and all in all, did a creditable job of playing host.

Ironically, it was the presence of Dr. Wynant which made even this much of a triumph possible for Elizabeth, and which then turned it into disaster. The doctor was an eminent surgeon, stocky and gray-haired, with an abrupt, positive way about him. Despite his own position in the world, he seemed pleased as a schoolboy to meet Raymond, and in no time at all they were thick as thieves.

It was when Hugh discovered during dinner that nearly all attention was fixed on Raymond and very little on himself that the mantle of good host started to slip, and the fatal flaws in Elizabeth's plan showed through. There are people who enjoy entertaining lions and who take pleasure in reflected glory, but Hugh was not one of them. Besides, he regarded the doctor as one of his closest friends, and I have noticed that it is the most assured of men who can be the most jealous of their friendships. And when a prized friendship is being encroached on by the man one loathes more than anyone else in the world . . . ! All in all, by simply imagining myself in Hugh's place and looking across the table at Raymond, who was gaily and unconcernedly holding forth, I was prepared for the worst.

The opportunity for it came to Hugh when Raymond was deep in a discussion of the devices used in effecting escapes. They were innumerable, he said. Almost anything one could seize on would serve as such a device. A wire, a scrap of metal, even a bit of paper—at one time or another he had used them all.

"But of them all," he said with a sudden solemnity, "there is only one I would stake my life on. Strange, it is one you cannot see, cannot hold in your hand—in fact, for many people it does not even exist. Yet it is the one I have used most often and which has never failed me."

The doctor leaned forward, his eyes bright with interest. "And it is . . . ?"

"It is a knowledge of people, my friend. Or, as it may be put, a knowledge of human nature. To me it is as vital an instrument as the scalpel is to you."

"Oh?" said Hugh, and his voice was so sharp that all eyes were instantly turned on him. "You make sleight of hand sound like a department of psychology."

"Perhaps," Raymond said, and I saw he was watching Hugh now, gauging him. "You see, there is no great mystery in the matter. My profession—my art, as I like to think of it—is no more than the art of misdirection, and I am but one of its many practitioners."

"I wouldn't say there were many escape artists around nowadays," the doctor remarked.

"True," Raymond said, "but you will observe I referred to the art of misdirection. The escape artist, the master of legerdemain—these are a handful who practice the most exotic form of that art. But what of those who engage in the work of politics, of advertising, of salesmanship?" He laid his finger along his nose in the familiar gesture, and winked. "I am afraid they have all made my art their business."

The doctor smiled. "Since you haven't dragged medicine into it, I'm willing to go along with you," he said. "But what I want to know is, exactly how does this knowledge of human nature work in your profession?"

"In this way," Raymond said. "One must judge a person carefully. Then, if he finds in that person certain weaknesses, he can state a false premise and it will be accepted without question. Once the false pre-

mise is swallowed, the rest is easy. The victim will then see only what
the magician wants him to see, or will give his vote to that politician, or
will buy merchandise because of that advertising." He shrugged. "And
that is all there is to it."

"Is it?" Hugh said. "But what happens when you're with people who
have some intelligence and won't swallow your false premise? How do
you do your tricks then? Or do you keep them on the same level as
selling beads to the savages?"

"Now, that's uncalled for, Hugh," the doctor said. "The man's
expressing his ideas. No reason to make an issue of them."

"Maybe there is," Hugh said, his eyes fixed on Raymond. "I have
found he's full of interesting ideas. I was wondering how far he'd want
to go in backing them up."

Raymond touched the napkin to his lips with a precise little flick,
then laid it carefully on the table before him. "In short," he said,
addressing himself to Hugh, "you want a small demonstration of my
art."

"It depends," Hugh said. "I don't want any trick cigarette cases or
rabbits out of hats or any damn nonsense like that. I'd like to see
something good."

"Something good," echoed Raymond reflectively. He looked around
the room, studied it, and then turned to Hugh, pointing toward the
huge oak door which was closed between the dining room and the living
room, where we had gathered before dinner.

"That door is not locked, is it?"

"No," Hugh said, "it isn't. It hasn't been locked for years."

"But there is a key to it?"

Hugh pulled out his key chain and with an effort detached a heavy,
old-fashioned key. "Yes; it's the same one we use for the butler's pan-
try." He was becoming interested despite himself.

"Good. No, do not give it to me. Give it to the doctor. You have faith
in the doctor's honor, I am sure?"

"Yes," said Hugh drily, "I have."

"Very well. Now, Doctor, will you please go to that door and lock
it."

The doctor marched to the door with his firm, decisive tread, thrust the key into the lock, and turned it. The click of the bolt snapping into place was loud in the silence of the room. The doctor returned to the table holding the key, but Raymond motioned it away. "It must not leave your hand, or everything is lost," he warned.

"Now," Raymond said, "for the finale. I approach the door, I flick my handkerchief at it"—the handkerchief barely brushed the keyhole—"and presto, the door is unlocked!"

The doctor went to it. He seized the doorknob, twisted it dubiously, and then watched with genuine astonishment as the door swung silently open.

"Well, I'll be damned," he said.

"Somehow"—Elizabeth laughed—"a false premise went down easy as an oyster."

Only Hugh reflected a sense of personal outrage. "All right," he demanded, "how was it done? How did you work it?"

"I?" Raymond said reproachfully, and smiled at all of us with obvious enjoyment. "It was you who did it all. I used only my knowledge of human nature to help you along the way."

I said, "I can guess part of it. That door was set in advance, and when the doctor thought he was locking it, he wasn't. He was really unlocking it. Isn't that the answer?"

Raymond nodded. "Very much the answer. The door *was* locked in advance. I made sure of that, because with a little forethought I suspected there would be such a challenge during the evening, and this was the simplest way of preparing for it. I merely made certain that I was the last one to enter this room, and when I did I used this." He held up his hand so that we could see the sliver of metal in it. "An ordinary skeleton key, of course, but sufficient for an old and primitive lock."

For a moment Raymond looked grave; then he continued brightly, "It was our host himself who stated the false premise when he said the door was unlocked. He was so sure of himself that he would not think to test anything so obvious. The doctor is also a man who is sure, and he fell into the same trap. It is, as you now see, a little dangerous always to be so sure."

"I'll go along with that," the doctor said ruefully, "even though it's heresy to admit it in my line of work." He playfully tossed the key he had been holding across the table to Hugh, who let it fall in front of him and made no gesture toward it. "Well, Hugh, like it or not, you must admit the man has proved his point."

"Do I?" said Hugh softly. He sat there smiling a little now, and it was easy to see he was turning some thought over and over in his head.

"Oh, come on, man," the doctor said with some impatience. "You were taken in as much as we were. You know that."

"Of course you were, darling," Elizabeth agreed.

I think that she suddenly saw an opportunity to turn the proceedings into the peace conference she had aimed at, but I could have told her she was choosing her time badly. There was a look in Hugh's eye I didn't like—a veiled look which wasn't natural to him. Ordinarily, when he was really angered he would blow up a violent storm, and once the thunder and lightning had passed he would be honestly apologetic. But this present mood of his was different. There was a slumbrous quality in it which alarmed me.

He hooked one arm over the back of his chair and rested the other on the table, sitting halfway around to fix his eyes on Raymond. "I seem to be a minority of one," he remarked, "but I'm sorry to say I found your little trick disappointing. Not that it wasn't cleverly done—I'll grant that, all right—but because it wasn't any more than you'd expect from a competent blacksmith."

"Now, there's a large helping of sour grapes," the doctor jeered.

Hugh shook his head. "No, I'm simply saying that where there's a lock on a door and the key to it in your hand, it's no great trick to open it. Considering our friend's reputation, I thought we'd see more from him than that."

Raymond grimaced. "Since I had hoped to entertain," he said, "I must apologize for disappointing."

"Oh, as far as entertainment goes I have no complaints. But for a real test—"

"A real test?"

"Yes, something a little different. Let's say, a door without any locks or keys to tamper with. A closed door which can be opened with a fingertip, but which is nevertheless impossible to open. How does that sound to you?"

Raymond narrowed his eyes thoughtfully, as if he were considering the picture being presented to him. "It sounds most interesting," he said at last. "Tell me more about it."

"No," Hugh said, and from the sudden eagerness in his voice I felt that this was the exact moment he had been looking for. "I'll do better than that. I'll *show* it to you."

He stood up brusquely and the rest of us followed suit—except Elizabeth, who remained in her seat. When I asked her if she wanted to come along, she only shook her head and sat there watching us hopelessly as we left the room.

We were bound for the cellars, I realized when Hugh picked up a flashlight along the way, but for a part of the cellars I had never seen before. On a few occasions I had gone downstairs to help select a bottle of wine from the racks there, but now we walked past the wine vault and into a long, dimly lit chamber behind it. Our feet scraped loudly on the rough stone, the walls around us showed the stains of seepage, and warm as the night was outside, I could feel the chill of dampness turning my chest to gooseflesh.

When the doctor shuddered and said hollowly, "These are the very tombs of Atlantis," I knew I wasn't alone in my feeling, and felt some relief at that.

We stopped at the very end of the chamber, before what I can best describe as a stone closet built from floor to ceiling in the farthest angle of the walls. It was about four feet wide and not quite twice that in length, and its open doorway showed impenetrable blackness inside. Hugh reached into the blackness and pulled a heavy door into place.

"That's it," he said abruptly. "Plain solid wood, four inches thick, fitted flush into the frame so that it's almost airtight. It's a beautiful piece of carpentry, too, the kind they practiced two hundred years ago. And no locks or bolts. Just a ring set into each side to use as a handle." He pushed the door gently and it swung open noiselessly at his touch. "See that? The whole thing is balanced so perfectly on the hinges that it moves like a feather."

"But what's it for?" I asked. "It must have been made for a reason."

Hugh laughed shortly. "It was. Back in the bad old days, when a servant committed a crime—and I don't suppose it had to be more of a crime than talking back to one of the ancient Loziers—he was put in here to repent. And since the air inside was good for only a few hours at the most, he either repented damn soon or not at all."

"And that door?" the doctor said cautiously. "That impressive door of yours which opens at a touch to provide all the air needed—what prevented the servant from opening it?"

"Look," Hugh said. He flashed his light inside the cell, and we crowded behind him to peer in. The circle of light reached across the cell to its far wall and picked out a short, heavy chain hanging a little above head level with a U-shaped collar dangling from its bottom link.

"I see," Raymond said, and they were the first words I had heard him speak since we had left the dining room. "It is truly ingenious. The man stands with his back against the wall, facing the door. The collar is placed around his neck, and then—since it is cleverly not made for a lock—it is clamped there, hammered around his neck. The door is closed, and the man spends the next few hours like someone on an invisible rack, reaching out with his feet to catch the ring on the door which is just out of reach. If he is lucky he may not strangle himself in his iron collar, but may live until someone chooses to open the door for him."

"My God," the doctor said. "You make me feel as if I were living through it."

Raymond smiled faintly. "I have lived through many such experiences, and, believe me, the reality is always a little worse than the worst imaginings. There is always the ultimate moment of terror, of panic, when the heart pounds so madly you think it will burst through your ribs, and the cold sweat soaks clear through you in the space of one breath. That is when you must take yourself in hand, must dispel all weakness, and remember all the lessons you have ever learned. If not . . . !"

He whisked the edge of his hand across his lean throat. "Unfortunately for the usual victim of such a device," he concluded sadly, "since he lacks the essential courage and knowledge to help himself, he succumbs."

"But you wouldn't," Hugh said.

"I have no reason to think so."

"You mean"—and the eagerness was creeping back into Hugh's voice, stronger than ever—"that under the very same conditions as someone chained in there two hundred years ago you could get this door open?"

The challenging note was too strong to be brushed aside lightly. Raymond stood silent for a long minute, face strained with concentration, before he answered.

"Yes," he said. "It would not be easy—the problem is made formidable by its very simplicity—but it could be solved."

"How long do you think it would take you?"

"An hour at the most."

Hugh had come a long way around to get to this point. He asked the question slowly, savoring it. "Would you want to bet on that?"

"Now, wait a minute," the doctor said. "I don't like any part of this."

"And I vote we adjourn for a drink," I put in. "Fun's fun, but we'll all wind up with pneumonia, playing games down here."

Neither Hugh nor Raymond appeared to hear a word of this. They stood staring at each other—Hugh waiting on pins and needles, Raymond deliberating—until Raymond said, "What is this bet you offer?"

"This. If you lose, you get out of the Dane house inside of a month, and sell it to me."

"And if I win?"

It was not easy for Hugh to say it, but he finally got it out: "Then I'll be the one to get out. And if you don't want to buy Hilltop I'll arrange to sell it to the first comer."

For anyone who knew Hugh it was so fantastic, so staggering a statement to hear from him that none of us could find words at first. It was the doctor who recovered most quickly.

"You're not speaking only for yourself, Hugh," he warned. "You're a married man. Elizabeth's feelings have to be considered."

"Is it a bet?" Hugh demanded of Raymond. "Do you want to go through with it?"

"I think before I answer that, there is something to be explained." Raymond paused, then went on slowly, "I am afraid I gave the impression—out of false pride, perhaps—that when I retired from my work it was because of a boredom, a lack of interest in it. That was not altogether the truth. In reality, I was required to go to a doctor some years ago, the doctor listened to my heart, and suddenly my heart became the most important thing in the world. I tell you this because while your challenge strikes me as being a most unusual and interesting way of settling differences between neighbors, I must reject it for reasons of health."

"You were healthy enough a minute ago," Hugh said.

"Perhaps not as much as you would want to think, my friend."

"In other words," Hugh said bitterly, "there's no accomplice handy, no keys in your pocket to help out, and no way of tricking anyone into seeing what isn't there! So you have to admit you're beaten."

Raymond stiffened. "I admit no such thing. All the tools I would need even for such a test as this I have with me. Believe me, they would be enough."

Hugh laughed aloud, and the sound of it broke into small echoes all down the corridors behind us. It was that sound, I am sure—the living contempt in it rebounding from wall to wall around us—which sent Raymond into the cell.

Hugh wielded the hammer, a short-handled but heavy sledge, which tightened the collar into a circlet around Raymond's neck, hitting with hard, even strokes at the iron, which was braced against the wall. When he had finished, I saw the pale glow of the radium-painted numbers on a watch as Raymond studied it in his pitch darkness.

"It is now eleven," he said calmly. "The wager is that by midnight this door must be opened, and it does not matter what means are used. Those are the conditions, and you gentlemen are the witnesses to them."

Then the door was closed, and the walking began.

Back and forth we walked—the three of us—as if we were being compelled to trace every possible geometric figure on that stony floor. The doctor with his quick, impatient step, and I matching Hugh's long nervous strides. A foolish, meaningless march, back and forth across our own shadows, each of us marking the time by counting off the passing seconds, and each ashamed to be the first to look at his watch.

For a while there was a counterpoint to this scraping of feet from inside the cell. It was a barely perceptible clinking of chain coming at brief, regular intervals. Then there would be a long silence, followed by a renewal of the sound. When it stopped again, I could not restrain myself any longer. I held up my watch toward the dim yellowish light of the bulb overhead and saw with dismay that barely twenty minutes had passed.

After that there was no hesitancy in the others about looking at the time, and if anything, this made it harder to bear than just wondering. I caught the doctor winding his watch with small brisk turns, and then a few minutes later saw him try to wind it again, and suddenly drop his hand with disgust as he realized he had already done it. Hugh walked with his watch held up near his eyes, as if by concentration on it he could drag that crawling minute hand faster around the dial.

Thirty minutes had passed.

Forty.

Forty-five.

I remember that when I looked at my watch and saw there was less than fifteen minutes to go, I wondered if I could last out even that short time. The chill had sunk so deep into me that I ached with it. I was shocked when I saw that Hugh's face was dripping with sweat, and beads of it gathered as I watched.

It was while I was looking at him in fascination that it happened. The sound broke through the walls of the cell like a wail of agony heard from far away, and shivered over us as if it were spelling out the words.

"*Doctor!*" it cried. "*The air!*"

It was Raymond's voice, but the thickness of the wall blocking it off turned it into a high, thin sound. What was clearest in it was the note of pure terror, the plea growing out of that terror.

"*Air!*" it screamed, the word bubbling and dissolving into a long-drawn sound which made no sense at all.

And then it was silent.

We leaped for the door together, but Hugh was there first, his back against it, barring the way. In his upraised hand was the hammer which had clinched Raymond's collar.

"Keep back!" he cried. "Don't come any nearer, I warn you!"

The fury in him, brought home by the menace of the weapon, stopped us in our tracks.

"Hugh," the doctor pleaded, "I know what you're thinking, but you can forget that now. The bet's off, and I'm opening the door on my own responsibility. You have my word for that."

"Do I? But do you remember the terms of the bet, Doctor? This door must be opened within an hour—*and it doesn't matter what means are used!* Do you understand now? He's fooling both of you. He's faking a death scene so that you'll push open the door and win his bet for him. But it's my bet, not yours, and I have the last word on it!"

I saw from the way he talked, despite the shaking tension in his voice, that he was in perfect command of himself, and it made everything seem that much worse.

"How do you know he's faking?" I demanded. "The man said he had a heart condition. He said there was always a time in a spot like this when he had to fight panic and could feel the strain of it. What right do you have to gamble with his life?"

"Damn it, don't you see he never mentioned any heart condition until he smelled a bet in the wind? Don't you see he set his trap that way, just as he locked the door behind him when he came to dinner! But this time nobody will spring it for him—nobody!"

"Listen to me," the doctor said, and his voice cracked like a whip. "Do you concede that there's one slim possibility of that man being dead in there, or dying?"

"Yes, it is possible—anything is possible."

"I'm not trying to split hairs with you! I'm telling you that if that man is in trouble every second counts, and you're stealing that time from him. And if that's the case, by God, I'll sit in the witness chair at your trial and swear you murdered him! Is that what you want?"

Hugh's head sank forward on his chest, but his hand still tightly gripped the hammer. I could hear the breath drawing heavily in his throat, and when he raised his head, his face was gray and haggard. The torment of indecision was written in every pale, sweating line of it.

And then I suddenly understood what Raymond had meant that day when he told Hugh about the revelation he might find in the face of a perfect dilemma. It was the revelation of what a man may learn about himself when he is forced to look into his own depths, and Hugh had found it at last.

In that shadowy cellar, while the relentless seconds thundered louder and louder in our ears, we waited to see what he would do.

RON GOULART

# IT WAS BAD ENOUGH

They only believed he was the Son of Satan killer for a day or so. Then the police realized they'd made a mistake and shouldn't have gunned him down in the middle of Sunset Strip like that.

Too late to do Beans Katzman much good. He was already lying in state in a satin-lined coffin in one of the most prestigious funeral chapels in the Los Angeles area by that time, surrounded by impressive funeral wreaths. The fancy send-off was mostly Juliet's idea. Once he was dead and gone, she seemed to feel a bit more kindly toward Beans, and quite probably she realized a lavish funeral would get the sort of media attention that'd provide some publicity for her upcoming book and movie.

Beans was preoccupied with that book of hers, and the possible movie, when I had lunch with him on a mild, hazy spring day a little over three weeks ago. The restaurant was a small, narrow vegetarian place a block or so from the forlorn peach-colored apartment building in a bleakly run-down section of Hollywood Beans was living in at the moment. It was called Disgustingly Healthy and had only recently moved into what had been a surplus store. Signs offering *Knapsacks at Low, Low Prices* and *Desert Boots ½ Price!* still decorated the pocked plaster walls.

Beans came in out of the haze and did his swish wave. "Oh, there you are, sweets. God, but I'm glad you could ditch the wife." He switched into his truck driver and walked through the tangle of shaky tables toward where I was sitting. "Where you want that truckload of avocados?" he inquired of the lean young man with the mustache who ran the restaurant.

"How are you today, Mr. Katzman?" the young man inquired, grinning.

"How vas I? How vas I?" he inquired in his Dutch accent. "Mine poy, I'm disgustingly healthy, dot's how I vas." Bouncing twice, he settled into the chair opposite me.

As a matter of fact, he did look in pretty good shape. Nowhere near as good as he had when he'd starred on *The Funny, Funny Hour* on television nearly thirty years ago, but better than he had the last time my ad agency had tried to use him for some commercials.

"Beans," I told him, "I think I'll be able to persuade them to give you a chance to audition for the part of Mr. Mildew in our Kildew Spray spots that are—"

"Sure, sure," he said, reaching into an inside pocket of his eleven-year-old sport coat. "Did you see this? Do you know what those gumballs are planning to do to me now?"

"Which—?"

"Ex-wife." He withdrew a folded-up copy of *Daily Variety* and waved it in the air. "Let me be more specific. Since my ex-wives are legion. I mean Juliet—Juliet Fairly. Gad, how could I have wed a wench with a name like that? Well, I was fifty at the time, and fifty is a dangerous— Listen, sis, are you giving me the come-on?" He'd noticed a thin girl in jeans and sweatshirt at the next table.

Putting down her sprout-and-mock-meat-loaf-on-pita-bread sandwich, she glanced over at him. "You were addressing me, gramps?"

"Never mind, I realize now it's only a tic." Beans dropped the trade
paper on the tabletop and smoothed it out. "Waiter, cancel that mag-
num of carrot juice for the beauty at the next table. Where was I?"

The girl was watching him. "You look vaguely familiar. Were you
somebody once?"

"Was I somebody?" His eyebrows quivered as he reached again into
his coat.

I figured the wallet was coming. "Beans, listen, I have to be back at
the agency fairly soon. So let's just have lunch and then discuss the
possibility of your doing—"

"Take a gander at that, girlie." The fat wallet was in his hand. He
flipped it open and two dozen plastic-coated photos came unfolding out
to dangle between the tables. "There I am as Dr. Dingledangle during
the 1954 premiere show of *The Funny, Funny Hour*. Next you see me
politely fondling Marilyn Monroe when she guested on—"

"Oh, yes. You're Beans Katzman." She returned to her sandwich.

"I can help your show-business career, my child. I know a first-rate
bordello down in Tijuana that specializes in ginks with a skinny fetish.
If I put in a good word, they'll hire you like—"

"Beans," I cut in, "the client is worried you may not be dependable
enough for a series of TV commercials that—"

"Not dependable? Me?" He fished in the pictures of his past career
triumphs and folded them up into a neat packet. "I'm completely
straightened out now. The bad days done been here and gone. I am off
booze, off pills, off broads. I am a prince of good fellows. Boy Scouts ask
*me* to help *them* across the street." He held out his hand and made it
quiver like a hummingbird's wing. "See how steady that is?"

"Seriously, Beans," I said, "when we used you on the KleanJon
commercials, you fell into the bathtub on the set not once but—"

"Three damn years ago is not now. I swear to you I haven't had a
drink in over a year. Truly."

"There'll have to be an audition. About two weeks from now, if you
can—"

"Squint at this item, will you." He jabbed his forefinger at an inner page of *Daily Variety*. "This is going to do more harm to my career than falling into a tub."

"What?"

"Here I am, at long last, on the comeback trail." He glanced around the nearly empty room, then lowered his voice. "I am not just being considered for demeaning parts in kitchen- and bathroom-product commercials anymore, my lad. Nay, I am in contention for a lead role in a new sitcom that'll—well, I'm obliged not to give out details. The thing is, I'm still only fifty-seven. My best years are—"

"You're sixty-one," I reminded.

"Not anymore. For the sake of my career I've gone back to fifty-seven. I'm fifty-seven, off the sauce, and by next week I have a full head of hair." He walked his fingers through the thinning spot at the back of his head. "I have my damn feet on the ladder again and then these gumballs come along to foul me up."

Picking up the trade paper, I skimmed the item he'd been jabbing at. "'Juliet Fairly, actress and author.' I didn't know she was an author."

"She scrawled her name and phone number on a lot of phone-booth walls in her youth—'Call me for a hot time.' That's the extent of her literary career."

"'Penning *I Married a Funny, Funny Man*, autobiog of her hectic life with once top comedian Beans Katzman. Publishers in Manhattan fighting over book . . . ' You were only married to her for about three years."

"Two and a half, but I made the fatal error of confiding all of my past sins to her. I mean, she was my fourth wife and I figured it was my last go-round."

"Fifth wife."

"No, no. I never counted Irene."

"'. . . Lonnie Sheck, Junior, dynamic prez of Paragon Pictures, is near to optioning book for a major biopic to be called *Funny, Funny Man*. When last heard from, Beans Katzman was doing the dinner-theater circuit in Nebraska and—' "

"You've already reached the heart of the item." Beans snatched the paper out of my grasp. "Do you see what they're doing? First off, there'll be a book wherein I appear as a drunken, pill-popping monster who broke windows and kicked down doors in my palatial Beverly Hills mansion, carried on with dozens of showgirls, busted my wife's arm, and behaved like a vile sot."

"Maybe a lawyer can—"

"How's a lawyer going to stop her from telling the truth? In those days I *was* a drunken, pill-popping monster who broke windows and kicked down doors in my palatial Beverly Hills mansion, carried on with dozens of showgirls, and busted my wife's arm—twice in fact." He stuffed *Variety* away in a coat pocket. "Then just as the last damaging afterglow of her nitwit book fades and I once again try to overcome the vicissi . . . the vissywissy . . . the bum breaks of life, the damn motion picture hits the fan. There, in a twenty-million-dollar production, I'll be seen breaking arms, pinching fannies, snorting coke, rolling in the gutter all over again. It'll ruin me for good and all." He pointed a finger at the low ceiling, like a movie senator delivering an oration. "And, my fellow Americans, do you know what is even worse? I'll tell you what is even worse. They're stealing my life! My life! Juliet steals it and makes it into a book. Next Lonnie Sheck, Junior, steals it and makes it into a movie!"

"Have you actually talked to an attorney?"

"Three of 'em. They say I haven't got a chance to stop it."

"Maybe it'd be best to leave the whole thing alone," I suggested. "A book and a movie might actually help your career. Years ago *The Jolson Story* gave Al Jolson a whole new career as—"

"Juliet isn't going to show me down on one knee singing 'Mammy,' " Beans pointed out.

"Even so, Beans, the best thing to do is let it alone and—"

"Nix, amigo. I've already devised a surefire plan to get Juliet to cease her pranks. Yes, I intend . . . what is it, lad?"

The proprietor, who also acted as waiter, was hovering beside the table. "Might I take your orders, gentlemen?"

"I'll have the overalls," said Beans, pointing at a sign on the wall. "Two pairs for the price of one. Yum yum."

"Always kidding, huh, Mr. Katzman?"

"'Tis me life's work, laddy. Did I ever show you the pictures of me on my—?"

"Several times."

I said, "I'll have the mock chop."

Beans took up his menu, brought it close to his face, adjusted a nonexistent monocle. "Mock chop . . . phony burger . . . fake steak . . . " he muttered. "Is this a real fake steak, old chop? I mean old chap. Wouldn't want a bloomin' fake fake steak, wot?"

"Well, it's made out of lentils, soybeans, carrots, and kelp."

"Ah, that's exactly how my dear old mammy down in Alabammy used to make it. I'll risk that and a glass of your Disgustingly Healthy Veggie Juice Cocktail Number 2. That's Number 2, mind you, not Number 1 or Number 3. And most certainly not Number 5."

The owner hurried off.

"As I was saying," said Beans, "I've concocted a clever scheme. Now, I admit that when we separated, Juliet was a bit nasty—"

"She had the police drag you out of the house in a straitjacket and manacles—"

"That was a bit nasty, wasn't it? Ah, but despite that, Juliet, of all my many wives, really was fond of me. Yes, my son, Juliet Fairly is a sucker for the ample Katzman charm. Therefore, I intend to persuade her to give up all thought of selling this tome."

"It's going to take a hell of a lot of persuasion. They're talking about offering her something like five hundred thousand for the hardcover rights, according to this story in—"

"You underestimate my charm." Beans spread his arms wide. "Look at me—feast your orbs. I'm fit and trim again as well as completely reformed. If I put my mind to it, I can woo Juliet into abandoning the whole foolhardy venture."

"Maybe," I said, far from convinced.


The next day the agency sent me up to Seattle to do a little troubleshooting. One of our clients was introducing a new diet-aid pill called Fataway Plus, and some unexpected problems had popped up. Nearly twenty percent of the people who tried the new pills not only cut down on their food intake, they ceased eating altogether. Nearly ten percent of these people also became very militant and declared they were on hunger strikes in support of various extremely radical causes.

The Fataway advertising manager had also flown to Seattle, which caused me an extra problem. I had to give out soothing stories to the media, come up with some quick radio commercials minimizing the dangers of the pills, supervise the quiet withdrawal of every damn bottle of the stuff from the shelves, and keep anybody with a camera of any sort from getting a shot of that ad manager. Pictures of a 360-pound diet-aid executive wouldn't do us much good. All in all, I was in Seattle for ten long days. It rained a lot while I was there.

Meantime, Beans Katzman had commenced his assault on Juliet. It was, I learned from him later, a complete and absolute flop. Since throwing him out of their mansion in Beverly Hills, she'd had a high stone wall built all around the grounds. There was an electrified iron gate, and according to Beans, chunks of jagged bottle glass all along the top of the wall. When Beans, clad in his newest suit, a conservative banker's-gray model from 1971, arrived at the gates on a clear morning two days after our vegetarian lunch, he found himself being scrutinized by a video camera mounted up above the electrified gate.

"Your business, please?" inquired a metallic voice that came barking out of a speaker embedded in the stone wall.

"I've come to pay my respects to the lady of the house." Beans waved the bouquet of yellow roses he was toting at the eye of the camera.

"Name, please?"

"Don't you recognize me?" He started to reach for his wallet full of pictures. "I'm Beans Katzman."

"Ben Katzman?"

"Beans! As in 'full of!' "

A silence followed.

The camera used the time to look him up and down.

"Beans?" A new voice came out of the speaker.

"Ah, Juliet, it does this old heart good to hear your lovely dulcet—"

"Get the hell off my property or I'll call the law!"

"Juliet, my sweet, I wish merely to—"

"I'm going to count to ten. Make that fifteen, for old times' sake. I'm going to count to fifteen and then turn the dogs loose. One . . ."

"Dogs, m'love?"

"Killer dogs," amplified Juliet. "Mean and rotten killer dogs who go for the throat."

"I doubt they can get at me through the iron bars in the gate." He jiggled the bouquet up in front of the video camera. "Take a look at these posies, Juliet. Yellow roses, your favorite most—"

". . . four . . . five . . . "

Sensing it wasn't the proper moment to launch his romantic campaign, Beans bowed to the camera eye. "I'll withdraw until you're in a better mood," he announced. "You may keep the flowers."

He bounded up closer to the gate, tossed the dozen bright-yellow roses over the high iron gate. There was a sentimental note attached, and Beans hoped that might melt Juliet's heart a bit.

". . . fifteen!"

An alarm bell started ringing somewhere up near the mansion. Metal doors clanged and he heard a loud galloping noise.

Seconds later, two huge, black, and evil hounds came charging down the well-kept lawn where once, in better days, Beans had strolled hand-in-hand with Juliet. One dog flung itself, snarling and slavering, at the gate. The other dog paused to worry the roses, ripping blossoms, wrapping paper, and tender note to shreds before joining its partner at the gate.

Shrugging philosophically, Beans sauntered down to his rented car and drove home.


Beans concluded that if he couldn't launch his romantic assault on Juliet at her home, he'd have to begin his campaign elsewhere. He considered himself a master of characterization and disguise, a fact attested to by his string of photos that showed him in sundry roles. He rented, on the cuff, a chauffeur's uniform and borrowed an impressive Mercedes sedan from his onetime agent, who still owed him a few small favors. Beans took to cruising through Juliet's posh neighborhood at various hours of the day and night. A few times he risked parking near the gates of the estate.

On his third day of this scouting, he saw the gates come rattling open and Juliet come barreling out of the drive alone in a silvery Jaguar. Discreetly, he followed her. It was midday and Beans assumed she was on her way to lunch. If he casually approached her, after doffing the disguise, in a public restaurant or cocktail bar, she certainly couldn't set the cops or those dogs on him. And Beans was confident that once Juliet got an up-close look at him, her old affection would blossom once again.

It was probably while trailing his ex-wife through the narrow, winding streets that he listened to the news on the car radio and was inspired with the alternative notion that was to prove so unfortunate to him.

" . . . The Son of Satan has struck again and stabbed two to death. That story after these messages," a handsome-voiced newscaster was saying as Beans followed Juliet.

"Skip the commercials, give me the gory details," whined Beans in his adenoidal teenager voice.

After spots for SweetiSink, Fat Ed's Homecooked Frozen Pizza, Nat and Phil's, Tallman's Clothing Warehouse, and the very funeral parlor he'd be buried out of, the news of the world returned.

" . . . Santa Monica police believe the crazed self-styled Son of Satan killer has claimed two more unfortunate victims, this time in a quiet residential section of Santa Monica. Late this morning, the bodies of Roberta M. Weaver, thirty-seven, and her husband, Mark L. Weaver, forty-two, were found in the couple's Santa Monica home. Both had been stabbed numerous times, and all the usual tokens had been left behind: the grim crimson Halloween mask representing the face of the Devil, the three black candles placed at the head of each victim in small silver holders, the brand-new set of carving knives left at the feet of the final victim. The Son of Satan killer also, as has been his gruesome custom in all seven of his previous murders, left a bloody message scrawled on the Weavers' wall. In the blood of his victims, he wrote, 'Why don't you stop me?' Acting Police Chief Alan Alch says the police are—"

Shaking his head, Beans found a soothing music station. "All the goofy people hereabouts aren't in show business," he observed, returning his full attention to his former wife's car.

Juliet seemed to be heading for the ocean. She must be meeting someone for lunch at one of the beachfront restaurants along the Pacific.

Juliet didn't go to a restaurant, though. Instead, she drove down to the beach town of San Amaro, some fifteen miles below Santa Monica. She drove up into the low hills and swung into the driveway of a modest shingle cottage. As Beans drove by, he saw a man come out of the little house, run across the browning lawn, and put his arms around Juliet.

"I'll be damned," he remarked, recognizing the small blond man who was kissing his former wife.


I'd hoped to return to Los Angeles in time to sit in on Beans's audition for our Kildew Spray commercials, but another agency field job came up and I had to fly directly from Seattle to Detroit. The new trouble involved our Mother Malley's Zippy Zoop. There was evidence that some crank was visiting supermarkets in and around Detroit and tampering with packages of the new instant-soup mix. The problem was that most of the customers who got the tampered-with packages swore the soup tasted better than it ever had before. My assignment was to get a tampered package, have it analyzed, and find out what the devil the crank had added. I was also to come up with a series of radio spots designed to persuade the crank to give himself up. Our client wanted to offer him a job in the Mother Malley test kitchens. That kept me away from home an additional two weeks, and I didn't get back until after Beans was buried. I had my wife send flowers—yellow roses—but I would've liked to attend his funeral.

The day after the auditions, I phoned Beans from Detroit to find out how he'd done.

"I didn't bother to show up," he informed me, sounding unusually chipper.

"Why? Is something wrong, or—"

"Something is right, my lad," he said. "That deal I alluded to when last we dined at that compost heap masquerading as a restaurant has come through. I'm going in to sign the contracts next week, with thirteen weeks guaranteed. The tide is turning."

"Great. What is it? A sitcom?"

"It's *Amos 'n' Andy*—a new version with an all-white cast. I'm going to be the Kingfish."

"Well . . . that's terrific, Beans. And you're certain it's set?"

"Just about," he said. "The only little snag is they want a notarized letter from Juliet in which she swears she's never going to write a book about me or a movie. See, if it looks like a lot of negative stuff about me is going to come out, even though I'm completely reformed, the people behind the show feel it'll screw up the sales potential."

"You sound pretty elated," I said. "So you must've won Juliet over. Did your campaign—?"

"It was a total flop."

"Then how are you going to get her to—?"

"Juliet is carrying on a torrid romance with someone," he said. "It turns out, believe it or else, to be that gumball who's going to make the movie."

"Lonnie Sheck, Junior? But he's married to Tuffy Kash, the girl who plays the second nymphomaniac on *Outskirts of Houston*. One of our client's co-sponsors that—"

"Since ven don't married peoples fool mit a liddle hanky-panky, mine poy?"

Beans then proceeded to explain to me, mostly in his Dr. Dingledangle accent, all he'd been up to since last we'd met—how he'd tailed Juliet to the hideaway she and the producer were using in San Amaro, how he'd followed her there several times and confirmed she was in the throes of a torrid affair, how she wasn't about to cease and let Beans win her over to his cause.

"I was quite taken aback when I saw who it was Juliet was fooling around with," Beans told me, back in a near approximation of his true voice. "First Lonnie Sheck, Junior, stole my life. Now he steals my ex-wife and my chance to woo her out of the idea of publishing that damn book.

"Remember that old Fred Allen radio routine? Probably before your time. The judge is asking the defendant why he killed his rival. Turned out the dead man had borrowed this guy's money, his car, his clothes, and so on. He then swiped his best suit, and sneaking into the guy's room at night, he stole his false teeth out of the glass beside his bed. The routine ends with the poor guy saying, 'It was bad enough, Judge, him using my money and my wedding suit. It was bad enough he married my girl, using the ring I'd bought for her. It was bad enough when he drove her off on their honeymoon in my car. It was bad enough when he stopped beside me on the street and rolled down the window of my car to razz me. But, Judge, when he laughed in my face with my teeth, I up and lost my temper.' That's about how I feel, my boy."

"Wait now," I said, sensing a smug note in his voice. "You aren't planning something criminal, are you? Like blackmail?"

"Me? *Moi?* Do something *crooked?* Why, that'd break the little hearts of the millions of freckle-faced boys who look to me as a role model," he answered in his handsome-nitwit voice. "Besides, blackmail won't work."

"How do you know?"

"Let us merely say I did some nosing around. Turns out Tuffy knows about the affair and doesn't give a hoot."

"Then what's left to—?"

"Not to worry, Guv. Be assured I'm not going to miss this last chance to get back into the limelight."

"C'mon," I told him, "this isn't your last chance. If the show doesn't pan out, you'll always—"

"This one will come through," Beans assured me. He hung up.


Obviously, Beans never confided in me what his intended solution to his problem was. I'm nearly certain, though, from what he did tell me and from what came out in the papers and on television after he was shot down in the street, that my conclusions come pretty close to the truth.

After watching Juliet for a while longer, he was able to work out a fairly accurate schedule of when she and Lonnie Sheck, Junior, got together. He knew that one of the times they always got together in the cottage in San Amaro was on Thursday nights about ten. He picked Thursday night to make his move—who knows? maybe because Thursday was the night *The Funny, Funny Hour* had been on television back in the 1950s.

What Beans would do was simple. He would kill both Juliet and Lonnie. He wouldn't be caught or even suspected, because he'd make it look like the Son of Satan killer had struck again. He bought the carving knives at a cut-rate hardware store in Los Angeles, the candles at an occult bookshop out in Glendale. The devil mask, the purchasing of which would've probably made somebody suspicious, he swiped from a costume shop he used to patronize back when he was doing his show.

Beans didn't feel he'd have much trouble bringing himself to kill either of them. After all, he'd done a lot of fairly violent things in his time, back in the days when he was on booze and pills. He had himself one hell of a motive, too. Not only were Juliet and her lover trying to steal his very past from him, they were on the verge of botching up the best chance he'd ever had for a comeback. Nope, he was dead sure he could knife them both and leave a messsage in blood on the wall afterwards. Nothing to it.

To make absolutely certain he was in the proper nasty mood, Beans decided to have a few drinks before driving out to San Amaro to get rid of all his problems.

That may be why things went the way they did.


At any rate, at a few minutes before nine Beans dumped all his Son of Satan props into a cardboard box and hopped into the borrowed Mercedes. He set the box on the front passenger seat beside him and drove on up to Sunset.

"The decline and fall of the West is commencing right here," he murmured to himself as he turned onto the gaudy Strip. "Hookers and hustlers by the yard."

An ebony sports car cut in front of him and came to a sudden dead stop alongside a gaggle of six or seven young women in shorts and high heels who were congregated in front of a club called Yellow Fever.

Beans hit the brakes, yelling, "Conduct your business elsewhere, gumball!"

He smashed right into the tail of the black sports car.

The driver was a tanned man of thirty-one. He leaped free of his car and came charging back toward Beans. "You old coot, why in the bloody blue blazes don't you watch—?"

"Me? Listen you ding-a-ling gumball," boomed Beans, climbing clear of his car, "in my day, hookers and their johns did business behind closed doors."

"How'd you like to pick your choppers up off the asphalt, Gran'pappy?" inquired the young man, waving a tanned fist near Beans's nose.

"A sawed-off beach bum like—? Hey, sis, get the hell out of there!"

A very pretty young blonde, possibly mistaking Beans for a potential customer, had slid into the car by way of the door closest to the sidewalk. Giggling, she was poking around in his cardboard box. Just as she held up the devil mask, two uniformed cops drove up, stopped, and eased out of their patrol car.

"What's the frumus all about, folks?" asked the younger one. He looked just exactly like a TV cop—blond, tan, handsome, and grim.

"Nothing, officer," said the sports-car driver. "This old gentleman and I are friends and we simply stopped to exchange a few pleasant words."

Beans wasn't paying attention to the conversation. He was watching the girl stumble out of the car with the crimson mask in one hand and the set of carving knives in the other.

Both policemen saw her now.

The older officer asked, "Who does that stuff belong to?"

The girl, whose face was pale now, said, "Him. The old guy."

"Mind if we ask you a few questions, sir?" asked the younger cop.

Shaking his head, Beans moved toward the Mercedes. "Let's just forget the whole thing," he suggested over his shoulder.

"Halt, sir," ordered the young cop.

"It's him!" decided his partner. "It's the Son of Satan! We got him!"

Angry, Beans spun around to face the cops. "Don't either of you gumballs know who I am?" He started to reach inside his coat for his wallet full of pictures.

"He's going for a gun!"

Both policemen fired at him. The older cop hit him once in the stomach. His handsome partner got Beans twice in the chest.

As I said, they realized their mistake after a day or so—but it was too late to do Beans much good. Juliet was already giving him his fancy send-off.

# JOYCE HARRINGTON

# DEATH OF A PRINCESS

"I think I know who killed her," the old gentleman whispered. The candles flickered, shooting distorted shadows across the bare stage. "I think I know the one man behind it all. They've tried to hush it up, make it seem like the inevitable result of old age. She wasn't that old. She had a lot of good years left in her."

"She's not dead yet," the boy muttered fiercely. "Tell me who you think it is. We'll go and talk to him. We'll make him save her."

"She's dead, son. She's dead. Nothing can save her now. She's as good as in that coffin over there."

The old man laid a gnarled hand on the boy's shoulder, and they both glanced across the stage to where the black coffin rested on two sawhorses. The candles gleaming at its head and foot provided the only light on the stage, and soon they would be guttering out. The backstage area and the void beyond the proscenium lay in thick, dusty blackness.

"Tell me," the boy insisted.

The old man shifted in his creaking folding chair and leaned across the space between them. He whispered a name in the boy's ear.

The boy leaped to his feet. "But that's impossible! We talked to him already. He promised."

"So he did. And his promises put everyone's fears to rest. The few who cared went about their business thinking she was safe. Everyone but us. Now all we can do is be her chief mourners."

"I can't believe it," the boy murmured. "How did you find out?"

"Work it out for yourself. Ask yourself who benefits. He wants her property. It's a valuable bit of land. He's a big man in this town. He can get just about anything he wants. Not much you and I can do to stop him. He'll get away with it, all right."

"It's criminal!" the boy shouted, his voice eddying away through the darkened house. "He's a liar, a cheat; and—and a murderer! We'll write to the Governor."

"We already did that."

"Well, let's telephone him. Let's do it right now." The boy dashed to the edge of the stage and started down the steps at its side.

"Hold on, son!" the old man called. "You're young, but you'll be a lot older, and maybe even wiser, before this business is finished. The Governor knows what's going on here, and he's not about to interfere. Now come back here and sit down, and let's get on with this wake. Show some respect for the dead."

The boy sloped reluctantly back to his chair, adjusting the black armband that had slipped down ihe sleeve of his jacket.

"I remember," the old gentleman began in a soft voice; "I remember her in her young days. Oh, she was a beauty then. All decked out in red velvet. We were all in love with her, and she entertained us royally. I think we were a little astonished that she'd settled in among us. This was just a sleepy little river town, and she was bright and lively and sophisticated.

"The riverboats used to stop here in those days, and people would come from far and wide just to see her. Even from as far away as Pittsburgh. Well, I know that doesn't seem like much nowadays when you can get to Pittsburgh in twenty minutes on that dinky little puddle jumper that flies out of here. But the riverboats were a way of life then, gracious and stately and fun for small boys pretending to be Mark Twain. You can't pretend to be anything but nervous strapped into a low-flying tin can for twenty minutes of bone-jarring and tooth-rattling." The old man shook his head.

"There's still the *Delta Queen*," said the boy.

"Yes. There's still the *Delta Queen*. Once or twice a year." The old man sighed. "To get back to our Princess. She entertained us royally, as I said, and all the great ones visited her. The Barrymores, and Mrs. Fiske, George Arliss—I have his autograph—Jeanne Eagels, and even the Divine Sarah. I was just a boy then, younger than you are now, but I was faithful to our Princess and never missed a single one of her entertainments."

"Tell me about the magicians."

"The magicians, is it? Well, she was very partial to the magicians. Always gave them a fine reception. Houdini, Blackstone, Elmo the Magnificent, who was a dwarf but had some pretty incredible tricks up his tiny sleeve. Lots of others, all forgotten except by her and me. Now there'll be only me, and I won't last too much longer."

The boy started to protest, but the old man sat stiffly alert in his chair and cried, "Hush, listen! It's beginning!"

The two craned upward, searching the dim decaying catwalks, the frayed ropes and rusty pulleys, the shreds of rotting canvas for the first breakthrough—the beginning of the end. There came a faint scraping sound, a thump, another thump, and then a muffled crash, followed by a shower of gritty dust. The boy blinked and swore, and if a tear or two rolled down the old man's cheek it was naturally because of the dust in his eyes. One of the candles flickered and went out.

A door at the back of the house flew open and a shaft of daylight flooded the aisle.

"Henry! Mama says come home right away. Mama says you're playing the fool and embarrassing her. Anyway, lunch is ready."

"My sister," the boy apologized. "Go home, Jessie," he called out.

"Tell Mama I can't come right now. I have to stay with Mr. Cooper—and the Princess."

"Mama says you're crazy and he's crazy and the Sheriff's gonna come and arrest you both and put you in the loony bin if the roof don't cave in on you first."

"Maybe you'd better go, boy." The old man sighed. "There might be trouble."

"No, sir. I'll stick it out. Maybe it won't do the Princess any good, but I wouldn't feel right about leaving now."

Another crash reverberated through the house, and somewhere backstage a grinding, groaning sound began, accompanied by the tinkle of breaking glass. The girl in the doorway shrieked and began hopping about on one foot and then the other.

"Henry! You better come right now. You're just dopey enough to let yourself get buried alive because *he* says so. I'm gettin' out of here."

"That's right, girlie. You skedaddle, and I'll take care of our two heroes."

The shaft of light from the doorway was perceptibly diminished by the bulk of the man who now appeared.

The girl skipped away, chanting, "Henry is a hero. Henry is a hero. Yah, yah, yippee, yah, yah."

Sheriff Gaines lumbered down the aisle, not speaking until he reached the foot of the stage. Then he growled, "Alden Cooper. You're an old fool." He paused and spat toward the first row of moth-eaten seats. "But you're a brave old fool, and I admire that. Take my advice and git on out of here. You and the boy both. The Princess is a dead duck and there's nothing you can do about it."

"She may be dead, Sheriff, but she's no duck. A swan, maybe, or a bird of paradise, but never a duck."

The old man's quiet reproach was followed by a clatter of falling plaster, and another choking cloud of dust floated toward them from the back of the stage.

"Alden," the Sheriff pleaded, "if you don't budge, I'll have to arrest you for your own safety. I've got a warrant in my pocket. I don't want to do it, but the big man is after your hide. You've caused him one heap of trouble."

"Sheriff," the boy piped up, "they won't go ahead while we're still in here. Will they?"

"Boy, according to them they don't know you're in here. And if you are, you're trespassing. That's a fine of five hundred dollars. Each."

"I haven't got any five hundred dollars." The boy wavered. "But I'm staying as long as Mr. Cooper stays." He folded his arms, pressed his rump more firmly to his chair, and glared at the Sheriff.

There was an awkward pause while the Sheriff fiddled with the zipper on his flight jacket and the old man retreated into his thoughts. At last he spoke.

"Maude Adams flew here, and we all shouted, 'I believe!' Maybe I should have scoffed and said, 'She's just hanging from a wire and I don't believe at all.' Maybe there's nothing left to believe in. Maybe I am just an old fool hanging on to a world of make-believe. The real world has no room for Princesses anymore."

He rose, suddenly seeming much older. "Come on, boy. You take one end of the coffin and I'll take the other. This wake is now declared officially over. The interment is about to begin."

The Sheriff grinned, relieved. "I thought you'd see the light, Alden. No point in standing in the way of progress."

But the boy leaped to his feet in agonized protest. "Mr. Cooper! You can't give up now. You said so yourself. 'We'll fight this to the bloody end.' That's what you said. Don't desert her now. Please, Mr. Cooper."

"This is the end, son. Unless I miss my guess, those catwalks are going to come loose from their moorings in a matter of minutes. Your mother wouldn't thank me if this turned out to be your funeral as well."

The pounding and crashing on the roof had continued unabated throughout the old man's deliberations.

"Well, all right. If you say so. But not because of my mother," the boy mumbled. But then he brightened. "We'll take the coffin out on the street. We'll sit down with it and stop the traffic. We'll make people notice. We can do it, Mr. Cooper."

"Come on, you two," the Sheriff growled, back once more in his official manner. "Blow that candle out, Alden. Don't want to start a fire, do you?"

The old man blew out the last candle, and the stage was left in darkness. Then, guided by the shaft of light from the open door, they heaved the coffin up the aisle and out into the mild spring afternoon.

The boy's hopes of creating a demonstration or at least a traffic jam were doomed to failure. Traffic had been diverted and the sidewalk fenced off. The few passersby on the other side of the street hurried by and for the most part ignored the boy and the old man seated side by side on a coffin in the middle of the street. Those who noticed them snickered and made joking remarks.

At first the boy waved a crudely lettered placard and exhorted the passing shoppers and businessmen to SAVE THE PRINCESS. But when this had no effect, he subsided onto the coffin beside the old man and grimly watched the progress of the toilers on the roof.

All afternoon they watched, and were watched in turn by a young policeman ordered by the Sheriff to see that they committed no further mischief. At last, when the sun was setting on the chimneys of the western side of town, the sledgehammers approached the noble gray stone pediment that arched across the brow of the forsaken building.

Chip by chip, curlicue by curlicue, letter by letter, the legend that had proudly informed one and all that here stood the PRINCESS THEATER— 1896 fell crashing to the sidewalk below.

"Well," said the old man, "I guess it's time to go home. I can only hope that whatever building takes the place of the Princess will be worthy of the sacrifice. Perhaps we can arrange to have a plaque commemorating her birth and death placed on the front of the new building. We can start work on that tomorrow."

He patted the boy's shoulder and turned to the young policeman who still watched them attentively, on guard against possible misdemeanors. "Tell me, young man. In your official capacity, have you any news of what the powers that be in this town plan to erect on this property?"

The young man gawped at him and cleared his throat. "You mean what they gonna build here?"

"Indeed that is what I mean. I trust it will be a fitting memorial to the gracious lady whose death agony we have just witnessed."

"Hell, Mr. Cooper," the young officer replied. "They ain't gonna build nothin' here. It's gonna be a parking lot. We surely need it."

# A SLIP OF THE LIP

Harry Boswell, Detective Third Grade, was slow. He thought slow, talked slow, and moved slow. On the other hand, nobody had ever accused him of not being thorough.

Take music, for instance. He played the fife in the police band and the clarinet in his neighborhood chamber-music group. He could handle a trumpet, a sax, or a flageolet, and he could tell you right off the difference between a pommer and a bombard—if any. All of which bears, more or less, on the triple murders of Bucconi, Santangelo, and Rodman.

Janet Boswell, however, was as quick as her husband was slow, and her approach to most matters was at the opposite end of the rainbow from Harry's. Still, they had many things in common, and music in particular. While Harry was a woodwind specialist, Janet went in for strings, and night after night they worked through all the cello-and-clarinet duets they could find. And they might have gone on like that forever, she with her loveliness huddled over the fingerboard of her cello and he sitting a couple of feet away and playing at and with her as the music moved him.

They were not particularly good musicians, either of them, but the interest they shared kept them close, and they spent their leisure listening or playing: all of which transcended the need to talk. For talk breeds argument, and argument can ruin a marriage—as it almost did theirs.

The trouble started with the Bucconi murder, a knife job that occurred right in front of their own building.

"Harry," Janet said on the first day of the investigation, "you must have seen him—you must have noticed things that nobody else did. You must have some inside information."

"I didn't and I don't."

"But there has to be something. Think about it, Harry."

"What for?"

"Because it's a challenge."

"Why?"

"Because it happened right here—on your own doorstep."

"It happened in the courtyard, and I never met the man."

"Harry, I just don't understand you."

"Agreed," he said. And that evening his clarinet and her cello stayed in their respective cases while Janet and Harry argued. Or at least, they argued until 9:00 P.M., when the New York Symphony came on.

The rift between them, however, was not deep, and the following night they played a Pape duet and merely mentioned the Bucconi case in passing. After all, what was a murder compared with a duet for cello and clarinet? And since Harry had only a small part in the homicide investigation, the next evening he was able to take his usual place in the chamber-music group that met every second Wednesday night.

● ● ●

The following week Santangelo was killed. Like Bucconi, he had been stabbed, and, like Bucconi's, his body was found in the courtyard of the Edward Everett Hale Housing Development, where the Boswells lived. That was too much for Janet.

"You knew him," she said to Harry. "You rode up and down in the elevator with him."

"I never did."

"How can you be certain?"

"Because we're on the third floor," he said, "and I walk."

"You walk down, but not up," Janet said knowingly. "We'll all be killed. There's a murderer in this building and you won't even take the trouble to find him."

"I," Harry reminded her, "am not on the homicide squad."

"Does that mean you don't care who gets killed? It might be me."

Harry studied her. Her skin was fair, her eyes were blue, and her hair was the color of raw honey. "They're pretty sure there's a gang war behind this, so you're safe."

"You're telling me gangsters don't kill women?"

"Not without a motive. Why would they harm you?"

"How can anybody be safe when there's a madman with a dagger around?"

The madman theory was reinforced when the third murder victim turned out to be one John Rodman. Until then, the inhabitants of the housing development had leaned to the belief that the murders were the work of an Italian terrorist organization that pursued its enemies around the world and exacted vengeance once a week, with the precision of a metronome. But Rodman wasn't Italian.

Except that he was. The police discovered that John Rodman had been christened Giovanni Romano and had Americanized his name. As a result, the community was again convinced that the Italian terrorist organization was responsible and that ordinary people were helpless against it. Anti-Italian feeling was widespread, and to combat it and to preserve the good name of Italo-Americans, the Christopher Columbus

Society posted a $10,000 reward for anyone solving the triple murders. And by special dispensation, police officers were eligible.

"You're in a particularly good position to get that reward," Janet told her husband. "You can speak to people in the building. You're a neighbor—they'll tell you things that they wouldn't tell a police officer."

"But I *am* a police officer."

"*They* don't know it."

Harry looked down at his shoes and studied them carefully. "I think they'd guess," he said.

"Try it."

"It wouldn't do much good." Harry pondered the matter. "If I took the elevator," he said, "so did you. And if they'd speak to me as a neighbor, they'd talk to you too."

"But I'm not a policeman," Janet said.


The murders haunted both of them, and their marriage was not as before. Janet was just as comely, Harry was just as slow, and they played the same duets as before, but the pucker had gone out of the vinegar. Life was flat—unaccountably, the world had changed.

The wheels of justice, however, were turning, and certain facts emerged. It had taken months of intensive, painstaking investigation to work them out, but there they were—incontrovertible proof, beautifully analyzed and perfectly dovetailed.

Thanks to the combined efforts of the local police, the state Bureau of Investigation, Interpol, and the police departments of Naples and Palermo, plus an assist from Scotland Yard and the French Sûreté, the story emerged of a vendetta that had begun with a seduction in a small Sicilian village and ended in the three slayings at the Edward Everett Hale Housing Development.

Blowing his soul into the reed that produced the soft, fluid notes of a Beethoven sonata transcribed for clarinet, Harry thought dreamily of the idyll back in that village, and he seemed to see Maria Turano, dark-eyed and lovely, walking barefoot to the village pump, where she filled the pails she'd brought from the stone cottage where her family lived.

Harry was convinced that every young man in the village came rushing to the pump hoping to earn the privilege of carrying Maria's burden back to her house. But Francesco always won the honor, just as he won the privilege of walking alongside her in the village square on the warm, balmy evenings that quickened the blood and sent wild, heady impulses coursing along the nerve paths to end up in summer madness. Exactly how the pair evaded the eyes of their parents and managed a moonlight tryst no one knew, but Maria's pregnancy was ample evidence of what had happened.

Surely Francesco must have been ready to cherish and wed—but what was he? A shepherd who wasted his time blowing on a reed when he should have been tending his flocks. Although a born musician, he was unworthy of the hand and soul of Maria. As a result, three of her cousins set upon Francesco and did to him what had been done to Abelard so many centuries before. And having done this, they fled to America.

There was evidence to the effect that someone in Francesco's family had been notified, and it was also on the record that his family was spoken of as a musical one. The heredity of Pan and his way with a reed was spread liberally through the entire tribe, but with that trickle of information—the murderer was a musician, and he was of Italian extraction—the trail ended.

Meanwhile, the $10,000 reward hung like an Aeolian harp in the branches of a eucalyptus tree, and Janet, sitting on the couch and holding hands with Harry while they watched the great orchestras of the world perform on TV, spoke often of the case.

"To think he's living right here in this building and the police are doing nothing!" she said one evening while they were listening to the All-American Symphony Orchestra. Her breast heaved with emotion, but eased off as she listened to the opening strains of Schubert's *Unfinished Symphony*. She stared at the conductor, but some gesture of his aroused her indignation and she returned to her theme. "Why," she said, "don't the police go through the whole building apartment by apartment and make people tell them the truth?"

"You can't just walk into a house and start asking questions," Harry said. "You need a warrant."

"If I ever see that man in the elevator," Janet said furiously, "I won't bother with all your rules."

"How will you know him?"

"From his eyes. They'll be like ice, and I'll shiver all the way down my spine."

"I doubt it," Harry said. "Shh! Just listen."

"If you could only—"

But Harry grabbed her hand and sat up excitedly. "Look!" he said. "Look!"

"At what?"

"At him. Don't you notice anything?"

"Nothing in particular. Why? What?"

"His lip," Harry said in an awed voice. "His upper lip!"

"What of it?"

"He's a fraud," Harry said slowly. "All-American Orchestra! Nonsense!"

His doubts triggered off the investigation into the background of Owen Frowley, clarinetist. Born in Omaha, Nebraska, he had studied wind instruments at the Longy Institute. He'd been a member of the WMFH Symphony for three years and had appeared as guest soloist with a great many different groups.

Harry studied the man's rap sheet, made various phone calls, and then went to talk to the Chief. As a result, one week later, Owen Frowley—Francesco—was arrested and charged with the three homicides.

That night Harry came home wearily, but with a check for $10,000.

"It took a lot of work," he said. "He'd covered everything but the one piece of evidence that finally broke him."

"What was that?"

"The thing I noticed in the first place. He claimed he was an American and had studied at the Longy Institute under James Weirton, now deceased. He figured it would be hard to prove he hadn't studied at the Longy when his supposed teacher was dead. He thought he was safe."

"But how—"

"At the Longy, as well as everywhere else in this country, we're taught to blow with the reed pressed on the lower lip—but in Sicily they blow with the reed pressed against the upper lip. So I knew he came from somewhere in Italy, and Sicily was a good guess."

"But suppose he claimed he'd had an Italian teacher before he even went to the Longy—then what?"

Harry considered the point carefully. "I never thought of that," he said finally. "But neither did he."

# GERALD TOMLINSON

# SNOOKERED

At least, the alumni didn't stage torchlight parades and burn the coach in effigy. Spence College was too small for that. Not that the alumni, as well as the faculty and students, wouldn't have liked a winning football team. There was plenty of discouragement in all their hearts, which was understandable in view of the fact that the Bulldogs' best record over the past decade was 3–7–1. Even 0–11 seasons were not unknown.

The coach had been around a long time and, despite his dismal performance, was in little danger of losing his job. He smoked the same kind of briar pipe that the revered professor of chemistry did, he went to the fraternities' beer busts, and he seemed to have adjusted well to perpetual defeat.

Mark DeVore had not adjusted well. He saw things differently. DeVore, whose title was Publications Director at the Alumni Office but who also acted as the Sports Information man, was sick unto death of phoning in 35–0 scores to *The Times* so that well-to-do alumni would see Spence College's name in print—if they ignored the alphabetical list of Midwestern winners and scanned the losers' column instead.

Ten years out of Spence College himself, DeVore saw little future in his job. While the football coach beamed and guzzled beer, Mark DeVore fumed. He had taken the job as an escape from teaching junior high school English. His wife liked the little Ohio college town better than she had liked Cleveland. Everyone at Spence claimed to be pleased with the work DeVore was doing.

But he hated it. He wanted to write, really write; write creatively. Churning out little tan brochures that begged for money held scant appeal for him. Oh, now and then he could do a piece of amusing nostalgia for the alumni newspaper, but on the whole he felt his life was becoming as dull and pointless as the copy he produced. He remembered that H. L. Mencken had written about those who believed "they would have graced a profession far gaudier." That was how DeVore felt.

And then he had an inspiration.

It was not the kind of inspiration that leads one to write *Moby Dick* or even *How to Coach Winning Football*. It was one that led instead to self-satisfaction, to the feeling that there was, after all, something he could control personally.

What he did, shorn of all its embellishments, was create a football team—an electrifying but imaginary football team. He also created a league. And a star.


The first step was hardly more than a joke. On the Saturday that Spence College lost to tiny, oft-beaten Olander, he picked up the phone, called *The Times*, the Columbus *Bulletin*, and the half-dozen others on his regular list, and forthwith reported something happier than the truth. Speaking factually, he would have informed them, "Olander 34, Spence 7." Instead he said, with a certain touch of pride, "Avery College 56, Williamson Tech 0."

Now, a glance at any standard list of American colleges and universities will show you that Avery College doesn't exist. Neither does Williamson Tech. But they sound as if they *could* exist—and, sure enough, come Sunday morning in *The Times*, the *Bulletin*, and other newspapers, they *did* exist. Every sports page picked up DeVore's bogus listing under Midwest, a location he had specified so as to make all their lives easier.

Emboldened by his success, he ignored the Spence Bulldogs' traditional losing effort the next Saturday too, and gave Avery College a comfortable 27-0 win over Braxton A&M. For the final game of the season (he regretted not having developed his team sooner), he phoned in a 44-0 win over Thayer College.

He followed up the Avery–Thayer game with a brief press release, mailed on Avery College stationery ($20.00 for a hundred letterhead sheets and envelopes). He sent this press release, with a post-office-box address, from nearby Wheelersburg. It read: "Avery College, winless at the start of the current season, ended in a blaze of gridiron glory by taking its last three games from strong, favored opponents: Williamson Tech, Braxton A&M, and Thayer College. Coach Tab Howell said most of the credit belongs to a sensational freshman running back, Wayne Snooker, from Bull Shoals, Arkansas. 'He's just phenomenal,' enthused Howell. 'You'll be hearing a lot about him next season.' "

Was Tab ever right!

Avery College started the next season with a 38-0 trouncing of Ligonier College. A three-line press release on Wayne Snooker followed, as well it might. Snooker had rushed for 278 yards.

Two of the newspapers DeVore phoned didn't print his scores, nor did they run his press release. He began to wonder. Had someone checked? He hoped not. This was the first season in quite a long time that he expected to enjoy.

Partial reassurance came in the form of a note from a TV station in Akron. It arrived in the post-office box on Friday just before the Avery College Phantoms' big game with arch-rival Braxton A&M. It said: "Hey, Avery C. No phone? That's what I call small. Who's this Snooker? Available for interview with top Akron sportscaster Bob Rice? Please phone." It was signed *"Bob Rice."*

"Hey, Bob," he said with breezy assurance. "Mickey Devlin here. Sports publicity for Avery College. Where's Avery, you ask? Southern Ohio, that's where. The Phantoms. Yeah, sure, I know. It's a fairly new school. Mostly West Virginia colleges in the league. Okay, so it's no Oberlin, but never mind the accreditation. Think football. We're in the Monongahela Conference. We're tiny, sure, but hey, Bob, we're coming up in the world. And you should see this guy Snooker. I mean, he's Big Ten caliber. He's just running all over everybody down here. An interview? Uh, well, I don't know, Bob, he's not—let me say this—he's not too articulate. You don't care? Well, if you don't care, if you're willing to interview a bump on a log, sure, why not?"

They set a time for the interview, three days away.


He had to produce a live body. Fortunately, this guy wouldn't have to say much.

He told his wife there was an annual convention of small-college publicists in Akron and that he'd be staying at Akron's Holiday Inn Downtown for the next two nights.

The drive north on Sunday couldn't have been more pleasant. It was a golden autumn day with a slight bluish haze, the kind of day on which he had been interviewed for his job at Spence College. He sometimes wondered if the weather makes a difference in life-changing decisions like that. If there had been a chilling rain, as there often is during the fall in southern Ohio, would he have finished the interview, slipped into his trench coat, pulled on his gloves, and said, "Sorry, but I can do this same kind of work in Chula Vista"?

No matter. He was now a fixture at Spence College, although busily publicizing not the Bulldogs but the Avery College Phantoms, along with their backwoods backfield sensation, Wayne Snooker.

All he had to do was find a plausible Wayne Snooker. He had taken $300 from the Spence petty-cash box to cover the trip and the cost of Snooker's TV debut. He knew it was wrong, illegal even, but the mood was on him. The day before, Avery had buried Braxton A&M under a 54-0 score. Although Snooker was billed as a tiger on offense, he seemed to be inspiring the hitherto shaky defense as well. Since Snooker's rise to stardom, not only had he rushed for phenomenal yardage on the Phantoms' behalf, but no team had crossed the goal line against the new Avery powerhouse.

After DeVore checked in at the Holiday Inn, he wandered down to the bar to have a martini and a look around. No Snooker there—mostly uptight-looking business types who must have read somewhere that you are what you wear.

He drove to a run-down downtown bar. It was called the Terminal

Tavern—appropriately, he thought, because most of the customers looked as if they were lost cases who probably made it their bounden duty to arrive at three in the afternoon and leave at three in the morning. Some were drinking cheap wine, some beer, and a few were putting away boilermakers. It was not the kind of place where you ordered Kir or Perrier or a Singapore Sling. DeVore ordered a double shot of bar whiskey. It brought tears to his eyes and fire to his stomach.

He began sorting out the clientele. In general, the gang here was too old. Pensioners maybe. Vets on full disability. Some Social Security graybeards. Not very many recruits for the Avery College Phantoms.

But there were two. One sat four stools down from him and gazed with a wise philosopher's eyes into his muscatel. He couldn't be over twenty-one, but he looked as if he had been studying that vintage for most of his life. He was pink all over, but not baby pink or sissy pink— more like boozehound pink. And even pink, he looked tough.

DeVore walked over to him. "Can I get you a refill?"

"You queer?"

"No, I'm a businessman. I want to talk business."

"If I wanted to talk business, I'd go down to the union hall. Get lost."

"It's worth a hundred dollars for ten minutes' work."

"And a lifetime worrying that my old lady will see the pictures? That it? No thanks, Mac."

At this, DeVore gave up on Kid Pink and tried the guy at the other end of the bar. Number Two didn't look a whole lot like his mental picture of Wayne Snooker. He looked more like Lou Costello, but at least he was the right age.

"Mind if I join you?" The stool beside Lou was empty.

"It's a free country."

Lou had a double-shot glass in front of him which he let sit there until the beer chaser arrived. Then he tossed them both off in two flicks of his wrist and used the third flick to point to the two empty glasses. "Barkeep!" A pile of bills crumpled in front of him proved his solvency.

"My name's Mickey Devlin," DeVore said to Lou.

"Is that so? Did I miss you on the *Today* show or something?"

"No, no. Just trying to be friendly. I'm a stranger in town."

"We're all strangers in town, Mick. If we weren't, we'd find other ways to blow our bankrolls."

"Well, let me say this, Mr.—"

"John."

"That's your last name?"

"You writing a biography? The name's John. That's all you need to know to talk to me. Call me John and I'll call you Mick. And if we get tired of talking, we'll clam up."

DeVore thought about trying another bar. John here and Kid Pink down the way were the only two prospects, and they didn't look like solid-gold possibilities; but time was a factor to consider. He had to find Wayne Snooker tonight. The interview was to be taped at eleven in the morning. He wasn't going to locate a running back after sunup tomorrow. He needed him now. He decided to stick with John.

"John, I've got a problem."

"Me too. I drink too much. I'll bet I look sober to you right now, don't I?"

"More or less."

"I'm loop-legged. If I stand up at this precise moment in time, I fall down. Humpty Dumpty. And I'm still ordering boilermakers. What's your problem?"

"I need somebody to go on television for me. To get himself interviewed."

John whistled. "This ain't Central Casting, Mick. I think you're in the wrong church, wrong pew."

"Don't be so sure. This guy doesn't have to say anything."

"That should be a dynamite interview. Pure TNT."

"This guy I need will be impersonating a football player. A running back, not much of a talker."

"I played football once. Warren G. Harding High. I was no good. Drank too much, I guess." He tossed off the whiskey.

"Look, John. The interview's at eleven in the morning with Bob Rice."

"Bob Rice!" He tossed off the beer.

"Right."

"He's big stuff, Mick. The local sports guru. Who does he think he's interviewing?"

"A football star from a little downstate college."

"What's the scam?"

"The guy in question doesn't exist. There's no such player. I made him up as a joke, after I made up his college. Now I've got to produce him for TV. You interested?"

"You mean I get interviewed by Big Bob Rice? I just nod and smile and say I owe it all to my mom and my kid sister? And yeah, I can run the hundred in nine flat, but shucks, half the fellows in Woodchuck Hollow can do the same?"

"John, that's great. You can do it. Just don't ham it up too much. Let me show you this guy's press clippings. His name is Wayne Snooker, by the way. That's really the main thing to remember. But it can't hurt to know all the rest, everything there is to know about him. You can make up more if you want. But it's got to be believable. Otherwise, no hundred bucks."

"Hundred bucks? Hey, Mick, I was about to do it for nothing. You just watch Wayne Snooker tomorrow. King of the gridiron. Fourteen yards a carry. Now, for tonight, could you just ease me off this stool and maybe hang on to my arm till we hit the cool air?"

"John, I don't want to lose you between now and tomorrow. I think you'd better come back to the Holiday Inn with me and sleep there. I asked for a single, but I got two big double beds. I want to make sure Wayne Snooker is on hand for his big break."

"You're the boss, boss. I'm a valuable property. Hey, I used to have a good arm. Do I ever pass for touchdowns?"

"No. You just run."

"Got it." He sagged as he stood, but DeVore held him upright and walked him, left foot, right foot, left foot, to the car.


Sober, fresh-faced, a little blubbery for a backfield sensation, John No-Name, a.k.a. Wayne Snooker, wowed Bob Rice and the crew at the videotaping session—not to mention Mark DeVore. The guy had read his press clippings in the motel room, and he fielded every question well. He embellished his story to a turn. Yes, he was just a poor country boy who'd picked up running speed as a kid by showing his heels to angry, snorting bulls. His high school was so small they played five-man football—"if you've ever heard of that, Mr. Rice"—and the real star of the team was a big crybaby named Goodykoontz, who was later killed in a car crash while running a load of white lightning down to Little Rock. No, young Snooker didn't have a girlfriend; he was too busy getting a good education at Avery College. His ambition was to teach phys. ed. back home in Bull Shoals. A pro career? Naw, he was too little, and— pinching the roll of fat above his belt—he figured he liked the training table too well.

At the end of the interview, Bob Rice congratulated Snooker on the air and then thanked DeVore off the air for bringing his star all the way up to Akron. ("Not articulate?" he whispered, as if the two of them shared some kind of happy secret.)

DeVore said, "They'll like this interview back home in Wheelersburg."

"You tell 'em all down in Wheelersburg I said hello," Rice boomed, turning to greet an angular seven-foot beanstalk who DeVore assumed played basketball.

He pressed a hundred dollars into the palm of his own star, who seemed reluctant to take it. John shook his head, muttering, "That's a snootful of bar whiskey."

DeVore stayed in Akron overnight and checked out the next morning. He drove south at a leisurely pace. Since Wheelersburg was not far off his route, he decided to look in on the Avery College p.o. box. He didn't expect to find anything, but surprises abounded. There was a card in the box (blank but beckoning), and two plainclothes policemen were hovering nearby.

"Mr. Devlin?"

"You must be mistaken," he said, trying to keep down an unreasoning panic. "My name is Mark DeVore. I have identification."

"Did you know Wayne Snooker?"

He didn't like the sound of that word *did*. "Snooker?"

"There's no need to playact, Mr. Devlin. Bob Rice can identify you easily enough. He gave us this box number."

"Why?"

"That's what we'd like to know. All we know at the moment is that Wayne Snooker was murdered outside the Terminal Tavern at about two this morning. He was rolled. His wallet, if he had one, is missing. He had no identification."

DeVore started to say, "There's no Wayne Snooker, fellows," but instead found himself asking, "If there was no identification, how did you know who he was?"

Both cops looked incredulous. "That wasn't much of a problem," the older one said. "Half the force saw Snooker on last night's Bob Rice show. As soon as we turned the body over, Cy Jefferson, or maybe it was O'Duffy, says, 'It's him. It's that football player who runs the hundred in nine flat and looks like a butterball. What's his name?'

"O'Duffy says, 'Snooker, isn't it? Zane—no—Wayne Snooker.' "

"So he was rolled," DeVore said. "That's all."

"Your star running back, the great Wayne Snooker, was rolled at the Terminal Tavern in Akron. *That's all?* That's plenty. And where were you, Coach?"

"At the Holiday Inn Downtown."

"Any witnesses?"

Any witnesses? Now, there was a poser. DeVore decided to avoid any more snappy comebacks. "Are you arresting me?"

"We're taking you in for questioning, Mr. Devlin. Or is it DeVore? Whichever. Young Snooker said some very strange things at the bar last night. He claimed you were his college coach, his mentor, the man who taught him all he knows about football. Which is practically everything. Bob Rice says phooey to all that—you're in publicity. But the little running back, he said you're the Avery College coach, the downstate genius who outbid Arkansas and Ohio State for his services. He said you taught him a vicious trick of the running game, something called the Slashback Maneuver, that can break collarbones like matchsticks. Said he broke a few guys' bones himself—two in last year's game against Williamson Tech."

DeVore said, "I can explain everything."

"You can? You think so?" The younger cop sounded doubtful. "Snooker said you'd kill him if he ever got caught boozing it up. It's bad for the wind, he said. Keeps those legs from pumping, too. That's what Cal Miller, the Terminal's bartender, overheard. Cal got quite an earful last night. Your running back really held forth. Bought a few rounds for the regulars."

"Look," DeVore said quietly, "there is no Wayne Snooker. There never was. I made him up."

The cops showed no sign of being impressed.

"There's a body in the Akron morgue," said the older cop flatly. "He's been identified by a dozen of our men and a TV sportscaster as the football player Wayne Snooker. Do you think we made *him* up?"

DeVore went with them without argument. He wasn't actually worried—not yet. He could explain. He really could. But it began to look as if the homecoming game with Thayer College would have to be canceled. Too bad. He figured the Avery Phantoms to win it by a thumping 63-0.

# HENRY SLESAR

# THE LAST ESCAPE

They lashed the heavy braided cord about Ferlini's wrists and knotted it tightly. Of the two men, the smaller was the more belligerent; he yanked and tugged until the cord seemed to bite through flesh. Grunting, they put the leg irons on his ankles, slamming the thick metal locks shut and testing their security. Finally, panting with their exertions, they stood over their victim and seemed smugly satisfied with his helplessness.

Then the woman was putting the screen in front of Ferlini's bound body. In less than a minute, it was thrown aside by Ferlini himself, the cord and the irons upraised triumphantly in his outstretched hands.

The audience of the small supper club gasped, and then exploded into tumultuous applause. Ferlini glowed at the sound of it. He was fair-skinned, almost albino; even the desert sunshine failed to alter his color; but an audience approbation could tint his cheeks with the red flush of gratified vanity.

The two volunteers from the audience, shaking their heads and grinning sheepishly, returned to their tables and their jeering companions, and the six-piece band swung into a traveling theme. Wanda, Ferlini's wife and professional partner, moved mechanically across the floor to pick up the screen and carry it backstage. There were some catcalls and a scattering of light applause, but she knew it was only in appreciation of her bare-legged costume. She was over forty, and her face was dependent on increasing layers of theatrical makeup for its passable beauty, but her legs were still long, lithe, and without blemish.

On her way to the dressing room, Baggett stepped in front of her and displayed his soulful eyes. "Let me help," he said, putting his hand on the screen.

"It's all right," Wanda whispered. "You better not, Tommy."

"They liked him tonight, didn't they?"

She frowned, putting cracks in the thick makeup. "It's that kind of crowd," she shrugged. "They'll like you too."

"Thanks," Baggett, an aging crooner, said drily.

"No, I didn't mean it that way." She placed the screen against a concrete wall and swayed toward him, her eyes dreamy. "You know what I think of you, Tommy. Your singing, I mean."

"Is that all you mean?"

"I better go," Wanda said.

When she entered the dressing room, she found her husband in a good mood, and it was the mood she liked least. He was staring into the mirror and rubbing his shoulders vigorously with a towel, his face split into a wide smile that showed every one of his large, strong teeth. "Yeah, it was good tonight, it was good," he said happily. "I could have gotten out of steel boxes tonight, that's how I felt. You see that little guy?" He guffawed and slammed the dressing table with his palm. "Little fella thought he was gonna fix me. You see how tight he worked the rope? I tell you, the little guys, they're the worst. It's a pleasure to fool 'em."

He swung around and looked at his wife, who was staring at nothing. He made fists of his big hands and flexed his exaggerated muscles, swelling out his chest to display the vast expansion that was so important to his art. "Look at that, hah—will you look at that? You think anybody'd ever take me for forty-six? What do you say?"

"You're a Greek god," Wanda said bitterly. "Only speaking of Greeks, we're invited out to dinner tonight. Roscoe's treat."

"Ah, that Phil, he spoils my appetite," Ferlini said, still with a grin.

"You hear him talk, the escape business is dead. He should have seen that crowd tonight, that's all I say. He'd know different."

"He booked you in this job, didn't he? He ought to know if it's dead or not." She yawned, and began to change into street clothes. Then she remembered something, and came to her husband's dressing table, wiping at her makeup. "Listen, when we see Phil tonight, don't start up again about that water business, huh? I'm sick of hearing about that."

"Aah," Ferlini said, waving his hand. "You're gettin' old, Wanda, that's your trouble."

"Look who's talking! You're no chicken either, Joe, and don't forget it!"

He turned to look at her, grinning shrewdly. "I count ten new wrinkles on you since last week, sugar. You take a good look at yourself? Go on, take a look—you got a mirror."

"Aw, go to hell."

"Go on, look!" Ferlini shouted suddenly. Then his muscular arm whipped out and caught her wrist. He bent her down toward the lighted mirror on his table, forcing her to face it. She looked up at her reflection, at the streaked orange makeup on her forehead and chin, at the age lines around her mouth, the puffy flesh beneath her eyes. She turned her head aside, and Ferlini's grip tightened cruelly.

"Stop it, Joe! For God's sake!"

"Who you callin' an old man, hah? I'm younger'n you, understand, on account of I keep in shape! Don't call me no old man, you hear me?"

"All right, all right!"

He released her, with a growl of disgust. His good mood was dissipated. Wanda, tears blurring her sight, went to the other side of the room and completed dressing.

"Not everybody thinks I'm so old," she whispered. "Not everybody, Joe."

"Shut up and get dressed. We're supposed to go to dinner, let's go to dinner. Besides," he said, standing up and slapping his flat stomach, "I want to talk to Roscoe about something. About the water trick."

Wanda said nothing.

● ● ●

The restaurant Roscoe had picked was just like Phil Roscoe himself: past its prime, seedy, congenial, and well lit. Roscoe held Wanda's chair gallantly for her, but Ferlini dropped heavily into a chair, reached for a roll, and tore it in half. With his mouth stuffed, he said, "Hey, you should have seen me tonight, Phil; I was the best. You tell him, Wanda: ain't it true?"

Wanda smiled weakly. "It was a good crowd."

"Good? I had three curtain calls!" Ferlini said, forgetful that he worked without curtains, and without encores. "I'm tellin' you, Phil, the escape business is comin' back with a bang. And I'm gonna be right on top when it does. Especially after we do that water routine—"

"What, again?" Phil groaned. "Look, we haven't even had a drink, and you're talking about water."

Ferlini roared with laughter, and shouted for the waiter.

For Wanda, the meal was tiresome from first course to last. Ferlini and his manager did the talking, and she had heard it all before.

"Look, Joe," Roscoe said, "you know as well as me that times are different. Few years ago, a good press agent could ballyhoo an escape guy right onto the front page. Only Houdini's dead, Joe—don't forget it."

"Sure, Houdini's dead. Only I'm alive!" He thumped his chest. "Me, Joe Ferlini!"

"That's one thing about you, Joe, you never had any trouble with false modesty."

"Listen," Ferlini grated, "what could Houdini do I can't? I work with ropes, chains, irons. I can get out of bags, boxes, hampers, chests. I can do handcuff routines. That bolted-to-a-plank stuff. I can do that Ten Ichi Thumb Tie. I can do the straitjacket. I can do escape tricks Houdini never even *thought* of. Besides, you know he used a lot of phony trick stuff—"

"And I suppose you don't?" Wanda snorted.

"Sure, sometimes. I mean, I got my skeleton keys and my phony bolts and that other junk. But you know me, Phil: I do my best tricks with muscle. Am I right?"

"Sure, sure," the manager said wearily. "You're the greatest, Joe."

"I keep in shape—you ask Wanda here. One hour a day, I'm with the barbells. I still got a terrific chest expansion. I can do this water thing, Phil. It'll be great!"

"But it's been *done*, Joe: that's what I'm trying to tell you. People don't get excited about it no more."

Ferlini made a noise of contempt. "You drink too much, Phil; your brain's soft. Sure, it's been done, only how many years ago? There's a whole new generation now. Right? And the way you handle things, it could be a real big deal. What do you say?"

Roscoe sighed, and it was a sigh of surrender.

"Okay, Joe, if you really want it. How do you want to work the act?"

Ferlini beamed. "I figure I'll do it up good. First I'll let 'em handcuff me. Then the rope around my body, about fifty feet, and the leg irons. Then they put me in a sack and tie it up good. Then they put the whole business in a big iron chest and dump me into Lake Truscan. How does that sound?"

"Like sudden death. How much is trick and how much is muscle?"

"The rope is muscle; I'll just give 'em the chest-expansion routine and the whole thing'll slip right off me. I'll have a skeleton key to the handcuffs in a double-hemmed trouser cuff. Once I get them off, I'll take a razor and slit the bag open. The chest'll have a phony bottom; I push it open and swim to the surface; the whole works sinks and I come up smelling like a rose." He gave Phil his victory grin.

"How good a swimmer are you?"

"The best. Don't worry about that part. When I was a kid, I wanted to go over and swim the Channel, that's how good I was."

"We could drop you by motorboat, and pick you up the same way. That'll lessen the risk."

"Sure, it's a cinch. I knew you'd see it, Phil."

"I see it," the manager said, "but I still don't like it. Hey, waiter! Where's that bourbon?"

From their third-floor room in the apartment hotel, Wanda could look out the window and see her husband stroking rapidly across the outdoor pool in the courtyard. He moved like a shark through the water, his graying hair slicked back and crinkling at the edges, the thick muscles in his back and shoulders rippling with every smooth motion of his arms. Once, fifteen years ago, she would have been rapt with admiration. Now she knew better. The great Ferlini needed only one admirer, and he saw him in the shaving mirror every day.

With a sigh, she came back into the room, sat down, and listlessly turned the pages of *Variety*. There was a timid knock on the door a few moments later, and she called out permission to enter. When she saw Baggett in the doorway, she caught her breath in surprise and guilt.

"Tommy! What are you doing here?"

"I had to see you, Wanda. I knew Joe was in the pool, so I thought it would be a good time. Looks like he'll be there the rest of the day."

"You're probably right."

She was flustered, but tried not to show it. She offered him a drink, but he said no. She tried to make small talk, but he wasn't interested. In the next minute, she was in his arms. But she was uncomfortable there, and soon broke from him and started to talk about her husband.

"You just don't know what he's like. Every year he gets worse; every day. All he thinks about is the act; night and day it's escape, escape, escape. Sometimes I think I'll go crazy, Tommy, I mean it. When we were in Louisville, last year, I actually went to a headshrinker for a while—did you know that? For three months I went, and then he got the job in Las Vegas, so that ended that."

"If you ask me," Baggett growled, "he's the one that's crazy, treating you the way he does."

"You know he even escapes in his sleep sometimes? No kidding. He wakes up in the middle of the night, throws off the covers, and takes a bow." She laughed without a change of expression, and then the tears flowed. Baggett surrounded her in his arms again. "Sometimes I wish he'd get tied up where he *can't* escape. Not ever."

"What do you mean?"

She looked up at him.

"You know the water trick, where he gets thrown in a lake? He's going to do it in a couple of weeks. You know what I've been thinking about, ever since he decided on it?"

She went to the window, looking down at the pool where Ferlini was still stubbornly plowing the water.

"I was thinking that maybe something would go wrong. He's good; I know that. He can escape from almost anything. But if one little piece of the act doesn't work right—he'd drown. Do you think I'm terrible, having a thought like that?"

"I don't blame you for a minute!" Baggett said loyally.

Moving slowly, Wanda went to the bureau and opened the second drawer. From a welter of paraphernalia, she removed a pair of steel handcuffs and two small metal objects. She brought the handcuffs to Baggett, and said:

"Do me a favor, Tommy? Put these on?"

He blinked. "You mean it?"

"Please."

He held out his wrists willingly, and she clamped the cuffs around them, pushing the lock into place.

"Now try and get out," she said.

Baggett, a thin, romantic type, strained mightily, until the blood rushed up in a crimson column on his neck.

"I can't do it!" he panted.

"Of course you can't. Nobody could, not even Ferlini, unless he happened to have this on him somewhere." She held up a small key, and handed it over. "Now try it," she said.

Twisting his fingers, his tongue tucked into the corner of his mouth, Baggett managed to insert the tiny key into the hole. He turned it, but nothing happened.

"It's not working," he said. "The key doesn't turn."

"No," Wanda said dreamily. "It doesn't, does it?"

"But why not? What's wrong?" There was a hint of panic in Baggett's voice.

"It's the wrong key," Wanda said. "That's the problem. This is the right one." She held up a second key, then came over and inserted it herself. The lock sprang free, and the handcuffs came off. Baggett, rubbing his wrists, looked at her questioningly.

"I think you better go now," Wanda said.


Phil Roscoe was pleased with the results of his publicity campaign. Four local newspapers in the Denver area were touting the event, and one major news service had put it on the wire. But the great Ferlini wasn't so easily pleased; his visions had been of television coverage, national magazines, and Hollywood offers, but these were sugarplums that Roscoe had been unable to obtain.

"For the love of Mike," Roscoe told him, "don't expect the moon out of this. It's not big news anymore, not since Houdini did it. Be satisfied with what you got."

Ferlini grumbled, but was satisfied.


On the day of the event, Wanda Ferlini woke up looking older and more haggard than ever before. It had been a bad night; her husband had twice startled her out of sleep with his wild dreams of incredible escapes. But it wasn't only sleeplessness that dulled her eyes and slowed her responses. It was anticipation, the dread of something going wrong.

Roscoe had hired a chauffeur-driven, open-top Cadillac for the occasion; they drove up to the site of Ferlini's performance in style. Wanda, sitting beside Roscoe in the back seat of the car, wore her best dress and had never looked worse. Roscoe, flushed with excitement and bourbon, held tightly to her hand. Ferlini, riding the high seat of the Cadillac, waving his arms to the crowd, wore a full-dress suit with a white tie, his muscular shoulders stretching the glossy fabric almost to the point of bursting seams.

If Ferlini had any further complaints about Roscoe's publicity buildup, they were forgotten now. The crowd on the edge of Lake Truscan numbered in the hundreds. Roscoe's efforts to enlist the mayor in the program had failed, but there were a city councilman, the chief of police, the assistant fire commissioner, and two of the town's leading businessmen in attendance. The supper club had supplied the affair with its full six-piece orchestra, and their ragtime marches made the occasion seem more festive and significant than it really was. Best of all, there were a dozen newsmen and photographers.

Roscoe had planned it all well, but there were still some disappointments. The public-address system developed a high-pitched squeal that made its use impossible, so there were no introductory speeches. The weather had seemed ideal in the early morning, but by one thirty a black-trimmed cloud had moved overhead. Wanda Ferlini shivered when she saw it. Roscoe, moving busily among the officials, tried to speed up the program before rain made Ferlini's escape attempt even more difficult.

They were ready to go at two.

The handcuffs were snapped on first, by the police chief; it seemed appropriate. The chief, a bluff man with a forced smile, examined the handcuffs carefully before placing them on Ferlini's wrists, and pronounced them thoroughly genuine.

The two businessmen were selected to wind the thick rope about Ferlini's body. He stripped off his tailcoat, his white tie, and his formal shirt, and then kicked off his shoes. In the T-shirt, his muscular chest drew admiring exclamations from the crowd's female element. The businessmen were both short and pudgy, and they were puffing by the time they had the fifty-foot rope coiled around Ferlini's body.

"Knot it, knot it!" Ferlini urged them, exposing the teeth made strong and sharp by years of tearing and biting at ropes. They knotted it, in odd, lumpy knots that accented the coil from head to foot. They were so busy that neither they nor the spectators were aware that Ferlini was pumping his lungs full of air, increasing the circumference of his chest by almost seven inches. He smiled complacently when they were through, confident that he could wriggle free of his bonds in only a few seconds.

The assistant fire commissioner was given the task of assisting Ferlini into the cloth sack. He rested it on the ground, and Ferlini was lifted over it; then the official pulled up the cloth until it covered the escape artist completely. The crowd murmured when the cloth was securely fastened over Ferlini's head.

But it was the sight of the huge iron chest that brought the sharpest reaction from the spectators. Somewhere in the throng, a woman screamed, and Roscoe grinned with pleasure. It was great show-manship. He sought Wanda's eyes to share the moment, but he found her face pale and drawn, her own eyes closed and her lips moving soundlessly.

Then Ferlini was deposited inside the chest, and the chest was locked and bolted by the city councilman. The committee examined it, declared it escapeproof, and then stood back as a quartet of hired mus-clemen lifted the chest from the ground and deposited it in the stern of the motorboat that was moored to the pier.

The supper-club orchestra struck up the funeral march, swinging the mournful melody. Roscoe stepped into the boat first, and then helped Wanda—who looked like a bereaved widow—aboard. The pilot of the craft, a jaunty crew-cut young man, waved at the crowd and unfastened the line. He started the engine, and moved the boat slowly out toward the deep of the lake.

"You all right?" Roscoe asked the woman.

Wanda murmured something, and reached for his hand.

When they were five hundred yards offshore, the pilot cut the engine.

"This okay, Mr. Roscoe?"

"This'll do fine." Roscoe trained binoculars on the edge of the lake, to see what the newsmen were up to. They were watching him just as eagerly; the photographers, some with telescopic lenses on their cameras, were hard at work.

"Let 'er go," Roscoe said.

Wanda cried out feebly, and the pilot grinned, put his hands against the iron chest, and tipped it over the side. It fell into the water with a splash that sprayed them all, and then vanished from sight, spreading a huge ripple all the way back to the shore.

Then they waited.

Roscoe looked at his watch. When thirty seconds went by, he looked at Wanda and smiled reassuringly.

Then they waited some more.

At the end of the first minute, the pilot's grin faded, and he began to whistle off-key. Wanda shrieked at him to be quiet, and he stopped.

At the end of the second minute, Roscoe could no longer look at the terrible chalk-whiteness of Wanda's face, so he lifted his binoculars again and studied the shoreline. The crowd had pressed forward to the water's edge by now, moving like some dark, undulating animal.

"My God," the pilot said. "He's not coming up, Mr. Roscoe!"

"He's got to come up! He's got to!"

Three minutes passed, but there was no sign of the great Ferlini.

At the end of six minutes, Wanda Ferlini moaned, swayed, and fainted. Roscoe caught her falling body before it struck the floor of the boat. Five minutes later, he ordered the pilot to head back for shore.

They recovered Ferlini's handcuffed body late that night.


Baggett tried to see Wanda on the day of the funeral, but it was Phil Roscoe who refused him admittance. Phil didn't care about Wanda's love life; he had too many problems of his own. But he was still a businessman, and Wanda was still a client, even without her famous husband. It just didn't seem smart to have Wanda appear as anything more than a tragic widow.

Wanda was playing the role well. By some strange cosmetic alchemy, her sorrow made her look younger. Her white-powdered face and pale lipstick contrasted well with her black mourning attire.

Roscoe had made the funeral arrangements, and they were almost as spectacular as the water escape itself. The turnout was large and well covered by the press; a horde of show people, not averse to being seen themselves, were on hand to mourn the passing of the great escape artist. The funeral procession wound slowly through the streets of the town, requiring a full half-hour to pass any one city block, but by the time Ferlini's coffin had reached the point of no return the crowd had thinned out considerably. Only a handful watched the final ceremonies in the graveyard.

Wanda sobbed against Roscoe's shoulder, and he patted her consolingly.

"It's the way he wanted it," he said inanely.

"I know, I know," Wanda said.

The eulogy, delivered by the town's most prominent clergyman, was brief. He spoke of Ferlini's courage, of his devotion to his art, of the pleasure he had given so many people in his lifetime. As he spoke, Wanda's eyes glazed oddly, and for a moment, Roscoe was fearful that she might swoon again.

They brought the coffin to the edge of the grave. The bearer in front, a waiter in the supper club, seemed puzzled by something, and murmured to the man beside him. Roscoe stepped forward, spoke briefly to them, and then conferred hastily with the minister. The conference piqued the curiosity of the solitary newsman on the scene, who came out of the sidelines to ask what was happening.

"I dunno," Roscoe said, scratching his head. "Freddy here thinks something is wrong. Says the coffin feels strange."

"How do you mean, strange?"

The waiter shrugged. "Light is what I mean. It feels too light."

"Really," the minister whispered. "I hardly think—"

"No, he's right," another bearer said. "Hardly weighs anything at all. And you know Ferlini—he was a big, hefty guy."

They looked at the coffin, waiting for someone to make a suggestion. It was Roscoe, finally.

"I hate to do this," he said softly. "But I think we'd better open it."

The minister protested, but they were already working on the lid.

"What's happening?" Wanda said. "What's going on, Phil?"

"Keep back," he pleaded. "I don't want you to see this, Wanda . . ."

But there was no way for her to avoid it. The lid was opened, and the truth was revealed to the sight of all. It sent a shock through the crowd as tangible as a blow.

The coffin was empty, and Wanda Ferlini was screaming like a high wind among the treetops.


Dr. Rushfield rolled a pencil along the blotter of the desk, and said, "Go on, Mr. Roscoe; I want to hear it all."

Phil Roscoe licked his dry mouth and wished he had a drink.

"You've got to understand how it is in my business, Doctor. Everything is showmanship, everything. That's why Ferlini made this deal with me, maybe ten, twelve years ago."

"And just what was this deal?"

"Nobody else knew about it, just him and me. It was crazy—I told him that. But you don't know how stubborn a guy like that can be. He made me promise that if anything ever happened to him, I mean if he died, that I would arrange for one last trick—something that would make him remembered even longer than Houdini. That's what it was, Doc."

"A trick?"

"A real easy one. I just slipped the undertaker fifty bucks, and he arranged to have Ferlini buried someplace in secret. Then he put an empty coffin in the hearse, and that was that. You see what I mean, don't you? Honest-to-goodness showmanship."

"I see," Rushfield said, frowning. "But I'm afraid that it had quite an effect on Mrs. Ferlini. I gather that she wasn't too well balanced before this happened, and now . . ." He sighed, and stood up. "All right, Mr. Roscoe. I can let you have one look at her, but I can't let you talk to her. I'm sorry."

Roscoe followed the doctor down the hall. They stopped at a door with a small barred window, and Roscoe looked inside. He drew back, appalled, at the sight of Wanda, her eyes round and unseeing, her arms straining uselessly to escape from the tight, unrelenting grip of the straitjacket.

# THOMAS ADCOCK

# NEW YORK, NEW YORK

Some. places where I
happen to spend a lot of my off-duty time are Yankee Stadium and any
Irish saloon you'd want to mention between The Bronx and the Battery.
At these fine establishments, they're forever playing Sinatra's rendition
of "New York, New York" on the juke or over the loudspeaker. Which
for some perverse reason seems to be just about everybody's cue to get
all gaga, especially during the part where Frank sings, "If you can make
it there, you can make it anywhere . . ."

I've got an uncle on the other side by the name of Liam who doesn't
think highly of this tune. He's Dun Laoghaire's premiere Anglo-Irish
workingman-philosopher, and once he visited New York, which he
proclaimed "enough indeed for any man, though surely not nearly
enough for the average beast." When he was in town, he heard the
Sinatra song exactly twice—once at the ballpark when Don Mattingly
homered in the sixth inning, and then shortly thereafter at one of my
favored pubs. He admired the game of baseball, which he quickly and

cogently assessed as an "unfathomable sport to the European since it puts into play that most peculiarly American sense of infinite chance and time."

But like I said, he did not so much fancy the Gotham ditty. "It's really quite a load of old codswallop, Neil, my boy," he told me between his fourth and fifth bottled Guinness stout, which he'd been well advised by mates back home was a nectar quite unsuited to travel, not to mention bottling, but which he drank nonetheless without the slightest complaint. "It's only so much booziness set to lyrics and melody, don't you see—a farrago of truth and lies meant to appeal to the most hopelessly hopeful amongst us."

I told him I couldn't agree more. That's because in my line of work I deal fairly exclusively with people whose sad and sometimes downright crummy lives turn the sentiment of the song inside out—people who couldn't make it anywhere else and wound up in New York.

It's been a long while since Uncle Liam's visit. I've thought about him, of course, but about that barroom chat we had on the topic of Old Blue Eyes' stale tune not until now have his words made so much sorry sense.

A couple of nights back, I had every reason to believe that I was about to launch a particularly rewarding new friendship with a particularly gorgeous new tenant in my four-story apartment building, an actress named Julie Todd who had recently taken a studio on the third floor. I saw her in the neighborhood spoon that morning and asked, "What's new?" She told me in a breathy rush how she'd won a role in one of those preciously arcane Off Off Broadway one-acts, something about cannibals and UFOs and Amway distributors as metaphors of the age.

Anyway, Julie was thrilled to a glow about it, and so I naturally decided the moment was right for me to make yet another pass. So I did, and the lady finally caught one.

We made a date for that evening to celebrate her success. I said I'd be by her place at eight o'clock with champagne and that I'd spring for some take-out Szechuan. I was ready by five. For three hours I killed time with the tube, which was an agony. First there was the early local

TV news and celebrity babble hosted by a pair of toothy dimwits; then there was the regular local news, anchored by a blond guy in a virtual helmet of hair spray; then there was Dan Rather and his sweater vest; then there came some sort of game show emceed by a moron in a three-piece suit who insisted on kissing everyone.

And then I made my way downstairs to Julie Todd's threshold, to whatever promise of womanly comfort lay beyond. The door was ajar, and soft music floated out into the hallway. I rapped lightly, then pushed the door all the way open.

Then, right about the time I would have been pouring us two flutes of Perrier-Jouët, I was doing what a cop does when he finds a corpse.

Take one guess what was playing on Julie's stereo.


Neil Hockaday is my name. Officer Neil Hockaday, N.Y.P.D.—but that's too formal for the way I look most of the time and for what I do on the job. Which is why almost everybody besides my Uncle Liam calls me Hock. Even Julie called me Hock. She heard the waitress at the spoon call me that one day and picked it up for herself.

I work out of a special borough detail the department calls Street Crimes Unit—Manhattan but cops like me call the SCUM patrol because it's good shorthand for what we're up against.

Forty hours a week—plenty more if my sergeant isn't being hard-assed about my overtime (he's the sort destined to fill out a wide chair behind a wide desk someday down at One Police Plaza)—I'm out there in the streets all dressed down for the occasion. At home, I've got a special closet for my professional wardrobe, which I get off the rack at a Goodwill over on First Avenue next door to a social club where old Puerto Rican gents play dominoes and collect policy slips. I'm entitled to deduct the price of the garments on my income-tax returns as unreimbursed business expenses. So every year on my 1040, I exaggerate like hell and claim a hundred bucks off the top for greasy chinos, chewed-up jeans, all manner of secondhand polyester togs, and the occasional military-surplus overcoat that I have slightly reshaped by an Orchard Street tailor in order to accommodate my .44 Charter Arms Bulldog and its shoulder holster.

I spend a lot of time above and beyond trying to be a good and effective cop—lots of off-hours cultivating snitches and that sort of thing. I don't mind that all this time doesn't show up on my paycheck; but my ex-wife minded for me.

I used to tell her, "Don't worry about it—there are lots of little noncash ways I make it up." This line never failed to set her mouth off and running.

"Like *how?*"

"Well, I'm not crooked, but I can be bent now and again."

"Oh, sure, sure. Like you claim that cockamamie hundred bucks on your taxes for those tourist clothes of yours and those smelly old bummy things you wear, too, and then you spend half the year convinced the I.R.S. is after you with a paddy wagon. Or you take a lousy provolone sandwich from the Greek at the deli and you're practically racing off to confession."

"They're not smelly."

Ignoring me, she'd continue. "Oh, and we mustn't forget all those swell Broadway tickets you're always getting from that screwy pal of yours, what's-his-name."

"Sid Fortune."

"You would have a friend named Sid Fortune, for godsakes. You'll have to thank Sid for those last ducats to *Moose Murders*, which was laughed out of town ten minutes after the curtain rose. How come you can't pal around with somebody who'd do you a little good for a change? Somebody like Eakin. You went to academy with Eakin, and you two were friendly enough then."

"What do you like so much about Eakin?"

"What's not to like? He's made lieutenant, he lives up in Rye in a house with a Jacuzzi, he's got three cars—"

"He's dirty," I added. "Someday the guy who holds the pad on him is going to collect. You've forgotten already about Knapp?"

"Oh, the hell with the Knapp Commission hearings. There were lots of crooked cops before those days; then a few of them became guests of the state. So what? I notice that New York's Finest still has a little room for goons and crooks. Don't be such a damn altar boy, Hock."

"You've got it way too simple. Before Knapp, you had no say about what kind of cop you were going to be. Now you've got the choice. You can be dirty or straight. And no matter which way you go, you're always sure of having at least one half the department behind you."

She clapped her hands. "A pretty speech, Hock. So?"

"So I'm saying there are shadows now. You want to be a good cop these days, you have to watch out which way the shadows are moving."

"Oh, to hell with your shadows."

It went on like this for years, until everything in both of us ached too much. So we split up and became a departmental statistic. Once in a while, I'd visit her in the house I used to own in Queens before a judge decided I didn't anymore. Whenever my alimony check bounced, she'd ring up my sergeant and leave a lovely message. The real joke of it was that I got so lonesome in my little East Village apartment that I missed even her.

Now, most cops will tell you *they're* never lonesome like me, how all kinds of women are chasing them all the time. Maybe they say that because it's what they've been telling each other for so many years in so many lonely cop bars they've actually come to believe it. Maybe I shouldn't begrudge a guy his bodyguard of cozy lies.

Anyway, the first time I laid eyes on Julie Todd I experienced a minor philosophical miracle—it hit me all of a sudden how it was the human race had managed to survive itself. Because as cynical as I am about life in general, and sometimes women in particular, there I was just plain knocked dopey by the sight of her. Julie Todd and her pretty face and her soft, slim shape and those devastating legs of hers walked right into the greasy joint down on the street where I have coffee and eggs most mornings and I was as flushed as a crew-cut kid on a Saturday night trying to pin a gardenia on some girl's spaghetti strap.

Julie was friendly enough, but only just so. You weren't likely to mistake her for a missy fresh from someplace where they put hot apple pies out on windowsills to cool off. She was what you'd call self-absorbed, which is like a lot of young women in New York—deadly serious about becoming the toast of Broadway and willing to do any-thing to stick around town until it happened. For instance, she took her coffee black, and from the look of her shapely hips she'd never so much as passed a Danish under her nose for a whiff. And she pored over the trades—*Variety* and *Backstage* and *The Hollywood Reporter* and *Show Business*.

The spoon is a small, intimate place. There's a beat-up marbled Formica counter and eight stools, a short-order cook with a lot of black hair curling out from the neck of his T-shirt, and tired waitresses who come and go, one at a time. Then it was Sonja, a motherly type with dimples in her elbows and a hairnet. Sonja took a big shine to Julie right off, for different reasons than mine, of course, and she got Julie talking about herself.

Of course, we guessed right off she was an actress. She'd done *The Best Little Whorehouse in Texas* on Broadway, she told us; she'd had a number of supporting roles in American movies and starred in a couple of European features; and she'd been one of the leggy chorus girls who dared to wear short-shorts in some TV commercial for a depilatory. There was more to her résumé, too, and we were suitably impressed.

For weeks, I tried for her. I even shaved on my days off and started wearing things from my other closet in case my ex was right about the work clothes being gamy. But like I said, Julie Todd was self-absorbed. It wasn't until she got a measly part in some measly play that she joined me on the same wavelength.

And then I found her dead . . .

Her body was slumped on an antique divan. She looked as if she might have been sitting at one end with a leg tucked up under her and then fallen sideways after being killed. Her head lay on an arm of the divan, her eyes wide and glassy. Blood trickled from her mouth down onto the rug. The current issue of *Backstage* lay crushed under her.

I've seen lots of corpses, and every time I do I'm struck by the calmness they bring to a room. There was calm enough in that room for me to sweep through it and the rest of her place for any material evidence that might be lying around to make the D.A.'s job easy (none), check the fire escape (empty), and question neighbors (nobody home besides me). Soon enough, I could get away to drink and maybe to cry.

I saw red welts on her slender neck. She'd been strangled, more than likely by a necktie, and it had been a quick, powerful job of murder. It had happened no more than two hours ago. Any longer than that and there would have been that oddly heavy odor of death that settles into your nostrils and stays around for days.

I used some of the tissue paper that was wrapped around the Perrier-Jouët to cover the telephone receiver before I picked it up and dialed 911.

All that night I was awake. I stared out the window, or else I watched my old Philco. (My favorite Reagan picture was on, the one where he gets his legs cut off. But I didn't enjoy it as much as usual.) I also knocked back a lot of Scotch and wished I lived a regular life. Maybe if I sold refrigerators at Sears, Roebuck or something like that I'd have a little predictability for a change.

I went down to the spoon when it opened at six, even though I wasn't particularly hungry. When I told Sonja what had happened, she almost dropped a dish of poached eggs. Crossing herself, she sobbed, "Mary, mother of Christ, no! Who done it?"

I told her what I could, which was only that the case was under investigation by the detectives of the Ninth Precinct.

"What are you goin' to do about it, Hock?"

"I'm going to stay out of it, Sonja, that's what. Homicide's not my line, except sometimes by accident. Besides, I don't like making the job personal. It's hard enough working with strangers."

"She told me she kind of liked you, Hock. I ain't sayin' it woulda been some heavy-duty number for you, if you know what I mean, but she didn't have no beaux in her life neither, so who knows? Anyways, she had a thing for you."

I was surprised that Julie had confided something like that to anyone at the spoon, even good old mother Sonja. "When did she say that?"

"Oh, Julie and me, we had plenty of nice talks." She wiped a tear from one eye. Then she undid her apron strings, pushed the net back over the top of her head, and ran a few fingers through her coarse red hair the way a moony teenaged girl might do it if she imagined herself a film goddess. "Maybe you won't believe it, but once a long time ago I was a dishy young thing myself. I wanted to be an actress too." She stood, her big homely head uptilted, that apron big enough to cover a

Kelvinator hanging loose, and she told the hairy cook, "I just can't go on today!" I wanted to laugh at her and felt lousy about myself for it.

I was punchy from shock and booze and no sleep, and I was trying to keep from thinking about Julie and who had killed her and why—and I had to be uptown at work in a few hours. Just my luck, I was posted that week on decoy duty smack in the heart of the theater world—Times Square.

I went upstairs to my flat and caught a few hours of shuteye, but it didn't help much dreaming about a dead lady. I woke up sweating and knowing it was all somehow going to get very personal and there was nothing I could do about it.

Decoy assignments come up for me once in a while, especially at the height of the summer tourist season when out-of-town marks go with Times Square like rednecks go with white socks. New Yorkers pretty much surrender the town to this crowd, whose interests are pretty much splashy musicals (so long as the casts have plenty of recognizable TV stars) and browsing for goods and services in the vicinity of Forty-second Street and Eighth Avenue, which contains most of what they're opposed to back home.

So there I was on what we call The Deuce, which is quite a Broadway show in itself. It's got comedy, drama, and tragedy, and all without rehearsals. For my ensemble, I'd chosen a powder-blue leisure suit that felt like fiberglass and a beige short-sleeved rayon shirt, open at the neck to display a vinyl shark's-tooth pendant. I'd blow-dried my hair and splashed Brut all over myself. I wore beige patent-leather shoes and a matching beige patent-leather belt with a buckle that said "CHUCK." I don't know what the outfit would go for out in Moline or Dubuque or Tulsa, but it set me back seven bucks and change at the Goodwill.

The possibilities for making money on The Deuce are many: mugging, boosting, check-forging, and dealing in drugs. Phony drugs, stolen merchandise, sex, blood, credit cards, telephone credit numbers, and gold chains. Mainly, I try to prevent street hustles from causing long-lasting damage by, among other things, offering myself as a "vic" (victim, tourist species) to the indigenous entrepreneurs of the Great White Way.

In my first three hours' loitering up and down The Deuce and around the corner on The Stroll (Eighth Avenue), I declined the opportunity to buy an assorted case of Valium, Placidil, Tuinal, codeine, and Tylenol No. 4 at a special closeout rate. I passed up a half-price offering on "collector's editions" of some magazine called *Spank Buddies*. I advised a pair of grannies from Topeka with beehive hairdos that it wasn't a good idea to bet the egg money on the three-card-monte game they were watching outside a fried-chicken parlor. And I gave a guy with a suit like mine (only his was lime green, with a Kiwanis lapel pin) directions to a place near the Seventh Avenue Nedick's called Mistress Tatiana's Temple of Titillating Terror. I also gave the brush to maybe a half-dozen transvestite prosses, which made me think back to the time a few years ago when some pup running for City Council said the cops weren't doing enough to clean up Times Square, which he described as having "a wide divergence between image and reality." He was from Staten Island, so you know he hadn't been on speaking terms with reality in years anyway.

All that time and I didn't come onto anyone throwing bricks—which on The Deuce means committing a felony—so just for the practice, I put the collar on a couple of young commuters from the South Bronx who were palming off lactose and Sugar Twin to some vic in an Ohio State windbreaker who was in the market for heroin. One of the perps said to me, "Hey, Murphy, have a heart, man! This stuff's just whack, dig? All we done is give this vic a whack attack. Man, all you got's a consumer rip-off on us." He had a good point—but then again, you never know what kind of good you might do the world by taking guys like this off the streets for an hour or so.

When I finished up with the punks at the Times Square station house, I bought a frankfurter and a cream soda from a street vendor who had a radio going on his cart. So what else? Sinatra was at it again with the opening lyric. "Start spreadin' the noooooooz . . ."

I didn't stick around to hear the rest. I wanted to see my friend Sid Fortune. He was someone who might help me answer some of the questions making knots of my brain—questions about the theater, about image versus reality, about Julie Todd.

Sid had two rooms over a magic shop on Broadway. Both those places have seen better days. The owner of the magic shop used to make props for Harry Houdini, but now most of his business comes from selling whoopee cushions to the spillover crowd from a nearby Hawaiian nightclub popular with folks who enjoy the wit and sophistication of drinks with little paper umbrellas in them. The guy in the magic shop also owns the building and feels a little sorry for Sid, so he gives him a break on the rent. That's a very lucky thing for Sid, who doesn't do so well anymore as the last of a breed of Broadway dinosaur—the independent talent agent.

"Everyone in the business is hooked up with I.C.M. or William Morris now," Sid complained to me once, "and you ought to see the twerps they have as agents at those big places. They look like insurance adjusters, and they don't even smoke."

I walked up the long hot dark stairway to the second floor and turned right. The gold leaf was mostly chipped away on the door marked "SIDNEY J. FORTUNE." I heard a television set droning on the other side and I smelled Sid's omnipresent Te-Amo cigar, so I knocked. "Door's open, unless you want me to pay up on my American Express!" he hollered.

The first thing he did when he saw me was make fun of my clothes. "I ain't seen nothin' like that since 'seventy-one. The only place you see that much baby-blue anymore is out in the country on a spring day, and then you gotta look up. A guy shouldn't go around lookin' like the sky, Hock baby. Maybe God don't like that so much, y'know?"

Then he gave me one of his cigars and lit it for me with a Zippo that leaked. I settled back in a cracked Naugahyde chair and told him how I was on decoy that day and all. Then I told him about Julie Todd's murder, and he listened closely.

"She really got to you, huh?"

"To me she was a classic. Like Garbo."

"Garbo! Listen, you seen Garbo lately? She just turned eighty, and she goes everywhere around town in one of them knit caps like guys up in Canada wear when they go ice-fishin'. I tell you, Hock, it's an ugly new age. Last time I saw Garbo, she was havin' coffee and a sinker at some dive over on Second Avenue next to the dog pound."

I changed the subject—so I thought. "What are you watching on the tube, Sid?"

"Talk about your ugly new age. I was watchin' this thing called *Lifestyles of the Rich and Famous*. It's hosted by some guy with the world's most annoying Australian accent—and take a wild guess who he just had on?"

I gave up.

"The curator of the Vatican art museum. The museum where the Pope lives! I mean, everybody's in show biz these days. I thought it was bad enough with the White House—but now the Vatican! See what I mean?"

No, I didn't quite see.

"Well, time was when there was lots of guys like Sidney Fortune you see sittin' here in front of you. We performed what you might say was a public service. Yeah, a real public service. By that I mean we were a barrier between the poor downtrodden audience and every harebrain from Nowheresville who thinks he's got what it takes to make it here in the Apple. I tell you, any act that got by the likes of me, *that* was entertainment!

"I used to tell some babe, fr'instance, 'I can make you a star, kid,' and lots of times I even meant it. Shoot, nowadays everybody thinks they're stars right off the bat because they were on the tube once maybe, or knew somebody who was. I don't know where it's going to end, I'm tellin' you." He slid the cigar from his lips and spat out some loose tobacco. "Wanna know the most ironical part of it?"

Yes, I did.

"The stars we got these days haven't got anything to do with guys like Sidney J. Fortune, which is somethin' you can look at two diff'rent ways—good and bad. *Bad* 'cause we got so many in the business like that so-called actress on *Dallas*—what's her name?—a skinny, no-talent dame who never woulda got past me to any audience anywhere. *Good* 'cause maybe I woulda made a mistake over a real artist like, say, De Niro.

"There's a laugh. Y'know where Robert De Niro lives? In a ratty loft down on East Houston Street is where, in a place that makes this here dump look like somethin' that hotel babe Leona Helmsley would grin about all over the magazines. You think that's how a star lives? Of course not. Nobody else does, neither.

"Confusin', ain't it? People got it all mixed up now about art and artifice, which used to be an art in my day. People in the business are confused, too. Youngsters mainly, but some who ain't so young anymore.

"The terrible part is everybody's in on the act. Everybody thinks they got what it takes which is because it don't take so much anymore. Just watch TV like I do and you'll see that. They just *say* they got it and everybody believes 'em."

I had to get back to work.

"Here's how this bunch stays afloat," Sid said. He spread open the latest issue of *Backstage* and pointed to the display ads. "There was a time when most of the ads in the trades was for parts. Nowadays most of the ads are for acting lessons and voice lessons and dance lessons, and cosmetics coaching and résumé preparation and eight-by-ten glossies, which we used to call 'sugar snaps.' Get my point?"

I didn't.

"Hell, the point is a good part of the money in show business in this town today comes from people makin' it off each other instead of off the stage. So what happens to the hopes and dreams we had in my day?

"That's why I'm tellin' you, it's ugly. Somethin's gotta give when you go and run over delicate dreams by makin' hope so cheap."

I picked up the *Backstage* and looked through it page by page until I came across exactly what I was afraid I'd find. Then I asked Sid if he'd be kind enough to check up on a few things Julie Todd had said about herself, and left his office at a dead run.

I got her address easily enough, and it traced to a scabby residential hotel full of half-crazy used-up working women over on Eleventh Avenue near where the city is tearing up everything in sight to make way for a convention center that will bring even more tourists to Manhattan. I woke an ancient crone who was the desk clerk of the place, showed her my I.D., and had her open up the room I was interested in.

She was gone, of course. "Smells like lavender in here," the desk clerk croaked. I saw why. The drawers all had sachets in them and were otherwise empty and left standing open, like she'd been in a big hurry to slip away.

There was a bed. It was a steel-spring number with a thin mattress, junior twin-sized to guarantee loneliness. It was heaped with the things she hadn't wanted anymore, parts of her life thrown away. Included among this detritus was the murder weapon, so I came to learn. I came across a photograph. It was of her and she'd marked the year 1949, month of November, around the crinkled white border in blue fountain-pen ink. She wore a studio page's uniform with a pleated skirt and a big smile. Milton Berle had his arm around her shoulder. She'd written below this, *"My first role, ha ha!"*

"Did she have any family anyone might know about?" I asked the desk clerk.

"Out of town, but I forget whereabouts." The desk clerk said this so slowly and deliberately I knew she was telling me the truth and that giving her ten dollars of the city's money for elaboration would be wasteful. "She didn't have nobody here in New York, I know that much. None of us here do no more, it seems. What'd she do, anyways, Officer?"

I ignored this. "Do you happen to know if she had any money to speak of? Any bank accounts?"

"You kiddin' me? With all it takes to pay thievin' doctors when you're an old biddy all by y'self?"

So there I was, at the end of a short trail. It's amazing, really, how very portable our lives can be. Even the biggest household can be packed up inside a truck and rolled off into the sunset. Lots can accomplish a vanishing act with the help of a couple of suitcases and a bus ticket. And those who are poor, alone, unattractive, and without friends can move with a special suddenness, and it will be a long time before we're missed.

It's been my experience that some of this sort make a final, common stop before leaving New York and its fables—the Times Square branch of Western Union, where they wait for money to be wired to them from towns they swore they'd never see again.

That's where I caught up with her that late-summer afternoon, after a quick phone call to Sid: in the airless black-and-gray Western Union office at Broadway and Fortieth Street, waiting on a long line of rumpled people talking like the last thing they needed in the world was financial help from home. Most on line had nervous friends along, forcing the laughs and mighty anxious to be blown to drinks and a meal, which maybe they hadn't had in a while. The tellers behind the bulletproof window cages counted out the money as slow as humanly possible and rolled their eyes when the only thing someone could show in the way of personal identification was a card from a walk-in medical clinic or the New York Public Library or Actors Equity. Larceny wasn't the only reason those teller windows had to be bulletproof.

Outside, I had an unmarked car idling at the curb and a couple of blue-and-whites nearby. I also had four uniforms hanging around for backup, but I knew that wouldn't be necessary. The detectives from the Ninth Precinct were on their way, so I'd be going to the mats with them pretty soon about who got the collar for the record.

She just stood on line all by herself with two elderly Samsonite grips on the floor in front of her. When I tapped her on the shoulder, she acted like she'd figured on bumping into me. I saw the air sort of go out of her and took my hand off the .44 tucked under the armhole of the leisure suit I planned on burning later. She was in a daze, somewhere far away from me and everybody else. She'd even forgotten to take off her hairnet.

"I suppose you had your reasons?" I said to her.

She looked at the floor and then raised her head melodramatically like she had that morning when I'd nearly laughed at her. "She tricked me."

"You mean she wasn't who she said she was?"

"If you mean she wasn't no workin' actress like she claimed, yeah, that's what I mean. She tricked me, just like all the rest. I checked up on her."

"Yeah, so did I. A friend of mine found out she never did that Broadway show like she said, never did any parts in any movies anywhere, and never even did any television. She wasn't a member of any of the unions."

"So what business did she have conductin' them classes with me up to her place, huh?"

"None at all."

"It wasn't just me she took money from. You see her ad in *Backstage*?"

"I saw it."

"Lies! All them credits she listed was nothin' but lies, right?"

"Yes, they were. People have to live, though, and she wasn't the only one in the world who's lied to do it."

"You have any idea how humiliatin' it is for an old nobody like me to be fooled like that? I shoulda seen that one. I shouldn't of fell for it, not after all I fell for in my life. Can you imagine?"

"I can imagine."

She folded her arms and we stood looking at each other for a minute.

"I forgot to give you the Miranda," I said.

"Yeah, I used to forget my lines all the time too. It's okay. Anybody asks, I'll tell 'em you did it right off. I was only goin' home after a long time away, and now that I think about it, a nice prison cell Upstate someplace is a better prospect than that."

"Did you use the apron strings on her?"

She looked down at the floor again. "Yeah, that's how I done it, and it didn't take long. Maybe you won't believe it, but I was sort of killin' myself.

"She looked kind of like me for a minute, sittin' there in that divan I liked so much and tellin' me about how she liked you. I already knew she was a fake, 'cause I'd checked up that day, and I couldn't help thinkin' how unfair it was that she had what she had. I mean, she's got this decent place to have a nice man come by and they can have somethin' to drink and just gas away a night. I never had that in all the years I spent hopin' for somethin' to come my way in the theater, y'know?

"Even so, I couldn't help but like her. I wanted to put her out of the misery that was sure to come to her. So I done it. I walked around behind her and she never knew what hit her.

"Yeah, I was mad at her—crazy mad—but honest to God, Hock, the other part of it was that she was such a sweet-lookin' young thing I just wanted to spare her the misery I knew she had comin'. I know that's sorta insane, but I think I'll just plead guilty and save myself from havin' to hope anymore."

I took her by the elbow and gently steered her to the door, where a couple of young officers in uniform took over. They cuffed her because it's regulation for homicide collars and put her in the cruiser.

It was then that I noticed how the Western Union office was hushed, how everyone had stopped to watch the strange drama Sonja played out for them.

She smiled at me from the backseat of the car. And from where I stood, she looked like she did in that old photograph she'd left behind for good in her sad little hotel room.

For a second or two before the car pulled away, she did look a little like Julie Todd. Despite her words, hopelessly hopeful, as Uncle Liam would have described her.

There was one thing Julie had told the truth about. She really had won a part in that measly play. It would have been her first role, and maybe she would have had somebody take a snapshot like Sonja had back in '49. And maybe that's as far as it would have gone for her, too. Go figure show business.

# JOHN F. SUTER

# A BREAK IN THE FILM

---

My family moved away from that town while I was still a kid. It was about two years before the movies changed from silent to sound. I've only been back once or twice since then. The place has changed, and I don't much care about going back, even if at the time it did just about kill me to have to leave there.

Sometimes I wonder about change. Old Time itself is the main thing, I guess. Time and death. Slow death and sudden death.

I don't want to go back, mostly because of the old Graphic Theater. Not that the Graphic made the town. Most of the town would have ignored the Graphic if it had been able to.

Every town has—or has had—a movie house like the Graphic. There's one right here, only instead of naming it Hippodrome or Grand or Bijou, they simply call it the Travers after the fellow who happens to own it.

You know what it's like: certainly not anything like a first-run or even like the best "neighborhoods." Strictly one cut above a dump. Nowadays there are carpets on the floors, and lights on the walls, and the seats have some stuffing (they're not plain hard wood, the way they used to be), but these places are all basically the same.

This was the Graphic, back when I was a kid: about the size of a large independent grocery store, but not so big as a supermarket. Hard seats, no wall lights, no carpets. So dark inside it hurt your eyes to come out into the street, especially because there wasn't any lobby. You paid your ten cents to Bessie Hawes in the little cubbyhole by the front door, she tore off a ticket and dropped it into a can, and you went in. The screen was on the front wall, and you walked past it and Joe Stockton, the piano player, and found yourself a seat in the gradually rising auditorium. Up at the rear there was a booth that doubled in brass: half was the projection room, the other half an office.

I was about nine when I started going to shows at the Graphic, and it was a battle to get started.

"I don't know whether I ought to let you go to that place or not," said Mom, staring at me as though she thought there was more to this than just my wanting to see a movie.

"Practically all the other kids go. Tommy Stewart does. If he goes, it's all right, ain't it?"

"*Isn't* it. Well, now—It's just that I've always heard it was such a dirty place. And you can't tell what might happen there."

But back in those days everybody in town knew everybody else's business, and they couldn't find anything to say against George and Bessie Hawes. Not then, anyway. And since George and Bessie ran the show, and since I kept at Mom, she finally gave in to me and I started going every Saturday.

If you went to the Graphic much, you met two people for sure, and maybe a third. Bessie Hawes you couldn't help meeting: she was always selling tickets. Bessie looked sort of middle-aged to me then, but I guess she was only somewhere between twenty-five and thirty. One of the first women I ever saw with short hair—short red hair that stood out ever so slightly from her head. Just a touch of powder and a suspicion of rouge, but enough to make her one of the town's first flappers. Lipstick too, of course. And she enjoyed life. Don't see how she could have, stuck in that ticket booth till all hours, but she always had a smile for you. Always.

Maybe what I remember most about the old Graphic is the front of it. Six-foot bills on each side of the building, with some kind of violent action going on in primary colors. Overhead, another big bill hanging, a square one, with more action screaming from it. William S. Hart in *Wagon Tracks*. Or Jack Mulhall in *The Social Buccaneer*. Or Art Acord, Antonio Moreno, Hoot Gibson—that crew. And there in that little ticket cubbyhole was Bessie Hawes, smiling. I remember that big poster flapping in the wind over Bessie's smile.

Joe Stockton, the piano player, was another one practically everybody knew. It was mostly because of his playing, I'm sure. Even in some of the better movie houses across the street, the organists sometimes fumbled it and were out of step with the film. Not Joe. He was always in there with something light during the comedies, like "Yes, We Have No Bananas," "It Ain't Gonna Rain No More," or "Barney Google," and he really bore down on it for the Westerns and serials. You hear all kinds of piano nowadays—boogiewoogie, sweet and sentimental, honky-tonk—but the kind I'd like to hear again is movie-house piano. With Joe Stockton playing it.

Saturday mornings, before the show opened at ten, Joe used to stand out front, and a lot of us kids would hang around and fuss over him. At the time, I thought Joe was a good guy being nice to us. Since then, I'm not so sure. Joe was only of average build, but he had pretty, almost white blond hair and a complexion like an old-fashioned rose. I wonder if he didn't stand out there for the women to look him over. A gang of hero-worshiping kids wouldn't have hurt him a bit. And there was talk that he was quite a man with the ladies.

Joe dressed well, too, for a piano player. The styles changed fast in those days, but he kept right with them. Always up-to-the-minute. I seem to remember a cigarette case, and that was in the days when most men either carried the pack plain or rolled their own. George Hawes remarked on Joe's clothes one day as he passed on his way to get the show started. "You must put all the money I give you on your back, Joe," he said, grinning. And because it was none of George's business, and Joe knew George knew it, Joe just smiled and shrugged. Then Bessie looked up from counting out piles of change and tacked on a postscript: "Joe'll amount to something someday. Anybody can see that. Won't you, Joe?"

I have always liked to find out how different machines work, and it wasn't long after I got to going to the Graphic that I decided to find out how the projector operated. So one Saturday I slipped up to the rear of the theater, nearly killing myself in the dark, and poked my head into the projection room. It wasn't much bigger than a Pullman washroom. Just room enough for the two projectors, a small worktable with a homemade splicing outfit and rewind reels, and George Hawes.

George looked down his long nose at me, but he didn't have a mean expression in his eye. All he said was "It'll cost you an extra dime to see this part of the show." When I pulled out the dime, he laughed and said to put it back in my pocket and come on in, if I could find someplace to squeeze myself.

Hardly anybody got to know George. They never saw him long enough. It was his theater, but he was up in the projection room all during the show, and in his little cheese-box office next to it before the show started. After the last showing at night, he stuck around to sweep up the candy papers, and sometimes he mopped the floors with soap and water and carbolic. Bessie helped once in a while, but usually she left at close-up time, to go home and get to bed early, she said.

George was a pretty nice guy. Not good-looking, but appealing. He had a long face—long in all dimensions—and his light brown hair wanted to soar off the back of his head as far as his face went down in front, even though his hair always seemed fresh-cut. A thin brown mustache gave him some distinction.

I learned about the machines fast, because he was entranced by them himself. I found out how to thread the film, how much loop to leave so there was no tautening and snapping, how and when to strike an arc with the carbons, how to splice and get the show going again after a break. All that I learned because George was delighted that somebody else wanted to know. He loved the movies and everything about them.

Finally he said, "You're a big help to me, Jeff. I feel I can step out of here once in a while without worrying. Can't stay in here all day, you know. Tell you what: You come around anytime you want to and Bessie'll let you in free. Only thing I ask is don't make this place a hangout. You're welcome company, but your folks won't thank me if you're down here more than you're at home."

The bargain stuck. If Mom and Dad ever got ideas about not liking what I was up to, they never let on. I guess nothing bad ever rubbed off George Hawes onto me. I don't think there was any bad to rub off.

As I say, George loved movies. At least, he loved Westerns, action pictures, serials, and comedies. The sticky and the complicated stuff was not for him. Keep it across the street in the other houses was his philosophy. His favorite was comedies. He always doled out generous helpings of Our Gang, Harold Lloyd, the chimpanzee Joe Martin, Felix the Cat cartoons, Ben Turpin, Harry Langdon, the Al Christie comedies (with the bone figures under the dialogue), the Hal Roach productions, Mack Sennett's stuff—all that. The titles alone would double him up, especially the takeoffs on the more serious shows: *Donkey, Son of Burro; Riders of the Kitchen Range; The Three Must Get Theirs.* They were funnier to me because George found them funny.

Early in the summer of the year when we moved from town, I was watching a William Duncan serial through one of the portholes of the projection room. The machine was whirring away, and Joe Stockton was giving the piano a good working-over, so I didn't hear anything at first.

Somebody said, "Mr. Hawes?"

I looked around. The door was open, and I saw a pudgy, dark-haired man standing in the doorway. I pegged him for a businessman by his stiff white detachable collar and cuffs. At that time soft shirts had taken only with workingmen and sports.

George squinted around the back of the projector. "Yes?"

"My name's Hurst. Could I see you in private? I have some business to talk about."

George glanced at me. "Jeff's not a licensed operator, so I can't— Oh, well, he's good enough; sure he is. Jeff, can you take her for a bit while this gentleman and I go into the office?"

I nodded.

"All right." He stepped around to the door and I squeezed around to the right of the projector. The reel in it had just started. "Anything goes wrong, you knock on the wall."

Just before it was time to switch to the other machine George came back alone.

"That," he said as he checked my threading on the new reel, "was an offer to buy this place."

I doubted I'd like this Hurst as well as I did George, just from the little I'd seen. I said, "You going to sell?"

He didn't answer until the new reel had started and he was cranking on the rewind. "You don't make up your mind that quick, Jeff, on things like this. Right now, I doubt it. He wants to put in a cut-rate men's-clothing store, he says. There's enough of them in town, and not enough entertainment." He slowed his cranking for a moment. "It was a good offer, though. Maybe too good."

I asked him what he meant, but all he said was "If you'd seen as many pictures as I have, you'd know that somebody who offers you more than a thing's worth is up to something."

I couldn't argue with him. He had the voice of authority. I went home not long after that.

The next week, when I went up to the ticket window to get Bessie to pass me in, she looked up and said, "Oh, Jeff. I want to talk to you. Let the rest of them go in first. D'you mind?"

I hung around until I was the last one. She motioned me over and put her face close to the hole in the glass.

"I want you to do something for me, Jeff," she said, low and sort of excited. "George has a chance to sell this place and make a lot of money. But he doesn't want to do it. I've tried to talk him into it and he won't listen to me. He might pay some attention if somebody else said the same thing. He likes you, Jeff. He might make up his mind if you talked to him. Would you, Jeff?"

Wouldn't listen to Bessie? I looked at her and, even in the early-summer heat, she looked a picture. If I were only a little older . . .

She was saying, "He wouldn't have to give up theater work. He could afford a bigger and better house, show better movies, if that's what he wants. It would be a step up. A big step."

But—*me* convince him? A kid?

"He seems to have some sort of prejudice against Mr. Hurst, Jeff. I don't know why. The Hursts are lovely people. Mrs. Hurst does get herself talked about, it's true. They say she's a little fast. And George fusses every now and then about the little bit I do, myself. But . . . Well, here I'm keeping you outside when you want to go in. Just talk to him, would you, Jeff?"

It wasn't easy; George didn't give me much opening. But I did finally get to ask him, as naturally as I could, if he'd decided to sell.

He was very casual. "No, Jeff," and he went on threading the projector as though there were nothing more to be said.

I thought a minute. "I'd sorta like to see you get a place like the Imperial, Mr. Hawes."

"Not my type. If I owned a house like that, I'd have to play the kind of show they do. This suits me fine, here."

"I hear this Mr. Hurst's made you a good offer." (I hadn't really. Just guessing from what Bessie said.)

"Yeah, and you know what I said before."

He started to say more, but then he stopped and mopped his face, which was wet with sweat in that hot little projection booth.

"Go get me a piece of ice to suck on," he said to me.

I went over and opened the bottom of the water cooler which he'd installed outside the door of the booth. But he'd forgotten to fill it with ice; there was only warm water in the ice section.

"You didn't put any ice in it today," I called.

"Well, get the ice pick and chip some up and fill it, would you? Then bring me a little piece of ice."

I ducked into George's office and reached up on the doorjamb where he kept the ice pick stuck in the wood. It was a sharp pick with a stout square steel handle. You could really put a drive behind it and make the chips fly if you wanted to.

I got George his ice from the little icebox nearby and popped a piece into my own mouth. By that time, I'd forgotten all about the business of selling the Graphic to Hurst.

I remembered it later in the day. Going down the street, I ran into Joe. Someone else had been filling in for Joe on the piano that day.

"Hi, Joe," I said, surprised. "I thought you were home sick."

He took a minute to place me.

"Oh, hi, kid. Naw, I had some business."

"They sure miss you up at the Graphic."

He grinned a little. "Anybody could pound 'em out good enough for that dump."

"Not like you, Joe." Then I thought of Hurst. "Suppose Mr. Hawes sells out, like they're trying to get him to? What'll you do then?"

When he grinned this time, it was sort of to himself. "I'm not worried, kid. Old Joe'll get along. Might even sell clothes for Hurst."

It wasn't but a couple of days when there was trouble at the Graphic. And a couple of days later there was more trouble. I got it in a roundabout way, so I decided not to believe it until George or Bessie said something about it.

When I showed up in the projection booth the next week, I could see that George wasn't his usual self. It could have been the heat, because the summer was working up to a scorcher. But it proved to be something else.

"Jeff, I'm glad to see you!" he almost yelled, grabbing me by the arm. "Come in here and get on these machines. I've been getting film breaks right and left, and it's just bum threading, that's all it is."

"Yeah?"

George was one of the few guys still left in the twenties who did their swearing by initials.

"H., yes! And who could thread right if he had to put up with all I've had to put up with the last few days?"

"What's wrong?"

I could already see he had his loops too small for the next reel. I started in adjusting.

"That g.d. Hurst, that's what's wrong! Tuesday, a fellow comes in here from the Board of Health. Inspection, to see if I keep a sanitary place. Says somebody—he wouldn't say who—had complained that the floor was filthy, that he'd seen rats running around the place. Now, you know, Jeff, that's a g.d. lie! This inspector had to admit, even if there's nothing fancy here, that I do keep it clean."

He stepped outside and fished a piece of ice from the cooler and came back talking around the ice in his mouth.

"As if *that* wasn't enough, on Thursday a guy from the Fire Department comes and says somebody's written them complaining that the Graphic is a firetrap. Well, now, that concrete floor's not gonna burn. There's no fancy carpets to go up like across the street at those other places. I keep fire extinguishers handy, too. Even the film nowadays is safety film and won't go up in a flash, the way it used to. Why, what in h., I even use a white wall for a screen, and that's something else won't burn! I told him all that. Oh, I told him good! Ended up, I have to put lights over the Exit doors. Well, that won't break my pocketbook."

"Anyway, they backed down, huh?"

"Oh, yeah. I'm not worried about any of that. It just gets me. I know Hurst is behind all this. He's trying to wear me down, make me sell."

"You know he is?"

"It's as plain as the nose on your face, Jeff. I've seen this same sort of thing, right there on that screen, a dozen times over. Next thing you know, he'll come around and he won't offer me as much as he did the first time. Just wait and see. But let me tell you, Jeff, the son-of-a-gun will have to burn the Graphic down around me to get me out. I can stand it as long as he can."

Neither of us was paying any attention. I was still checking the machine, and George was stooping over the film can under the table. There were several reels still in the can. Neither one had his eye on the door.

All of a sudden, George said, "What in the . . ." just as I caught a flicker of something out of the corner of my eye. I looked up quickly. George stooped still farther and grabbed something out of the can in a hurry. He threw it on the floor.

"Some stupid . . ." he shouted, and stamped down hard. I watched for him to take his foot away.

It was a cigarette butt.

"If that hadn't been safety film, I'd have been cooked," he growled; and he stepped outside fast. I looked, but all I could see was the dark. Whoever had pulled this poor excuse for a joke, or whatever it was, had gone. Even when George came back, baffled, and asked me, all I could say was that I hadn't seen who threw it. But for some reason, I remembered that butt.

That afternoon I was in Camp's Drug Store getting a soda when Mr. Hurst came in and pulled up the wire-legged stool beside me. He didn't know me from Adam, so I don't know why I said anything. Because I felt sorry for George, I guess.

"Mr. Hurst," I said.

He looked at me, sort of surprised.

"Yes?"

"Mr. Hawes won't sell the Graphic to you. Don't you know that? Why don't you leave him alone?"

He stared at me, then his face got kind of dark.

"I don't have troubles enough! Now I have kids trying to tell me my business! Didn't you ever hear kids should be seen and not heard?"

I was a little scared. Such a cowardly-looking guy, I'd thought, and here he was turning out anything but. I quickly sucked up my soda and left.

Three or four days later, I ran into Charlie Lester, who was in my grade in school, and he was asking me how last week's chapter of the serial came out. I told him. Then he said some funny things.

"Them Haweses is as good as the show, anyway."

He lived right next door to them, so I let him talk.

"Mostly we don't know they're around," he said, and I could see he was watching something in his mind. "But last night, late—I don't know the time, but it was late, because they woke me up—Old Lady Hawes musta just come in. First thing I knew, old George lets out a yell about where's she been? A woman's got rights, she says, or hasn't he heard about woman—woman suffer—suffer—well, something—hasn't he heard about it yet? Sure, you got rights, he says, but I've been hearing things, let me tell you. Why do you always leave the show before I lock up? he says. Tell me that. I have a right to some friends, she says. And what have you heard, anyway? I've heard plenty, he yells. But I always thought you could be trusted. Now I'm not so sure. You'd rather believe the lies? she asks him. Lies? he says, and he tames down some. Well, now, he says, I see it clearer. It's just some more of that Hurst's scheme, he says, sort of talking to himself. She doesn't say anything to that. I better not catch him spreading this stuff, old Hawes says. Let him watch his own backyard, from what I hear. He'd better mind his tongue about mine."

Charlie stopped and looked me over.

"Well?" I said. "What else?"

"That's all. They shut up then. At least, that's all I could make out."

Next Saturday was the last chapter of the serial, and I went down to the Graphic as usual. It was one hot day. I remember it for the heat as much as anything.

Bessie looked pretty wilted and burned-out when she passed me in. For the first time, I didn't think she was pretty. She wasn't smiling; maybe that was the reason.

"Go ahead, Jeff," she said, in a heavy voice. "When the last brick of this place falls to the ground, I'll be here selling tickets and you and George will be running the projectors. How's that seem to you as a future?"

I would have put an arm around her, the way I did to Mom when she was down in the dumps, but the booth was in between. I just went on in.

I looked to see if it was Joe at the piano. The playing seemed a little ragged. It was Joe, so it must have been the heat that threw him off.

George had his shirt off and was down to his BVDs. Nowadays, he'd be in his shorts, period, but then that was as far as he felt he could go and stay decent. He was sucking ice and mopping his face. Even his mustache had little water beads on it, and his face glistened with sweat.

He didn't bother to talk, just nodded and waved me to come in.

I looked around for something to do, but there wasn't anything. So I started watching the show through the porthole.

"This is a bum print they sent us this time," said George. "Film's old and rotten. A lot of splices already. We can look for it to break almost anytime."

"Like me and the Graphic," I said.

George was a little startled. "What's wrong?"

"Pop told us last night he's been transferred. We're moving out to Chicago by the end of summer. He's been made some kind of superintendent or manager. I don't know. I don't care. I don't want to go."

George reached over and slapped me on the back. "There are lots worse things, boy. You'll get over it."

Then he leaned over and squinted through the porthole. Was that Hurst coming in the front door, in that short burst of sunshine? As hot as I was, I wasn't sure of anything. It might even have been Bessie.

I forgot about it in the next minute, because there was a brittle snap and a sort of flapping. The film had broken. George and I acted together. I jerked the ONE MOMENT PLEASE slide over into position and threw it on the screen, while George teased the film out of the projector and went to work on a fast splice. He had the emulsion scraped, the cement on, and the patch made before somebody else could have realized what happened. In almost no time, we were back in operation.

When we had finished, George was dripping sweat, and so was I.

"Take her a little bit, Jeff," he said. "I'm going out in the alley and cool off. Then I'll spell you."

He left. I kept one eye on the screen and one on the film unreeling in the projector, if you can believe it. It can be done. Everything kept going all right, so I relaxed.

Then I got thirsty. I stepped to the cooler and drew some water. It was warm. I opened the ice compartment. No ice. All melted.

I stepped across to the office quickly and reached for the ice pick.

No ice pick.

I went and looked in the little icebox. Ice, but no ice pick.

Disgusted, I started back to the booth.

All of a sudden, down front, Joe came down on that old beat-up piano with a big jangling discord. It sounded like he was tearing the thing apart. I must have jumped a foot.

Kids were out of their seats all over the place. Somebody yelled, "Something's happened to Joe," and somebody went out the front door fast. The exit door to the alley opened and shut as somebody else either went out or came in. A hullaballoo started.

I did the only thing possible. I cut the machine and threw on the house lights.

Then the noise really got going. Kids were milling and shouting all over the place. George and Bessie were right in the middle of it, trying to shoo them out in orderly fashion. I left the booth and elbowed my way down to see what the trouble was.

Joe Stockton lay over the keyboard of his piano. A lot of the white keys were red. Out of the back of Joe's neck stuck the handle of the ice pick.

After a while the only ones there were George, Bessie, me, and the cops. George tried to ease me out, but the cops wouldn't let him.

They were asking questions, and George was bellowing.

"Who did it? That Hurst, that's who! He can't get me out any other way, so he murders my piano player to give the Graphic a bad name and get my license revoked!"

One cop, a leather-faced old guy with stripes on his sleeve, looked at George and shook his head.

"Maybe they do that in the movies," he said, "but I want to hear something more practical."

"He didn't do it himself," amended George. "He's too smart for that. He hired it done."

The cop turned to Bessie.

"Was anybody in here except kids?" She started to talk, but he went on. "Don't lie. I know that on Saturday afternoons you usually get 100 per cent kids."

Bessie gulped and nodded.

"That's what I thought," said the old cop.

Then George sort of collapsed.

"I was the one," he said. "I found out Joe was bothering Bessie here. My wife's a good woman, but Joe wouldn't let her alone. And this g.d. heat, I guess I just went crazy and stabbed him."

The cop looked satisfied.

"That's more like it. That makes sense."

So they took George away. It was like in one of his favorite movies, where the hero kills the villain to save the heroine's honor. And that's the way the papers wrote it up the next day.

As I say, we moved away by the end of summer and I've never had the urge to go back. For one thing, there's a big cut-rate drugstore where the old Graphic used to stand.

And life isn't as simple as in the movies George went for. It can be darned tricky.

Because I still remember that cigarette butt George fished out of the film can. It had lipstick on the end of the paper. Bessie almost never smoked, but there weren't any other grown women in the Graphic that day, so she must have been the one who tried to get rid of George. And she'd have succeeded, too, if she hadn't forgotten the film was safety film.

Of course, I can't prove that part. Any more than I can prove that Bessie'd been the one who complained anonymously to the Board of Health and the Fire Department when she thought Hurst was trying to buy the Graphic. She thought the pressure would force George to sell.

And when that didn't work, Joe looked even better to Bessie. A man like Joe could take her away from George and on up the ladder. Joe had a drive, she figured, that was missing in George.

I guess that's why George confessed. He must have thought that Joe wouldn't fall in with Bessie's plans and so she'd killed him—the woman scorned or the woman wronged. And maybe George felt responsible for driving Bessie into the whole thing. I don't know.

I do know George had nothing to do with Joe's death. The truth was pretty simple. Joe was playing around with Mrs. Hurst. She was even fool enough over him to give him money and little presents. Well, you know how gossip goes in a town. The gossip about his wife got to Hurst, but he didn't know just who "the guy at the Graphic"—as the rumors put it—was. Hurst's offer to buy was just an excuse so he could hang around the theater and smell out the identity of the guilty man. When he found out it was Joe, Hurst grabbed the ice pick he'd seen in George's office, and he let Joe have it.

How'd they find out all this? So simply, it's silly. People in the early Twenties weren't as fingerprint-conscious as today. Hurst just forgot to wipe the handle of the ice pick.

In some ways, we've changed nowadays. Progress, I guess you'd call it.

# EDWARD D. HOCH

# CAPTAIN LEOPOLD GOES TO THE DOGS

Eddie Sargasso was a gambler.

In his younger days he'd been known to bet on everything from the fall of a card to the virtue of a woman. Now that he'd passed forty, he was more likely to limit his wagers to recognized sporting events and games of chance, but he was still always on the lookout for an angle. He'd been in on the recent jai alai fixes until a grand-jury investigation broke the scandal wide open. Now it was greyhound racing that took his fancy.

Eddie Sargasso was fortunate to live in one of the few Northeastern states where dog racing was legal. If he'd resided elsewhere it wouldn't have stopped him from betting, but it would have kept him from arranging to meet Aaron Flake—by convenient accident—in the Sportsman's Lounge one Sunday evening in July.

Flake was a little man with thin blond hair and glasses that were too big for his face. He was sitting alone at the bar, nursing a gin-and-tonic, when Eddie slipped onto the stool next to him. "Hey, aren't you Aaron Flake, the guy from the dog track?"

The man smiled thinly. "I'm a licensed hare controller, if that's what you mean. You may have seen me at the track."

"Damn right," Eddie said, building it up. "You were pointed out to me as knowing more about greyhound racing than anyone else in the state."

"After working at something for sixteen years, I suppose it's natural that you learn some facts about it."

Eddie Sargasso whistled. "Sixteen years! It hasn't even been legal that long, has it?"

"I worked the Florida tracks before I came north. New England was a whole new territory for me and I figured to get in on the ground floor."

"You got a family here?"

Aaron Flake shook his head and took another sip of his drink. "Wife and kids stayed in Florida. They liked the sun. I'm divorced now."

"I do a little betting on the dogs," Eddie admitted.

"That's what we race 'em for."

"I like them better than horses because they're harder to fix, you know? You bet on a greyhound and you know it's going to be a good honest race."

"Well, there are ways of fixing them. Tampering with the dogs. I read a story once about dog racing in England and they had a dozen ways of making the dogs run faster, or slower, or whatever they wanted. We check 'em pretty careful over here, though."

Eddie signaled the bartender for two more drinks, and Flake offered no objection. It was a Sunday, after all, and he didn't have to work again till Monday night. "You control the mechanical rabbit, don't you?" Eddie asked, pretending an ignorance of the sport's basics. "How does that work?"

"I usually call it an artificial hare rather than a mechanical rabbit. There's nothing mechanical about it, really. It's a stuffed animal strapped to a device that moves around the track. It's powered by an electric motor, and my job is to maintain just the correct speed for the hare. If it's too slow the lead dog might catch it, and if it's too fast and gets too far ahead of the dogs they lose interest. Judges have been known to declare a no-race if that happens."

"How many dogs are there?"

"We race eight at a time in this state. Some places race nine."

"You can keep them all in view during the race?"

"Sure, it's not hard. I'm in a little booth overlooking the track."

"Which post position is best?"

"Number eight trap is on the outside of the oval, nearest the hare. That dog has to run a few more feet than the number one dog on the inside—but it's not enough to speak of. They usually bunch together after the start anyway. I wait till the hare's about twelve yards in front before I open the traps, and I try to maintain that distance. We have an electric-eye camera at the finish line to record the winner."

"Sure sounds exciting. I've only been a couple of times, but I think I'll drive out again tomorrow night."

Aaron Flake finished his drink. "You'll enjoy it," he said, sliding off the barstool. "See you around."

Flake had left suddenly, but that didn't bother Eddie Sargasso too much. At least he'd made contact, and with any luck he'd fare better than Marie did. Eddie and his wife lived in an expensive colonial house at the edge of the city, not far from the dog track, and driving home that evening he went over the possibilities in his mind. Somehow he needed an edge on the race fixing so he could get his cut of it and still avoid problems with the law. He had a lengthy arrest record over the years, and he knew there were some cops in the city just waiting for a misstep to nail him.

"How'd you make out?" Marie asked as he entered the family room, where she was watching television.

"Pretty good for the first meeting. If anyone knows when the fix is in, it must be Flake. Watching the races that carefully every night, he has to see something."

"I hope you do better than me. I couldn't get to first base with him. He never even phoned me!"

He bent over and kissed her. "Don't let it bother you. I guess he doesn't go much for the ladies. I thought you could talk to him about Florida, but it didn't work out."

"Are we going to the track tomorrow night?"

"Sure. I told him I'd probably be there. We can use the old system till we latch on to something better."

Monday was a warm night, and that brought out a good crowd. Marie wore her white pantsuit, and Eddie had on his lucky brown jacket. He studied the dogs through binoculars, watching them break from their numbered traps to pursue the motorized rabbit.

After the third race, he ran into Donald Wayne of the state betting commission. "Eddie! They haven't barred you from the track yet, I see."

"Come on, Donald. I'm a solid citizen."

"Sure, I know. Do you still make bets on things like whether the next girl into a bar will be wearing slacks or a skirt?"

"That was in my younger days, and I lost too much money. Now I try to bet only on sure things."

"I know. That's why we hate to see you at the dog tracks. We've had enough trouble with jai alai in this state."

"Would you be suspicious of a poker game at my place on Friday night?"

"That's more like it! Close up, I can keep my eyes on you."

Eddie chuckled and patted him on the shoulder. "Make it eight o'clock. I'll see who else I can round up."

It had been more than a year since the weekly poker games with Wayne and a few others. Eddie had stopped asking him when Wayne was appointed to the state betting commission, fearing it might somehow compromise his friend's position. But if Wayne didn't mind coming, why should Eddie?

He made a bet on the fourth race, buying his ticket from one of the totalizator operators in their distinctive dark red jackets. Then he stood for a time watching the odds change right up to post time. It was much like horse racing in that respect. There was always big money bet in the closing minute, and late changes to lower the odds often indicated inside information on a winner. Often when Eddie saw that happening he sent Marie out to stand in line at one group of windows while he went to a different selling location. When the odds changed on the totalizator screen, they'd each buy a $100 ticket on the horse whose odds showed a sudden last-minute drop.

He went back to his seat in time to see the greyhound wearing the bright blue racing jacket numbered 6 cross the finish line first. "There was last-minute betting on him," Eddie told his wife. "The smart boys are at it again."

"You want me to get in line for the next race?"

"I think so. Until we get more friendly with Mr. Flake, that's the only move we've got." He passed her a $100 bill. "Watch the odds, and be close enough so you can make a last-minute bet just before the machines lock."

"You don't have to tell me. I've done it a thousand times."

He watched her head for the downstairs bank of selling windows and he went back to the windows nearest their seats. As he stood watching the totalizator board, another familiar figure passed into his line of vision. It was Sam Barth, one of the track stewards. "Sam!" Eddie called out.

"How's it going? Where's your lovely wife?"

"Downstairs, Sam. How about a poker game Friday night? Donald's coming over."

"Wayne? That's great! I think I can make it, but not till I get out of here at eleven. That okay?"

"Fine. Come when you can, Sam."

He watched the slender man walk away, wondering vaguely if a track steward could be in on any fixing. Stranger things had happened.

He got into the shorter of the two lines then, hoping he was timing it right. "Hi, Eddie. How they running?"

He turned at the sound of the woman's voice and saw Joyce Train, a woman he'd known quite well in his younger days. "Joyce! Good to see you! How's the family?"

"Who knows?" She smiled and winked. "I'm back to work."

"You are? Since when?"

"The spring. I couldn't take being a housewife."

Eddie chewed at his lower lip. "I'll keep it in mind. I might have something for you."

"I'm at the old place if you need to reach me."

"Fine." She still had a great figure, and she knew how to show it off, wearing a dark brown jumpsuit with some frills at the neck and cuffs. A few years ago she'd quit the call-girl business to get married, but hardly anyone had thought it would last. Apparently it hadn't.

Thinking about her, Eddie wondered if he might try introducing her to Aaron Flake.

The totalizator screen was changing. He memorized the current odds and watched them shift. Minor changes, mostly, at one minute to post time.

Except . . .

Dog number 4 dropped from 8–1 to 7–2. That meant a big last-minute bet. He hoped Marie had caught it at the other windows.

"One hundred on number four," he told the ticket seller when he reached the window a few seconds later. He was just walking away when he heard the snap of the machines locking as the starter signaled the release of the hare. Then there was a roar from the crowd as the eight greyhounds burst from their numbered traps.

He made it back to his seat in time to see them rounding the first curve of the oval track. The dogs were closing in on the electric rabbit, and the lead one looked to be almost within striking distance. He'd never seen them that close before. Maybe Flake . . .

The dogs were onto the rabbit, straining at their muzzles and sending up growls of frustration. Instantly the steward and judges were on the track, signaling it was a no-race. The message flashed on the tote board that all bets were off.

Eddie Sargasso couldn't figure it out. He met Marie by the steps, and she was as baffled as he was. "What happened?" she asked.

"I don't know—but it'll probably cost Flake his job. We'll have to start all over with someone else."

They pushed their way through the crowd of disgruntled spectators, watching the trainers and track officials trying to bring some order from the confusion on the track. The dogs were growling and fighting among themselves, separating only reluctantly as the trainers pulled them apart.

The control booth for the hare was some distance away, near the starting gate, and by the time Eddie and Marie reached it he saw Donald Wayne coming out. His face was white as Eddie asked him, "What in hell happened?"

Wayne stared at him blankly, then seemed to recognize him and said, "Murder—that's what! Somebody stabbed Aaron Flake!"


Captain Leopold was not a gambler.

He'd been to the dog track once in his life, with Lieutenant Fletcher and his wife shortly after it opened. That night he'd managed to lose $12, enough to convince him he was no luckier with dogs than with horses. Now, as he pulled up to the main entrance with Fletcher at his side and the siren wailing, he wondered if he'd be any luckier this night.

"We should have gone home early," Fletcher decided, looking at the crowd of people. "Let the night shift handle it."

"Come on. Maybe it's an easy one—some drunk who's waiting to confess."

"Sure, Captain." Fletcher liked to use the title when he was being sarcastic. Most of the time they were good friends, and Leopold had been out to dinner at Fletcher's house twice so far during the summer. With Connie Trent away on vacation, they'd been spending more hours together in the office too.

"This way, Captain," a voice called to him as they entered the stands. Leopold recognized Sam Barth, one of the track stewards, whom he knew slightly. Barth stood at the top of a short flight of steps, wearing a dark red blazer like all the track personnel.

"What happened here?" Leopold asked. "The report said a homicide."

"That's it. Our hare operator, Aaron Flake, was stabbed in the back. It happened right during the race, and the dogs caught up with the hare!" That seemed to bother him more than the murder.

"All right, show us the way."

Leopold and Fletcher followed him to a little wooden booth overlooking the dog track. A husky man in a rumpled brown suit was there to greet them. "This is Donald Wayne of the state betting commission. He found the body," Barth said.

Leopold shook hands with Wayne and waited while the man opened the door of the control booth. Then he took a deep breath. The man they identified as Aaron Flake was slumped over in his chair, head down on the desk in front of him. Something—Leopold saw it was the evening's racing program—was pinned to his back with a bone-handled hunting knife.

"All right, Fletcher, get the photographer and the lab boys up here." Leopold glanced at the desk on which the body was slumped, and saw another racing program, an ashtray with one cigarette butt, some pencils, and a blank pad of paper. A pair of binoculars was mounted on a stand in front of the dead man's head.

He turned and looked at the door of the booth, observing a simple hook-and-eye latch. "Did he keep this door latched?"

Donald Wayne nodded. "It's something of an art, keeping that hare just the right distance ahead of the dogs. Flake didn't want anyone walking in during a race and ruining his concentration, so he kept the latch on. The door was unlocked when I found him, though."

"So he admitted his killer. It was someone he knew."

"Looks like it," Wayne agreed. "But that doesn't limit it very much. We have over fifty track employees, plus the owner and trainer of each dog. There are stewards, judges, a starter, a timekeeper, even a veterinarian. Flake knew them all. Plus he might have admitted any one of the spectators that he knew."

"Make up a list of track employees for me," Leopold suggested. "And try to indicate where each one would have been during the race."

Sam Barth, the track steward, was standing outside the little booth. "I can probably do that better than Donald. I work with them. He was just a visitor tonight."

"How's that?" Leopold asked the stocky man.

"Well, I'm on the betting commission and I figure I should go around to the tracks once a week or so. We don't have Thoroughbred racing in this state, but between the greyhounds and jai alai it keeps me busy."

"You were standing near this booth when it happened?"

"Not too far away," he told Leopold. "At first I couldn't believe my eyes! I've never seen the dogs catch the rabbit in all the years I've been coming here. It's something that just never happens! As soon as I realized something had gone wrong with Flake I hurried up here to the booth. But it was too late."

"Could you see the entrance from where you were standing?"

Barth shook his head. "You see the way these supporting girders stick out to hold the roof. There's a blind spot here, so the door to the booth can't really be seen from the stands. Anyone could have entered without being seen."

While Fletcher made notes of the booth's measurements and other facts, and the medical examiner set about removing the knife from the wound, Leopold went down to the track with Sam Barth. "Never had anything like this happen, Captain. I still can't believe it!"

There was barking from a few frustrated dogs as Leopold walked along the edge of the track toward the kennels. One trainer was leading his muzzled greyhound for a trot around the exercise track. "Think we'll be able to finish the rest of the card, Sam?" he asked.

"Not a chance, Matt. They've scratched it all for tonight. We'll try to get another hare controller up from Stamford for tomorrow's card."

"No one seems to be mourning the dead man too much," Leopold observed.

"Aaron Flake was a loner. Stuck pretty much to himself. Behind his back they called him Flaky, of course. He probably had that all his life."

"Was he married?"

"He told people he was divorced, but it may not have been true. He came up from the Florida tracks when we started dog racing here. There was some sort of trouble at his last track, but the state investigated and decided he wasn't involved."

"Trouble? Like fixed races?"

"No, something else. I don't know what."

"Have there been any fixed races here?"

"I couldn't say, Captain."

"All right," Leopold said. "I'll talk to you later."

He'd ordered the gates closed shortly after his arrival, but of course the killer had had several minutes to make his escape before the Captain's arrival.

Leopold watched the progress of the lines without spotting any familiar faces, then went back to the booth, where the medical examiner was just finishing. "What about the weapon?" Leopold asked.

"Standard sort of hunting knife. You can buy them at any sporting-goods or department store. Five-inch blade, about nine inches overall. Perfect for hiding in pocket or purse."

"And the program skewered to the body?"

"Beats me! A message of some sort?" He closed his bag and followed the stretcher out.

Fletcher came up the steps from the lower section. "I spotted an old friend of ours in the crowd."

"Who's that?"

"Joyce Train. Used to be a call girl working out of the Harbor Motor Lodge. Remember?"

"How could I forget? She's back in the business, isn't she?"

"So I heard."

"Let's go talk to her," Leopold decided.

They'd been given the use of Sam Barth's private office under the grandstand for questioning, and Fletcher brought Joyce in there. "Hello, Joyce. Enjoying the races?"

"Leopold! So there's been a murder?"

He nodded. "Aaron Flake. Know him?"

"I know him by sight. He wasn't one of my customers, if that's what you mean."

"What can you tell us, Joyce?"

"Nothing. I was out here betting on the dogs like everyone else."

Fletcher perched himself on the edge of the desk. "In your line of work it's good to give the police tips once in a while."

"You're not the vice squad!"

"But they're right down the hall at headquarters. Come on, Joyce. Think hard and give us some information. Who had it in for Flake?"

"I don't know a thing, honest!"

Leopold tried a different approach. "You said he wasn't a customer, and he didn't have a wife on the scene. Any chance he was homosexual?"

She shrugged. "Maybe. I saw him in bars with other men occasionally."

"How occasionally?"

"Last night."

"Who was the other man?"

She glanced away. "It was over at the Sportsman's Lounge. But it wasn't anything like that. This other guy's no queer."

"Suppose you let us decide that. Who was it?"

Joyce Train bit her lip and stalled for time. Leopold knew she would tell them the name, but she wanted to make it look like a difficult decision. "All right," she said finally. "It was Eddie Sargasso, the gambler."

"Sargasso!" Fletcher gave a low whistle. "Man, I'd like to hang something on him!"

"He's here tonight," Joyce added in a low voice.

"Here? At the track?"

She nodded. "You won't say it was me that told, will you?"

"Not unless we have to bring it out in court," Leopold promised. "He didn't see you at the Lounge last night?"

"No. I was in a booth with a—a friend."

"Thanks, Joyce. You've been a big help. We'll remember it." He turned to Fletcher. "Let's go find Eddie Sargasso before he gets away."


Eddie was standing in line with Marie, only three away from the officer taking down names and addresses of the personnel, when Leopold spotted him. He smiled and stuck out his hand. "Captain Leopold! This is a real pleasure!"

"Would you step into the office and have a word with us, Eddie? Your wife too?"

"And lose my place in line?" Sargasso asked with a try at lightness.

"You won't have to wait in line," Leopold assured him.

Eddie and Marie followed Leopold into a little office under the grandstand. He knew it belonged to Sam Barth, and wondered where the steward was.

"Now what's on your mind, Captain?"

"The murder of Aaron Flake."

"Terrible thing! Any idea who did it?"

"That's what we're working on. How well did you know him?"

The office door opened and Lieutenant Fletcher came in. That didn't surprise Eddie. He knew Leopold and Fletcher worked together. "Hardly at all," he answered. "I hardly knew him."

"You were having a drink with him last night in the Sportsman's Lounge downtown."

"Yeah? Hey, I guess that's right! Just happened to see him in there. That's the first time we ever talked, you know?"

"You're a gambler, Eddie, the sort who likes to gamble on sure things. There've been some shady races run at this track lately. Not the sort of thing you'd want to gamble on unless you had inside information."

"How do you fix a dog race?"

"That's what I'm asking you. Maybe you do it by bribing the hare operator."

"Not a chance! You saw what can happen if the hare isn't controlled just right. The dogs catch it, and there's no race. Those guys aren't licensed because they might be crooks. They're licensed because it takes a certain skill to run the hare at the proper distance from the dogs."

"I don't need any instructions on dog racing," Leopold said. "Suppose you tell me what you and Flake talked about."

"Nothing, I swear! Just barroom chat, that's all."

Leopold turned to Marie. "Were you with your husband at the time of the killing?"

She glanced sideways at Eddie, and his heart skipped a beat. They were really out to hang this on him! If only Marie would say the right—

"Not the exact instant," Marie admitted, and his hopes died. "I came up from the lower ticket window just after the race was stopped."

"She was placing a last-minute bet for me," Eddie explained.

"And what were you doing?"

"I was placing a bet too." He knew it sounded foolish, so he explained. "Sometimes people with inside information wait till the last minute to place big bets, so it doesn't cause a run on a certain dog and lower the odds too much. I watch the tote board and if I see a drop in odds during the final minute before a race I usually put a hundred on the dog. The same thing holds with horses. It's just smart betting."

"It's smart betting if you suspect something crooked."

"Well, yeah."

"Why wasn't your wife with you?"

"Sometimes you figure the length of the line wrong and get shut out when the machines lock. I figured with Marie and me in separate lines, at least one of us would make it to the windows in time."

"Did anyone see you there?"

He remembered Joyce. "Girl I know—Joyce Train. I saw her in line just before the board changed."

"But she didn't see you after the race started?"

"Well, no. I was on my way back to our seats."

Fletcher picked that moment to lean across to Leopold and hand him something. It looked to Eddie like an address book. "This was in the dead man's pocket, Captain."

Leopold studied the entry Fletcher had indicated, then passed it along to Eddie. "What do you make of this?"

*Marie S.*, it read, followed by a phone number. Eddie moistened his lips and said, "I don't know."

"Is that your number?"

"Yeah, I guess so."

He turned to Marie. "Mrs. Sargasso, do you have any explanation as to why the dead man had your name and phone number in his address book?"

"I—"

"Shut up, Marie!" Eddie barked.

Leopold leaned forward. "This is murder, Sargasso! And right now you're our prime suspect. You'd better let her talk."

Marie looked at him. "Eddie, we have to tell them what we know."

"Yeah," he agreed reluctantly. "I suppose so."

"Eddie wanted me to meet Flake and strike up an acquaintance. He knew there was something crooked going on at the track and we figured he'd be a good one to know about it. We'd seen him drinking alone at the bars around town, and I gave it a try, but I didn't get anywhere. I told him my name was Marie Sullivan and he wrote it down, but he never called me."

"How long ago was this?"

"Back in June, about a month ago."

"So last night I tried it," Eddie said. "I figured if he didn't like girls maybe I'd have better luck, just chatting with him over a few drinks. But nothing came of it."

"Something came of it," Leopold corrected him. "Aaron Flake was murdered."

"I don't know a thing about that."

Suddenly Marie had a thought. "Eddie, the tickets! We didn't cash them in yet. We've still got them!"

He saw at once what she was driving at. It just might be enough to save their skins. "That's right! The lines were so long we decided to wait till tomorrow night to get our refunds for the canceled race. I've got my hundred-dollar ticket on number four, and you can check the totalizator records to see that the odds on number four took a big drop in the final minute before the race. That was our signal to buy. You got your ticket, Marie?"

She nodded and dug around in her purse, finally producing it. Leopold took the tickets and studied them. "These were bought just before the race?"

"Less than a minute before. We didn't know which dog to bet on before that. And Flake was killed less than a minute into the race."

"I'll agree with that," Leopold said. "There's no way he could have run that rabbit with the knife in his back. It killed him almost instantly."

"Well, there! I couldn't have gotten from the ticket window to that booth in anything like two minutes. It's impossible!"

Leopold frowned and said, "Time it, Fletcher." He glanced at Marie. "Where did you buy your tickets?"

"Downstairs."

"Time it from where she was too. And see if there's a ticket seller closer to Flake's booth."

"Right, Captain."

"Those are the only two grandstand banks of windows," Eddie said. "There's another in the clubhouse, but that's way down at the other end. Besides, this number on the ticket identifies the machine that sold it."

Leopold nodded. "We'll see what Fletcher reports."

Eddie used the few minutes for chatter about the track, and about gambling in general. "There was a time when I'd bet on anything, Captain."

"Want to make a bet on whether I solve this case?"

"I might," Eddie answered carefully.

Fletcher came back shaking his head. "Looks like they're both in the clear, Captain. A fast walk from the upper windows to the booth took me two minutes and twenty-eight seconds. With the crowd here it would have been closer to three minutes. From downstairs where Marie bought her ticket it's even further—two minutes and forty-five seconds. They couldn't have bought these tickets and still gotten up to the booth in time to stab Flake."

Leopold sighed. "All right. You can go now."

Eddie got to his feet. "I'll lay two-to-one you don't crack this case, Captain."

"I'm not a betting man."

"That's too bad."


After they'd gone, Leopold and Fletcher went back to the kennel area, walking beneath the lights past row after row of barking dogs. "They're restless," he told Fletcher. "Unhappy, like me."

"You still think Sargasso's guilty, don't you?"

"He's a two-bit gambler who never did an honest day's work in his life. But we can't get a murder conviction on those grounds."

Up ahead they saw the man from the betting commission, and Leopold called to him. "Mr. Wayne, do you have a minute?"

Donald Wayne turned and waited for them to catch up. "Just talking to a few of the owners about what happened," he said.

"Do they have any information?"

"Nothing. No one can imagine Flake having an enemy. He was such a quiet guy."

"How about friends? Did he have any of those?"

"Not many, according to Sam Barth. He knew Flake better than I did, certainly."

"What's going on at this track?" Leopold asked. "They've been fixing races, haven't they?"

"What gives you that idea?"

"Eddie Sargasso told me a lot of money was being bet on certain dogs just before post time. And those dogs usually won."

"I wish he'd make his accusations to me."

"You a friend of Eddie's?"

Donald Wayne nodded. "From the old days, before I was on the betting commission. We used to play poker together."

"But not anymore?"

"Matter of fact, he invited me over for a game on Friday night. Don't know if I'll be going now."

"Who else was at these games?"

"Sam Barth, sometimes."

"Mr. Wayne, if there was a fix in at this track, how could it be worked?"

"Oh, lots of ways. They run twelve races a night, with eight dogs per race. That's nearly a hundred dogs each night. Of course, most dogs race every evening, and travel a circuit through the three New England states that have dog tracks. The owners get to know one another. Sometimes they get to know each other so well that a group of them will get together and take turns winning. The other owners or trainers hold back their dogs by various methods and one man wins. Then it's someone else's turn."

"Is that going on here?"

"To some extent." He spread his hands. "To some extent it probably happens at horse tracks—especially harness tracks—too. But that doesn't mean it led to Aaron Flake's death. He wouldn't have been a party to it."

"Except that he's watching the race very carefully through binoculars, every foot of the way. He knows the way greyhounds run, and he recognizes it when they're running different—either too fast or too slow. He could have been blackmailing somebody."

"Yes, I suppose so. But who'd be foolish enough to kill him like that, in the middle of a race? A blackmail victim would more likely choose a dark street after the race, when there was less chance of discovery."

"That's true," Leopold agreed. "It's almost as if the killer *had* to do it during the race."

"And leave that program pinned to his back with the knife," Fletcher reminded them. "If you ask me, it's some nut with a grudge against dog tracks."

"Except that Flake unlatched the door for this person."

"Couldn't the latch have been flipped from outside with a piece of plastic or a credit card?" Wayne suggested.

Fletcher shook his head. "I tried that. There's a strip of wood around the jamb that prevents it."

Sam Barth came hurrying up from the direction of the grandstand. "I've been looking for you, Captain. Here's that list of track personnel you requested. Any one of them could have gained admission to the booth."

Leopold glanced at the typewritten sheets. "I think we can rule out the ticket sellers and gate personnel. And any security guards with fixed posts. Likewise the judges, the paddock steward, the starter, and the timekeeper. None of those people could have left their positions during the race. That still leaves stewards like yourself, plus most of the owners and trainers, the veterinarian, and others."

"Plus Flake's friends."

"Yes, if he had any." Leopold was staring up at the grandstand, where the lights were beginning to go out.

"What are you thinking, Captain?" Fletcher asked.

"I'm thinking we should come back here tomorrow night."

Leopold spent much of the following day on the phone to the Florida police. When he'd finished, he thought he had the beginnings of an idea.

"Look here, Fletcher—Aaron Flake once worked at a dog track in Miami where an owner was knifed to death in his trailer."

"The same sort of weapon."

"Exactly. It's just possible that Flake was a blackmailer after all—but blackmailing a murderer instead of a race fixer."

"That still doesn't tell us who did it."

"Were there any fingerprints on the knife or the program?"

Fletcher shook his head. "Wiped clean."

"Blackmail or not, the killer still risked a great deal stabbing Flake during the race, when he knew people would rush to the booth to see what was wrong."

Fletcher brought in two cups of coffee from the temperamental machine in the hall. "Any chance the lever controlling the rabbit could have been turned on automatically, after the killer left the booth?"

"None at all. The starter signaled Flake to release the rabbit. He had to be alive then, even if the killer was standing right behind him in the booth."

Fletcher set the coffee cup on a square piece of cardboard that Leopold used as a coaster. Leopold stared at it in silence for a moment and then said, "You did that to protect the desk, in case the coffee spilled."

"What?"

"Just thinking out loud, Fletcher. I've got an idea who killed Aaron Flake, and I know how we can prove it at the track tonight."


News of the murder had obviously not hurt the dog track's business. By the time Leopold and Fletcher arrived, shortly after the gates opened, lines of people were pouring in.

"Curiosity seekers," Sam Barth said, standing in his red jacket just inside the entrance. "By next week they'll be onto something else."

"Have you seen Eddie Sargasso yet?" Leopold asked.

"Not yet, but he'll be here."

Leopold sent Fletcher to cover the lower-level ticket windows while he took the upstairs ones himself. Sargasso hadn't gone to the clubhouse the previous night, so he probably wouldn't go there tonight. It was just a matter of waiting.

"Looking for killers?" someone asked. It was Joyce Train, with a man the Captain didn't know.

"That's right," Leopold said. "I read somewhere they always return to the scene of the crime."

He chatted with her a moment and then glanced back at the lines. Eddie Sargasso was there, with his wife right behind him. Leopold hurried over, edging through the thickening crowd.

"Hello, Captain," Eddie said. "Break the case yet?"

"Just about."

Eddie reached the window and pushed a ticket through. "We're cashing in our tickets on the canceled race last night," he explained.

"I know," Leopold said.

Eddie took his $100 and stepped aside. Then, as fast as he could act, Leopold's hand shot out to grip Marie Sargasso's wrist. "Not so fast, Marie. I want to see that."

Eddie made a move toward Leopold. "What in hell are you doing?"

"You may not know it, Eddie, but it was your wife who murdered Aaron Flake, and the proof of it is here in her hand."

"You're crazy!" Sargasso growled. "Marie, tell him he's crazy!"

But the life seemed to have gone out of her. "It's true, Eddie," she said simply. "I killed him."

Later, in Sam Barth's office under the grandstand, Leopold explained. "These tickets were the key to it," he said, fanning eight tickets on the previous night's race across the desk. "Marie's alibi, like her husband's, rested on the fact that she was in line, waiting for the odds to change so she could make a last-minute bet on a certain dog. And sure enough, she and Eddie each produced a ticket on the number four entry. Fletcher timed it and verified they couldn't have bought the tickets and still reached the booth in time to stab Flake."

"So how'd she do it?" Barth asked.

"Simply by buying one ticket on each of the eight dogs in the race, as soon as she went downstairs. That gave her time to reach the booth and kill Flake, and still hold a hundred-dollar ticket on whichever dog showed that last-minute odds change. Sure, it cost her eight hundred dollars, but she knew better than anyone else the race would never be completed. She knew she could get her money back on the tickets last night or today. I heard Eddie say they'd do it today because the lines were too long last night. Of course, Eddie had no idea his wife was guilty. That was the main reason for her elaborate scheme. Most other people might have killed Flake in an alley, but Marie had to do it in such a way that she'd have a perfect alibi—not only for the police but for her husband!"

"But *why* did she kill him?" Sam Barth asked.

"We're digging into that. We think Marie killed a man at a Florida dog track years ago and got away with it. Eddie sent her to make Flake's acquaintance as part of their scheme to get inside dope on the fixed races. Flake recognized her from Florida and had some sort of knowledge connecting her with the prior killing. When he tried to blackmail her, she decided to kill him. She knew Eddie usually sent her to buy a last-minute ticket on the races, and she used that as her alibi. She went to the booth, pretending she had a blackmail payment for Flake, and he let her in. While his back was turned controlling the hare, she took the knife from her purse and stabbed him."

"Through the program?" Fletcher asked.

"I saw that coaster under my coffee cup today and I got the idea, Fletcher. The knife blade was sticking through the program when she stabbed him so it would act as a shield against possible bloodstains. That was the only likely explanation.

"So what did we know? The killer was someone Flake knew—either as a coworker or as an acquaintance. The killer found it necessary to murder Flake during the dog race, even with the risk involved. And the killer had to take great care to avoid even a speck of blood. Whom did that point to?"

"Couldn't it have been Sargasso as well as his wife?"

"Not likely. Eddie was wearing a dark brown jacket yesterday, remember? Likewise, Sam here and all the other track personnel wear dark red blazers. Even Donald Wayne had on a rumpled brown suit, and I think that girl Joyce wore brown too. Dark brown or dark red wouldn't likely show a bloodstain that obviously—not so the killer would find it necessary to use that program trick. But Marie Sargasso was wearing what?—a white pantsuit! Even a speck of blood would have been fatal to her."

"There must have been a thousand other women at the track wearing white or light summer colors," Fletcher protested.

"But their names and phone numbers weren't in Flake's address book. And they weren't from Florida, as Marie was."

"Why'd she wear white if she was planning the murder?"

Leopold shrugged. "Maybe Eddie liked it on her, and she couldn't attract his suspicion by refusing to wear it. The important thing was that she avoided any blood splattering from the wound by using the program as a guard."

Eddie Sargasso rode down to headquarters in the car with his wife and Leopold. She was silent and her head was bowed. Eddie held her hand all the way, and at one point he said, "You should have taken my bet, Leopold. You solved the case."

"I told you I wasn't a gambler."

"You gambled that she'd break down and confess. You had no real evidence against her."

Leopold thought about it and said, "I suppose there are different sorts of gambling, Eddie. When you put it that way, maybe we're not so different after all."

# JOAN RICHTER

# THE WASTE PILE AT APPLE BOW

He'd seen the destruction of the land from the air—the hills and hollows of the earth's flesh, scarred and scabbed under a helpless sun. But from the plane window it had been distant and unreal. It wasn't until the TV news correspondent had begun his climb up the steep mountain path, following the old miner, that he began to understand what the big mining interests had done to Appalachia.

By the calendar it was spring; but the only evidence of the land's rebirth was an occasional stalk of fern pushing up a clot of rotting leaves. His eyes smarted from the smoggy haze that hung like gray angel's hair from the branches of the unleafed trees. Steve Jaros licked his lips and felt the grime of coal dust rough under his tongue.

On the path ahead of him he heard the miner cough, and he listened to the lingering rattle in the old man's chest. It was the only sound in the stillness besides that of their footfalls on the trail. There were no birdsongs, no rustle of squirrels scurrying among the dead leaves. There was no sign of any animal life at all.

The strip mines and the smoldering piles of coal wastes that had been blackening the hills for years were now wrenching the last bit of life from the air and the soil.

He shifted the strap of his camera on his shoulder and undid the buttons of his suede jacket. Though the air was cold and raw, the exertion of the uphill climb had made him warm. Usually the camera wasn't his to carry; but when he'd learned that the mining company was refusing to talk to newsmen and that the miners were being equally silent, he'd decided to enter Apple Bow with a minimum of fanfare. He had come alone, leaving his cameraman and sound man back at the small hotel in Elkton, on the other side of the mountain.

The decision had one severe drawback. It meant he was limited to using the Filmo, a small camera without sound. Yet had Charlie and Usher and all their equipment been with him when he'd walked into the schoolhouse now converted into a rescue shelter, he would have met with an even colder wall of reserve. He wouldn't have got any answers at all. He wouldn't be headed now for what was left of the waste pile overlooking the hollow of Apple Bow.

At least, that was where he hoped Newt Boyd was taking him. But he wasn't really sure.

For more than half an hour they had been walking in silence, single file, following the steep rutted trail. Ahead of him, gun and game bag slung over his shoulder, the frail old man leaned into the steep incline. Now and again his shoulders shook with a fit of coughing.

When the trail showed signs of leveling off, Newt Boyd stopped and turned around. "Let's set here a minute." He moved off to the side and settled himself on a large boulder.

Across the way, Steve leaned back against the trunk of a tree. As he slipped the camera from his shoulder he saw Newt peering at him, faded blue eyes staring intently from under wrinkled, drooping lids. The miner cleared his throat, and Steve had the feeling that the pause in the trek up the hillside might have another purpose besides a rest.

"I suppose you heard the company's claiming that flood slide was an 'Act of God.' "

Steve nodded. He'd heard the no-liability position the company had taken, and he'd read the terse statement that used just those words— "Act of God."

"They're blaming the rains. Well, rains come every spring. But the company held off until the clouds were hangin' right in there between them hills before they did what they should have done months ago. The thunder and lightning was crackling so hard you couldn't hear nothin' on the radio. The rain was coming down in sheets. That's when they tried to blast, hoping to shore things up. But it was too late. There weren't nothin' that could have changed the course of that slide then."

"Are you saying the company *knew* that waste pile at Apple Bow was in danger of collapsing?"

"Sure they knew! Everybody around here knew it was restless. For more than a year we'd been listening to the rumbling and the shifting deep inside that heap, watchin' the water build up behind it, seein' it start to seep through. A survey done last year by some government inspecting team put Apple Bow on the list of piles to be shored up. But the company knew nobody was gonna come around to check, so they did nothin'—until it was too late."

Steve cast a frustrated glance down at the camera on the ground. It would do no good to film Newt Boyd without sound, and there was no point in wishing Charlie and Usher were with him now. If only he'd be able to get Newt Boyd to repeat later the things he was saying now . . .

The miner turned sideways and pointed toward a distant spot through the trees. "See off there. There's another pile just like the one at Apple Bow."

Steve's eyes focused on a blackened mound, hooded by a layer of gray cloud. That was what Apple Bow had looked like, before the water had gathered behind it and turned it into a hurtling avalanche of rock and mud and coal waste. One hundred twenty-four people had been killed, and more than three thousand left homeless.

"There's hundreds of others of them piles, scattered all over these coal hills, all sitting and waiting until somethin' starts them shifting. Once they start, there ain't nothin' that'll stop them."

There was no point in waiting any longer, Steve decided. Now was the time to broach the subject of filming the waste pile at Apple Bow. He could get what he needed with the Filmo. Later he'd try to persuade Newt to talk to him in front of the sound camera that Charlie and Usher had in Elkton.

"How about it, Newt? How close can we get to the pile at Apple Bow?"

The miner was gazing off in the distance, still looking at the other smoldering mound. His head turned slowly.

"You'd have to get mighty close to get any pictures of them boreholes where they put the powder when they tried to blast. The company's posted guards to make sure nobody comes snoopin' around. They got guns and orders to shoot anybody trespassing."

Steve knew about the guards, though he hadn't known they were armed. The way he saw it, the company's aggressive silence made it a sure bet it had something to hide. The miners weren't talking because they had something to fear. These suspicions, side by side, aroused not just his interest but his anger.

"There's going to be an official investigation in a few days, Newt. Then the company won't be able to keep anyone away; but I don't want to wait. I want that film now."

"Well, it ain't gonna be easy. Anybody going in there has a good chance of getting his head shot through. This ain't the first time a dam's broke in these parts and it's been the company's fault. It ain't the first time we had to go digging for our dead. There's always some hollerin' right afterwards, and politicians make a lot of promises, giving us to believe something's gonna be done. Nothin' ever is. You don't know how powerful these big companies are."

Newt looked away, and against the gray day his profile was sad and lonely. A scraggly beard camouflaged his sunken cheeks, but the loose brown coat did little to hide the dejection and fatigue in the thin rounded shoulders.

Up until then Steve hadn't been able to put his finger on the whole of what was driving him after this story—why, when he had met a wall of silence to his questions, he hadn't simply been satisfied with recounting the details of the disaster and letting it go at that, returning when and if an investigation turned up new information. That was what other correspondents from other networks had done.

But he was incensed by the company's arrogance, its pontifical stand that an "Act of God" had caused the collapse of the waste pile. He bristled at the company's self-exoneration while all around him he saw signs of its negligence and its culpability. His eyes swept over the gray-brown woodland, as barren as any he had seen in war zones, and he tried to imagine what it had been like before the mining companies had come, when springtime had meant trees in leaf, a ground cover of wildflowers, and small animals and birds stirring in the brush.

But there was yet another ingredient in the angry mix of his emotions which kept him after the story that lay buried in the rubble of maimed lives. It was what he saw in Newt Boyd's face now, in the droop of his shoulders and the set of defeat in his bones; what he had seen in all the faces at the rescue shelter, except in the girl's.

He remembered the toss of her blond head, the resolute set of her chin, and the fiery flash of determination in her deep blue eyes. Even if she were not one of the prettiest young women he'd seen in a long time, she would have stood apart from the others because of her spirit.

He couldn't rid himself of the feeling that she was responsible for Newt Boyd's coming forward, that it was because of her that Newt Boyd was talking to him now.

The old man shifted his position on the boulder and cleared his throat. "There's somethin' you might not know. The company's got a way of drying up a man's living if he's heard complaining. That's one of the reasons them folks at the shelter wasn't saying anything."

"Why are you taking the chance, Newt?"

The old man shrugged. "Fed up. Tired of letting them get away with things. I'm not young anymore. My family's grown. I got nothin' to lose."

Steve walked to where the miner was sitting and put his hand on his shoulder. "Newt, the public has been stirred up by what happened here. But people have a way of forgetting things that don't involve them directly. They have to be kept stirred up until the investigation gets started. If there are enough angry people around, demanding answers, the company's negligence and the government's ineffective inspection system won't get swept under the rug this time."

"How're you gonna go about doing that?"

"By keeping the story alive; by showing people what these hills look like close up; by letting them hear what the miners and their families have to say. To begin with, I want film of Apple Bow."

A light flickered in Newt Boyd's eyes, but in an instant it was gone. "You sure you understand what I've been telling you? Them guards have been hired to watch out for fellas like you. If they catch you spying, or trespassing, or whatever you want to call it, they'll shoot, just as if you was a crow sittin' on a fence. And if needs be, afterwards, they'll say that's what they thought you was, a crow."

"Damn it, Newt, what else are you going to come up with? Are you going to take me there, or do I go alone?" Steve picked up his camera and slung it over his shoulder.

A grin creased through the scraggly beard. There was no mistaking the brightness in the faded blue eyes now. "Lorny said you can't tell a bird while he's all sleeked and strutting. You gotta get him a little ruffled to find out what's under all them feathers. That silk neck thing and that fancy suede jacket you're wearing had me thinkin' you might be all show and no innards. Guess I was wrong. Lorny will be mighty pleased with herself when she finds out."

He got to his feet with a sprightliness Steve hadn't seen before and said, "Let's go."

But Steve put a hand on his arm.

"Who's Lorny?"

"My daughter. Seen you eyeing her at the shelter. Pretty thing she is, but sometimes she's got a mind harder than a hickory nut. She's waiting lunch for us, and I expect she's gonna be a bit fussed. We're late."

Steve wasn't about to be sidetracked. "What about filming Apple Bow, Newt?"

"Let's eat first and talk later. Lorny's got a plan."

Steve shook his head, exasperated. At least he'd been right about the girl. His curiosity mounted as he followed Newt back on the trail.

In a few minutes, they rounded a bend and he saw a small gray house set back among the trees.

"Needs painting," Newt said. "Lorny was all for starting it this week. Said it would be good therapy, but I've not been of a mind. Since she's come, she's set herself to ironing curtains and washing windows, between helping down at the shelter. Long time ago her brothers and me promised her ma we'd see she went away to school. Martha didn't want Lorny ending up like all the other women in the hollows, waitin' for their men to come up out of the mines. Lorny's been gone six years, graduated college most two years ago."

"Where does she live?"

"Up North; works in the big city. Came right down when she got the news. She's talking about stayin' on, but this ain't no place for her."

Their voices must have carried into the house, because the front door swung open and Lorna Boyd appeared in the doorway, blond head tossing, an impatient hand on a slim jeaned hip.

"I should have known noon would mean closer to two!" A smile softened the reprimand in her blue eyes.

"Now, let's not start in scolding, girl. I had a few things on my mind that needed straight'nin' out." He turned to Steve. "This here's my daughter, Lorna. Guess she knows you. Says she's seen you on TV. Can't say I have. Don't have a TV, and when I get a chance to see one, don't watch the news. Don't watch them hillbilly programs either. Makes us mountain folk out to be a bunch of dumb clowns."

Lorna Boyd smiled and held out a slim, smooth hand. "I thought you were still in Vietnam."

"I got back a couple of weeks ago. This is my first Stateside assignment in a long while."

"How does it compare?"

An honest answer would have plunged them into a lengthy and morbid discussion, so he avoided it. "Any place you haven't been before is strange. It helps, though, when everybody speaks the same language."

"Do we?" There was the unmistakable glint of mischief in her eyes.

He responded with a slow grin as he followed her into the house. "There *have* been moments when I've not been so sure."

In a bathroom down the hall, where fresh white curtains framed a window that faced a hillside of scraggy oaks and pines, Steve splashed some water on his face and pulled a comb through his dark curly hair. For a moment he stared at his reflection, smiling, wondering if "sleeked and strutting" had really been her words, if that was the impression he had made on Lorny Boyd.

Because her speech still held some traces of mountain twang, she presented an interesting mixture of sophistication and homeyness. Their brief exchange outside revealed a mind that was quick and pleasantly combative. Her time away from the hills must have changed her a great deal from the girl she had been. He liked the way her eyes sparkled, with a hidden challenge, and the way her yellow knit shirt hugged her gentle curves and fitted tidily into lean beige Levi's.

When he returned to the kitchen, she was at the stove taking a platter of fried chicken from the oven.

She glanced up and smiled. "I hope you're hungry."

"I didn't realize how much until I stepped in here." He sniffed the air appreciatively.

"Everything's ready, and Dad's waiting for you." She nodded toward a round table by the window where Newt was already seated and three places were set.

"How about a mite of whiskey?" Newt offered, and reached for a jug on the floor at his side.

"I can't think of anything I'd like more," Steve said agreeably.

Newt filled two small glasses. "Goes down nice and easy." He handed one to Steve and waited. Steve tipped the glass to his lips, bracing himself. He'd had mountain brew before. But he was pleasantly surprised and nodded his approval.

"Local?"

"Don't drink nothin' else," Newt said, with a grin. "Two's my limit, though. Doctor says I shouldn't drink at all account of the cough. But the few extra days it might give me ain't worth it."

Lorny joined them, adding a basket of warm buttered biscuits and a bowl of salad to the chicken that was already on the table.

"How did you manage all this?" Steve asked as she held the platter out to him. "You were still at the shelter when your father and I left."

She glanced quickly across the table and then back at Steve. "There's a shortcut. It takes only about ten minutes to get up here."

Steve raised an eyebrow and looked at Newt.

The miner shrugged. "There was some thinking I had to do. Some questions that needed answering. Takes a while to figure out a man. Ain't sure I got you figured all the way, but I got a pretty good idea. Wanted to give you enough chances to change your mind."

"One more and I might have."

"Don't think so. You're the kind, the harder it gets, the more you want it."

Steve smiled. "Could be."

"But I think it's time we stopped being cagey and got down to business. First off, there's somethin' you should know." Newt paused, his gaze lowered, hovering over his plate. Then his head came up. "Four of our kin were killed in that slide at Apple Bow—my two sons and my daughter-in-law and my four-year-old granddaughter. They was having the little girl's birthday party. I should have been there, only I'd been to Elkton to do some buying. Got held up because of the rain."

Steve drew in a long breath.

"Don't bother trying to say anything. There ain't nothin' anybody can say. But you gotta know from that I got no love for the company. And neither does Lorny. But up until you came along we weren't in agreement as to what to do about it. Right after it happened, before Lorny come down, I near went crazy. I took my gun and I went out looking for somebody to blame. I guess I would have shot the first company man I seen, except I got a bad coughing spell and could no more walk than I could shoot, so I come on home."

Newt looked toward a corner of the kitchen where the rifle and game bag stood. Steve followed his glance and felt frustration boil within him. A great story was unfolding before him. A newspaper reporter listened and went to a typewriter and wrote it down. But without film and a voice to go along with it, the story Newt was telling him was worthless for television.

"Lorny's got different ideas from the rest of us who've never been out of these hills. Mountain folk have always stayed to themselves, not mixing even with each other much. Lorny says we have to change our ways. Doing things alone ain't gonna get us nowhere now. We got to organize, she says."

Across the table, the smooth curves of Lorny's cheeks were touched with pink, and anger had once again crept into the deep blue of her eyes. She looked as she had at the shelter, determined and ready to fight.

She leaned toward Steve and spoke with quiet control. "You saw those people at the shelter today, patiently waiting to find out what was going to happen to them—women who had lost their husbands, miners who'd used their own picks and shovels to dig out their dead children. All of them homeless, victims of big-company negligence and power, grateful when a Red Cross worker gave them a bologna sandwich!"

Her blond head tossed, and her hand reached out and gripped his arm. "They don't know their rights or how to go about finding out what they are. Somebody has to help them! Someone has to show them how!"

Newt's head jerked in his daughter's direction. "Let's not start that again. I didn't send you up North so you could turn right around and come back here. This ain't no place for you, Lorny. Your mother will be crying in her grave."

She eased herself back in her chair and took her hand from Steve's arm. She looked at her father. "All right," she said softly. "We won't talk about that now."

"We're not gonna talk about it ever. Now, that's settled." Newt banged his empty glass on the table. "Now suppose we get on with explaining your plan."

Lorna Boyd's blue eyes left her father and turned to Steve. "I'll take you to Apple Bow. We'll leave before dusk this afternoon and get there by dark. We'll stay overnight so we can be there at dawn before the guards get up. You should be able to get all the film you want, without their even knowing you've been there. If Dad took you, he'd be sure to get one of his coughing spells."

Steve looked at Newt. The pieces were beginning to fit. Up until now he still hadn't been able to figure out the miner's reticence to take him to Apple Bow. Now he at least had some idea what was behind it.

"She's somethin', ain't she? Worked this all out herself, even before you showed up at the shelter. Claims she knew you were the kind who wouldn't be satisfied without digging into things."

"What do you mean before I showed up at the shelter? How did you know I was coming?"

Lorny's blue eyes sparkled. "The man who tends bar at the hotel in Elkton is my uncle. He overheard you talking with your crew."

Steve shook his head, grinning slightly. "You've got as good a spy system as I've seen anywhere."

Newt chuckled. "I didn't like the sound of this idea at first, but I guess it will work out all right. How's it strike you?"

"So far, so good; but Apple Bow isn't enough. I need you on film, Newt, saying the kinds of things you told me on the way up here, about the company knowing the pile was unstable and not doing anything about it until it was too late."

"Lorny said you'd want that. That's why I'm going to Elkton this afternoon and get those two fellas you left waiting there and that big camera."

"Is there anything you two haven't thought of?"

Newt shrugged. "Maybe. I'll get them and their stuff to the other side of Apple Bow, just across from where you're gonna be. Between the lot of you, you should get all the pictures you want. After that's done we can talk."

Steve looked at Lorna. "You the expert on TV equipment in this family?"

"I took an elective course in radio and TV techniques at college. I knew the camera you have with you now has no sound."

Steve eyed her appreciatively as she rose to clear the dishes from the table and returned with a pot of coffee. He forced his mind to return to the problem of the interviews he wanted. Now more than before, it wouldn't be enough to talk only to Newt. Four members of his family had lost their lives in the slide. It would be natural for Newt's objectivity to be questioned. He explained this.

"What will it take to get some of the other miners to talk to me?"

Newt's eyes narrowed and his thin lips pursed. A thoughtful expression came to his face. "After tomorra morning you won't have no trouble. I promise you."

A look of apprehension darkened Lorna's blue eyes. "What are you planning to do?"

"Ain't telling nobody. So there's no use your pesting." Newt pushed his chair back from the table and rose stiffly. "Since it's a long ways to Elkton, I'm gonna take a bit of rest. Wake me in an hour if I ain't up by then."

Steve called after him: "You can use the car I left a couple of streets away from the shelter."

Newt grinned. "I wondered if you'd get around to offering or if I'd have to ask. Blue Chevy, ain't it, parked just a few yards from the post office?"

Steve shook his head as the miner walked down the hall to his bedroom. Then he turned to Lorna. "I have to hand it to you two. You sure have led me up a mountain path."

But this time her responding smile was only fleeting, overpowered by the concern in her eyes. "What do you suppose he's up to?"

"You're asking me?"

While Newt slept, Lorna Boyd drew a sketch of the area around the Apple Bow waste pile, showing Steve where she planned to take him; she also mapped out the approach his camera crew would follow on the other side.

"I find it hard to believe if we got that far without being stopped, the three of us couldn't just walk up to that pile and start filming. Those guards can't shoot all three of us and say we were crows sitting on a fence."

"I do believe we are beginning to speak the same language." The sparkle was back in her eyes. "No, I don't think they'd shoot the three of you. But they wouldn't let you film, either. So what would that accomplish? The only way to do it is without their knowing."

She leaned toward him. "Steve, do you understand what this will mean to the miners? It will show them that the company can be challenged. Maybe their knowing that will be enough to convince them they should talk to you."

Her face brightened. "I bet that's what my father plans to do—take a few men along with him and let them see for themselves. You know people here don't know there's a difference between TV newsmen and

the men who put on those awful hillbilly programs. My father didn't. It
took a lot of talking to convince him. He didn't trust you. Why should
they?"

Steve shook his head. "You're right. Why should they? Why do
you?"

She wrinkled her nose at him. "I've been out in the big, wide world.
Besides, I need you to help me get things started here. My father doesn't
like the idea of my coming back. I'm not really sure I want to. But
sometimes I think it's the only right thing. To leave here and get an
education and not come back and help out—"

"And here I've been hoping to see you in New York."

"That would be nice." She smiled wistfully. "It isn't easy to decide."

"None of the big ones are."

While she did the dishes, he wrote a note to Charlie and Usher,
explaining what the plan was, enclosing the map she had made of the
area surrounding Apple Bow.

Newt had been asleep almost an hour when the sound of coughing
came from his room, deep and strangled. Lorna started down the hall,
but stopped outside his door. In a while she came back to the kitchen.

"He's lived with it for so long now. But someday . . ." She left the
sentence unfinished.

In a few minutes Newt joined them. "You got things ready for
tonight, Lorny?"

She opened the door of a cupboard and took out three bulging pil-
lowcases. "Blankets, food, and something to drink." She reached up to
a hanger and handed Steve a heavy woolen sweater and a worn leather
jacket.

"It will be cold tonight. What you're wearing won't be warm enough,
and besides, you don't exactly melt into the landscape."

He grinned. "I'll have you know I bought this jacket in Spain, and
the scarf came all the way from Bangkok."

"You don't say? Well, peacocks never were a part of these woods,
and if they were, they'd be mighty scarce by now. So you'd better
change your feathers or those guards will shoot you for the wrong
reasons."

Steve threw his head back and laughed. Then, with a deliberate glance that ticked off her yellow knit shirt and the trim Levi's, he asked, "And what are you going to wear?"

"You won't recognize me when I've changed."

"You want to bet?"

Newt cleared his throat. "Listen, you two, this ain't no picnic you're going on. Don't go getting carried away with that kind of nonsense."

"What nonsense?" she asked, the color in her cheeks deepening.

"Listen here, girl, I'm not dead yet, and besides, my memory is pretty good. I can see it's a waste of time saying anything else, so I'd best just be on my way." He thrust out a bony, callused hand at Steve. "Maybe when this is all over you can do somethin' about them hillbilly programs. Keep an eye on her. She thinks she knows it all, but she don't."

Lorna kissed her father's cheek. "I'd forgotten how ornery you can be."

Newt started toward the door, then stopped, walked back across the room, and hoisted his rifle and game bag over his shoulder.

Lorny's hand reached out. "Pa." In the one word her voice was a frightened child's whisper.

Newt patted her hand. "Don't go frettin' none. I've lived a long time, and I know what I'm doing."

In the middle of the night, Steve woke to a thick blackness all around him. There were no stars to be seen, only the dim shadows of the moon, hidden by a heavy layer of clouds.

Beside him Lorna Boyd stirred, and he felt her breath sweep past his cheek, the soft silk of her hair brush his ear.

He lay still, waiting for the horizon of the dark night to become fringed with the glow of a coming dawn.

Before they left the house, she had taken him around to the back where the spikes of crocus leaves had struggled up through the sour earth: the last of a garden her mother had planted years before. Lorny had pointed out the roof of the schoolhouse below and the winding path of the shortcut.

"When I was a little girl, there used to be bushels of violets to pick in the spring. My brothers used to go hunting for raccoon and squirrel and wildcat. One summer a flock of bluebirds flew into that tree over there. But nothing lives or grows here now—only human beings."

Her face had been turned away from him, her thoughts involved in a private memory. He remembered thinking how lovely she was, even in the baggy dark gray coat that belonged to her father. In another time, in another woods, he would have turned her toward him and taken her in his arms and kissed her. But instead, he reached for a stick and broke it in two.

Dawn now hovered below the horizon of the sky. He woke her, and they untangled themselves from the coverings and rose, stretching cramped limbs. She poured them steaming coffee from a thermos.

They were on the downward slope of the hillside, overlooking the high and the hollow of Apple Bow. As dawn lifted and the spread of light fanned upward into the sky, an ugly, sprawling black shadow took shape in the shallow valley not far below: the dregs of the waste pile.

Steve began to film at regular intervals, following the progression of dawn into day. While his eye was to the camera, a sudden beam of brilliant sunlight pierced the layers of cloud cover, and with the accuracy of an arrow finding its mark, it illuminated a string of boreholes at the base of the collapsed waste pile.

Beside him, Lorny touched his arm and pointed, exclaiming softly. He nodded and swept the area with the camera.

He lowered it and turned to her. "Look over there," he said softly, pointing to the opposite hillside. "Did you see that?" There was a sudden brief glint of light, there one instant, then gone, then repeated, with no set pattern.

"What is it?" she asked.

"Sun glancing off a camera lens. Your father got to Elkton. Charlie and Usher are where he said they would be." He wondered if Newt was with them. "Where are the guards?"

She held on to his arm and leaned forward, pointing to a spot just below them, still in partial shadow, not yet discovered by the sun. He could make out the shape of a lean-to.

He changed the film in the camera and put the reel he'd shot into a weatherproof bag.

"You stay here. I want to get a closer look," he said.

Her blue eyes defied him, and he knew there was neither time nor point to argument. Newt had warned him she was strong-willed.

The ground was soft from the recent rains, and any leaves left from previous years were damp and made no sound underfoot. The greatest hazard was the possibility of slipping, but there was enough low growth for them to catch on to as they made their slow descent.

Suddenly the murmur of voices reached them, and they stopped. Three figures emerged from the lean-to, burly men in heavy woolen coats. One had a shotgun, held lightly in his hand; the other two carried rifles. Steve raised the Filmo to his eye and followed the men as they fanned out into a semicircle and walked to a midpoint in the hollow.

As the three men spread out, Steve could see that their heads were raised, their eyes scanning the encircling hillside. For a moment he felt a pair of eyes looking directly at him, but they slid away without acknowledgment.

Across the way, the glint of sunlight came and went again. The man with the shotgun called out, and one of his partners lifted a pair of binoculars hanging from a strap around his neck and trained them on the hillside across the way.

Beside him Lorny's fingers grabbed and bit into his arm. But the camera was up to his face and he would not be distracted. The man with the binoculars let them fall to his chest and was bringing his rifle up to his shoulder.

"Steve!" Her voice beside him was an imperative hoarse cry. His eyes flashed toward her for an instant, and he saw her face chalk-white against the dark gray of her father's wool coat.

But Lorny was not looking at the man with the rifle. Her face was turned sideward, eyes wide with terror, focused on the small bent figure coming up from the mouth of the hollow.

Steve watched as Newt Boyd picked his way amid the rubble of the wash, heading in a straight line for the three armed guards.

Across the way, a sparkle of light glinted against the brown hillside. The guard's rifle was raised and aimed.

"Hey, what you fellas shooting at?" Newt's voice rang out clear as a shot in the hollow.

Three guns swung and fired. Newt Boyd staggered and fell still to the ground.

Over Lorny's agonized moan Steve heard the sound of gunfire coming from the woods below. A shower of black earth sprang up and spattered around the feet of the guards. Guns fell from their hands and their arms reached into the air.

A small band of miners started out of the woods, moving slowly across the blackened earth of the hollow.

Lorny buried her face against Steve's chest. He took her in his arms and laid his cheek against her hair.

On the opposite hillside came the familiar glint of sun off the camera's lens. Charlie and Usher were there, with sound and film. Steve was sure they had got it all.

Slowly she lifted her head and he looked into her upturned face, into blue eyes blurred by tears, filled with sorrow and uncertainty.

His voice was husky in his throat when he spoke, and his eyes stung. "Your father didn't plan it this way, but he knew it could happen—and he took the chance."

She nodded quickly, biting her lower lip. Then she reached for his hand, and in a while they started down into the hollow together.

# WILLIAM F. NOLAN

# SATURDAY'S SHADOW

First, before I tell you about Laurie—about what happened to her (in blood)—I must tell you about primary shadows. It is vitally important that I tell you about these shadows. Each day has one, and they have entirely different characteristics, variant personalities.

Sunday's shadow (the one Laurie liked; her friend) is fat and sleepy. Snoozes all day.

Monday's shadow is thin and pale at the edges. The sun eats it fast.

Tuesday's shadow is silly and random-headed. Lumpy in the middle. Never knows where it's been or where it's going. No sense of purpose to it.

Wednesday's shadow is pushy. Arrogant. Full of bombast. All it's after is attention. Ignore it, don't humor it.

Thursday's shadow is weepy . . . lachrymose. Depressing to have it cover you, but no harm to it.

Friday's shadow is slick and swift. Jumps around a lot. Okay to run with it. Safe to follow it anywhere.

Now, the one I really want to warn you about is the last one.

Saturday's shadow.

It's dangerous. Very, very dangerous. The thing to do is keep it at a distance. The edges are sharp and serrated, like teeth in a shark's jaw.

And it's damned quiet. Comes sliding and slipping toward you along the ground—widening out to form its full deathshape. Killshape.

I really *hate* that filthy thing! If I could . . .

Wait. No good. I'm getting all emotional again about it, and I must not *do* this. I must be cool and logical and precise—to render my full account of what happened to Laurie. I just *know* you'll be interested in what happened to her.

Okay?

I'll give it to you logically. I can be very logical, because I work with figures and statistics at a bank here on Coronado Island.

No, that's not right. *She* works there—worked there—at a bank, and *I'm* not Laurie, am I? . . . I really honest-to-God don't think I'm Laurie. Me. She. Separate. She. Me.

Sheme.

Meshe.

Identity is a tricky business. We spend most of our lives trying to find out who we are. Who we *really* are. An endless pursuit.

I'm not going to be Laurie (in blood) when I tell you about all this. If I *am* then it ruins everything—so I ask you to believe that I was never Laurie.

Am never.

Am not.

Was not.

Can't be.

If I'm not Laurie, I can be very objective about her. No emotional ties. Separate and cool. That's how I'll tell it. (I could be Vivien. Vivien Leigh. She died too. Ha! Call me Vivien.)

No use your worrying and fretting about who I am. Worry about who *you* are. That's the key to life, isn't it? Knowing your own identity.

Coronado is an island facing San Diego across an expanse of water with a long blue bridge over the water. That's all you *need* to know about it, but maybe you'll learn more as I tell you about Laurie. (Look it up in a California travel guide if you want square miles and length and history and all that boring kind of crap which does no good for anybody.)

It's a *place*. And Laurie lived at one end of it and worked at the other. Lived at the Sea Vista Arms. Rent $440 a month. Studio apartment. No pets. No children. (Forbidden: the manager destroys them if he finds you with any.) Small bathroom. Off-white plasterboard walls. Sofa bed. Sliding closet door. Green leather reclining chair. Adjustable bookshelves. (Laurie liked black-slave novels.) Two lamps, one standing. Green rug. Dun-colored pull drapes. You could see the bridge from her window. View of water and boats. Cramped little kitchen. With a chipped fridge.

She walked every day to work—to the business end of the island. Two-or-three-mile walk every morning to the First National Bank of Coronado. Two-or-three-mile walk home every afternoon. Late afternoon. (With the shadows very much alive.)

Ate her lunch in town, usually alone, sometimes with her brother, Ernest, who worked as a cop across the bay in San Diego. (Doesn't anymore, though. Ha!) He'd drive his patrol car across the long high blue bridge and meet her at the bank. For lunch down the street.

Laurie fixed her own dinner, alone, at her apartment. Worked all week. Stayed home nights and Saturdays. Never left her apartment on Saturdays. (Wise girl. She *knew*!) On Sundays she'd walk to the park sometimes and tease Sunday's shadow. You know, joke with it, hassle it about being fat and snoozing so much. It didn't mind. They were friends.

Laurie had no other friends. Just Sunday's shadow and her brother, Ernest. Parents both dead. No sisters. Nobody close to her at the bank or at the apartments. No boyfriends. Kept to herself mostly. Didn't say more than she had to. (Somebody once told her she talked like a Scotch telegram!) Mousy, I guess. That's what you'd call her. A quiet, small, logical, mousy, gray person living on this island in California.

One thing she was passionate about (strange word for Laurie—passion—but I'm trying to be precise about all this):

Movies.

*Any* kind of movies. On TV or in theaters. The first week she was able to toddle (as a kid in Los Angeles, where her parents raised her), she skittered away from Daddy and wobbled down the aisle of a movie palace. It was Grauman's Chinese, in Hollywood, and nobody saw her go in. She was just too damned tiny to notice. The picture was *Gone With the Wind,* and there was Gable on the huge screen (*really* huge to Laurie) kissing Vivien Leigh and telling her he didn't give a damn.

She never forgot it. Instant addiction. Sprocket-hole freak! Movies were all she lived for. Spent her weekly allowance on them . . . staying for hours and hours in those big churchlike theaters. Palaces with gilt-gold dreams inside.

Saturday's shadow had no strength in those days. It hadn't grown . . . amassed its killpower. Laurie would go to Saturday kiddie matinees and it wouldn't do a thing to her.

But it was growing. As she did. Getting bigger and stronger and gathering power each year. (It got a lot bigger than Laurie ever got.)

Ernest liked movies too. When she didn't go alone, he took her. It would have been more often, but Ernest wasn't always such a good boy and sometimes, on Saturdays, when he'd been bad that week (Ernest did things to birds), his parents made him stay home from the matinee and wash dishes. (Got so he hated the sight of a dish.) But when they *did* go to the movies together, Laurie and Ernest, they'd sit there, side by side in the flickered dark, not speaking or touching. Hardly breathing even. Eyes tight on the screen. On Tracy and Gable and Bogart and Cagney and Cooper and Flynn and Fonda and Hepburn and Ladd and Garland and Brando and Wayne and Crawford and all the others. Thousands. A whole army of shadow giants up there on that big screen; all the people you'd ever need to know or love or fear.

Laurie had no reason to love or fear *real* people—because she had *them.* The shadow people.

Maybe you think that I'm rambling, avoiding the thing that happened to her. On the contrary. All this early material on Laurie is necessary if you're to appreciate fully what I'll be telling you. (Can't savor without knowing the flavor!)

So—she grew up, into the person she was destined to become. Her father divorced her mother and went away, and Laurie never saw him again after her eighteenth birthday. But that was all right with her, since she'd never understood him anyway.

Her mother she didn't give a damn about. (Ha!)

No playgirl she. Steady. Straight A in high school accounting. Sharp with statistics. Reliable. Orderly. Hardworking. A natural for banks.

Some years went by. Not sure how many. Laurie and Ernest went to college, I know. I'm sure of that. But their mother died before they got their degrees. (Did Laurie *kill* her? I doubt it. Really doubt anything like that. Ha!) Maybe Ernest killed her. (Secret!)

Afterward, Laurie moved from Los Angeles to Coronado because she'd seen an ad in the paper saying they needed bank accountants on the island. (By then, she'd earned her degree by mail.)

Ernest moved down a year later. Drifted into aircraft work for a while, then got in with a police training program. Ernest is big and tough-fingered and square-backed. You don't mess around with Ernest. He'll break your frigging neck for you. How's *them* apples?

Shortly after, they heard that their daddy had suffered an attack (stroke, most likely) in Chicago in the middle of winter and froze out on some kind of iron bridge over Lake Michigan. A mean way to die—but it didn't bother Laurie. Or Ernest. They were both glad it never froze in San Diego. Weather is usually mild and pleasant there. Very pleasant. They really liked the weather.

Well, now you've got all the background, starting with Saturday's shadow—so we can get into *precisely* what happened to Laurie.

And how Ernest figures into it. With his big arms and shoulders and his big .38 Police Special. If he stops you for speeding, man, you *sign* that book! You don't smart-mouth that cop or he puts one-two-three into you so fast you're spitting teeth before you can say Jack Robinson. (Old saying! Things stay with us, don't they? Memories.)

Laurie gets out of bed, eats her breakfast in the kitchen, gets dressed, and walks to work. (She'd never owned a car.)

It is Tuesday, this day, and Tuesday's shadow is silly and harmless. (No reason even to discuss it.) Laurie is "up." She saw a classic movie on the tube last night—*The Grapes of Wrath*—so she feels pretty chipper today, all things considered. She's seen *The Grapes of Wrath* (good title!) about six times. (The really solid ones never wear thin.)

But her mind was going. It's as simple as that, and I don't know how else to put it.

Who the hell knows why a person's *mind* goes? Drugs. Booze. Sadness. Pressures. Problems. A million reasons. Laurie wasn't a head; she didn't shoot up or even use grass. And I doubt that she had five drinks in her life.

Let me emphasize: she was *not* depressed on this particular Tuesday. So I'm not prepared to say what caused her to lose that rational precise cool logical mind.

She just didn't have it anymore. And reality was no longer entirely there for her. Some things were real and some things were not real. And she didn't know which was which.

Do *you*, for that matter, know what's real and what isn't?

(Digression: Woke up from sleep once in middle of day. Window open. Everything bright and clear. And normal. Except that a few inches away from me, resting half on my pillow and half off, was this young girl's severed head. I could see the ragged edges of skin where her neck ended. She was a blond, hair in ringlets. Very fair skin. Fine-boned. Eyes closed. No blood. I couldn't swallow. I was blinking wildly. Told myself: Not *real*. It'll go away soon. And I was right. Finally, I began to see through it. Could see the wall through the girl's cheeks. Thing faded right out as I watched. Then I went back to sleep.)

So what's real and what isn't? Dammit, baby, I don't even know what's real in this *story*, let alone in the life outside. Your life and my life and what used to be Laurie's life. Is a shadow real? You better believe it.

As Captain Queeg said, I kid you not. (Ha!)

So Laurie walks to work on Tuesday. Stepping on morning shadows, which are the same as afternoon shadows, except not as skinny, but all part of the same central day's primary shadowbody.

She gets to the bank and goes in and says a mousy good morning and hangs up her skinny sweater (like an afternoon shadow) and sits down at her always neat desk and picks up her account book and begins to do her day's work with figures. Cool. Logical. Precise. (But she's losing her senses!)

At lunchtime she goes out alone across the street to a small coffee shop (Andy's) and orders an egg-salad sandwich on wheat and hot tea to drink (no sugar).

After lunch she goes back across the street to the bank and works until it closes, then puts on her sweater and walks home to her small apartment.

Once inside, she goes to the fridge for an apple and some milk.

Which is when Alan comes in. Bleeding. In white buckskins with blood staining the shoulder area on the right side.

"He was fast," says Alan quietly. "Fast on the draw."

"But you *killed* him?" asks Laurie.

"Yes, I killed him," says Alan. And he gives her a tight, humorless smile.

"That shoulder will need tending," she said. (I'm changing this to past tense: says to said, does to did.) "It's beyond my capability. You need a doctor."

"A doc won't help," he said. "I'll just ride on through. I can make it."

"If you say so." No argument. Laurie never argued with anybody. Never in her life.

Alan staggered, fell to his knees in the middle of Laurie's small living room.

"Can I help . . . in *any* way at all?"

He shook his head. (The pain had him and he could no longer talk.)

"I'm going to the store for milk," she said. "I have apples here, but no milk."

He nodded at this. Blood was flecking his lower lip and he looked gray and gaunt. But he was still very handsome—and for all Laurie knew, the whole thing could be an act.

She left him in the apartment and went out, taking the hall elevator down. (Laurie lived on floor 3, or did I tell you that already? If I didn't, now you know.)

At the bottom, ol' Humphrey was there. Needed a shave. Wary of eye. Coat tight-buttoned, collar up. Cigarette burning in one corner of his mouth. (Probably a Chesterfield.) Ol' Humph.

"What are you doing here?" Laurie asked.

"He's somewhere in this building," Humph told her. "I *know* he's in this building."

"You mean the Fat Man?"

"Yeah," he said around the cigarette. "He's on the island. I got the word. I'll find him."

"I'm not involved," Laurie said.

"No," Humph said, smoke curling past his glittery, intense eyes. "You're not involved."

"I'm going after milk," she said.

"Nobody's stopping you."

She walked out to the street and headed for the nearest grocer. Block and a half away. Convenient when you needed milk.

Fay was waiting near the grocer's in a taxi with the engine running. Coronado Cab Company. (I don't know what their rates are. You can find that out.)

"I'm just godawful scared!" Fay said, tears in her eyes. "I have to get across the bridge, but I can't do it alone."

"What do you mean?" Laurie was confused.

"He'll drive us," Fay said, nodding toward the cabbie, who was reading a racing form. (Bored.) "But I need someone *with* me. Another woman. To keep me from screaming."

"That's an odd thing to be concerned about," said Laurie. "I never scream in taxis."

"I didn't either—until this whole nightmare happened to me. But now . . ." Fay's eyes were wild, desperate-looking. "*Will* you ride across the bridge with me? I'm sure I'll be able to make it alone once we're across the bridge."

Fay looked beautiful, but her blond hair was badly mussed, and one shoulder strap of her lacy slip (all she wore!) was missing—revealing the lovely creamed upper slope of her breasts. (And they *were* lovely.)

"He'll be on the island soon," Fay told Laurie. "He's about halfway across. I need to double back to lose him." She smiled. Brave smile. "Believe me, I wouldn't ask you to be with me if I didn't *need* you."

"If I go, will you pay my fare back across, including the bridge toll?"

"I'll give you this ten-carat diamond I found in the jungle," said the distraught blond, dropping the perfect stone into the palm of Laurie's right hand. "It's worth ten times the price of this cab!"

"How do I know it's real?"

"You'll just have to trust me."

Laurie held up the stone. It rayed light on her serious face. She nodded. "All right, I'll go."

And she climbed into the cab.

"Holiday Inn, San Diego," Fay said to the bored driver. "Quickly. Every second counts."

"They got speed limits, lady," the cabbie told her in a scratchy voice. "And I don't break speed limits. If that don't suit you, get out and walk."

Fay said nothing more to him. He grunted sourly and put the car in gear.

They'd reached the exact middle of the long blue bridge when they saw him. Even the driver saw him. He stopped the cab. "Ho-ly shit," he said quietly. "Will you look at *that*?"

Laurie gasped. She knew he'd be big, but the actual sight of him shocked and amazed her.

Fay ducked down, pressing close to the floor between seats. "Has he seen me?"

"I don't think so," said Laurie. "He's still heading toward the island."

"Then go *on*!" Fay agonized to the cabbie. "Keep driving!"

"Okay, lady," said the cabbie. "But if *he's* after you, I'd say you got no more chance than snow in a furnace."

Laurie could still see him when they reached the other side of the bridge. He was just coming out of the water on the island side. A little Coronado crowd had gathered to watch him, and he stepped on several of them getting ashore.

"You know how to find the Holiday Inn?" Fay asked the driver.

"Hell, lady, if I don't know where the Holiday is *I* should be in the back and *you* should be drivin' this lousy tub!"

So he took them straight there.

In front of the Holiday Inn, Fay scrambled out, said nothing, and ran inside.

"Who pays me?" asked the cabbie.

"I suppose I'm elected," said Laurie. She dropped the jungle diamond into his hand. He looked carefully at it.

"This'll do." He grinned for the first time (maybe in years). He juggled the stone in his hand. "It's the real McCoy."

"I'm glad," said Laurie.

"You want to go back across?"

Laurie looked pensive. "I *thought* I did. But now I've changed my mind. Screw the bank! Take me downtown."

And they headed for—

Wait a minute. I'm messing this up. I'm *sure* Laurie didn't say "Screw the bank." She just wouldn't phrase it that way. Ernest would say "Screw the bank," but not Laurie. And Ernest wasn't in the cab. I'm sure of that. Besides, she was finished at the bank for the day, wasn't she? So the whole—Wait! I've got this part all wrong.

Let's just pick it up with her, with Laurie, at the curb in front of the U. S. Grant Hotel in downtown San Diego, buying a paper from a dwarf who sold them because he couldn't do anything else for a living.

Gary walked up to her as she fumbled in her purse for change. He waited until she'd paid the dwarf before asking, "Do you have a gun?"

"Not in my purse," she said.

"Where, then?"

"My brother carries one. Ernest has a gun. He's a police officer here in the city."

"He with you?"

"No. He's on duty. Somewhere in the Greater San Diego Area. I wouldn't know how to contact him. And frankly, I very much doubt that he'd hand his gun over to a stranger."

"I'm no stranger," said Gary. "You both know me."

She stared at him. "That's true," she said. "But still . . ."

"Forget it," he said, looking weary. "A policeman's handgun is no good. I need a machine gun. With a tripod and full belts. That's what I really need to hold them off with."

"There's an army-surplus store farther down Broadway," she told him. "They might have what you need."

"Yep. Might."

"Who are you fighting?"

"Franco's troops. They're holding a position on the bridge."

"That's funny," she said. "I just came off the bridge and I didn't see any troops."

"Did you take the Downtown or the South Five off-ramp?"

"Downtown."

"That explains it. They're on the South Five side."

He looked tan and very lean, wearing his scuffed leather jacket and the down-brim felt hat. A tall man. Rawboned. With a good, honest American face. A lot of people loved him.

"Good luck," she said to him. "I hope you find what you're after."

"Thanks," he said, giving her a weary grin. Tired boy in a man's body.

"Maybe it's death you're *really* after," she said. "I think you ought to consider that as a subliminal motivation."

"Sure," he said. "Sure, I'll consider it." And he took off in a long, loping stride—leaving her with the dwarf, who'd overheard their entire conversation but had no comments to make.

"Please, would you help me?" Little-girl voice. A dazzle of blond-white. Hair like white fire. White dress and white shoes. It was Norma Jean. Looking shattered. Broken. Eyes all red in the corners. Veined, exhausted eyes.

"But what can I do?" Laurie asked.

Norma Jean shook her blond head slowly. Confused. Little girl lost. "They're honest-to-Christ trying to kill me," she said. "No one believes that."

"I believe it," said Laurie.

"Thanks." Wan smile. "They think I *know* stuff . . . ever since Jack and I . . . The sex thing, I mean."

"You went to bed with Jack Kennedy?"

"Yes, yes, yes! And that started them after me. Dumb, huh? Now they're very close and I need help. I don't know where to run anymore. *Can* you help me?"

"No," said Laurie. "If people are determined to kill you, they will. They really will."

Norma Jean nodded. "Yeah. Sure. I guess they will, okay. I mean, Jeez! Who can stop them?"

"Ever kick a man in the balls?" Laurie asked. (*Hell* of a thing to ask!)

"Not really. I sort of tried once."

"Well, just wait for them. And when they show up you kick 'em in the balls. All right?"

"Yes, yes, in the *balls*! I'll do it!" She was suddenly shiny-bright with blond happiness. A white dazzle of dress and hair and teeth.

Laurie was glad, because you couldn't help liking Norma Jean.

She thought about food. She was hungry. Time for din-din. She entered the coffee shop inside the lobby of the Grant (Carl's Quickbites), picked out a stool near the end of the counter, sat down with her paper.

She was reading about the ape when Clark came in, wearing a long frock coat and flowing tie. His vest was red velvet. He walked up to the counter, snatched her paper, riffled hastily through the pages.

"Nothing in here about the renegades," he growled. "Guess nobody *cares* how many boats get through. An outright shame, I say!"

"I'm sorry you're disturbed," she said. "May I have my paper back?"

"Sure." And he gave her a crooked smile of apology. Utterly charming. A rogue to the tips of his polished boots. Dashing. Full of vigor.

"What do you plan to do now?" she asked.

"Nothing," he said. "Frankly, I don't give a damn *who* wins the war! Blue or Gray. I just care about living through it." He scowled. "Still— when a bunch of scurvy renegades come gunrunning by night . . . well, I just get a little upset about it. Where are the patrol boats?"

She smiled faintly. "I don't know a thing about patrol boats."

"No, I guess you don't, pretty lady." And he kissed her cheek.

"Your mustache tickles," she said. "And you have bad breath."

This amused him. "So I've been told!"

After he left, the waitress came to take her order.

"Is the sea bass fresh?"

Laurie ordered sea bass. "Dinner, or a la carte?" asked the waitress. She was chewing gum in a steady, circular rhythm.

"Dinner. Thousand on the salad. Baked potato. Chives, but no sour cream."

"We got just butter."

"Butter will be fine," said Laurie. "And ice tea to drink. *Without* lemon."

"Gotcha," said the waitress.

Laurie was reading the paper again when a man in forest green sat down on the stool directly next to her. His mustache was smaller than Clark's. Thinner and smaller, but it looked very correct on him.

"This seat taken?" he asked.

"No, I'm quite alone."

"King Richard's alone," he said bitterly. "In Leopold's bloody hands, somewhere in Austria. Chained to a castle wall like an animal! I could find him, but I don't have enough men to attempt a rescue. I'd give my sword arm to free him!"

"They call him the Lion-Hearted, don't they?"

The man in green nodded. He wore a feather in his cap, and had a longbow slung across his chest. "That's because he has the heart of a lion. There's not a man in the kingdom with half his courage."

"What about *you?*"

His smile dazzled. "Me? Why, mum, I'm just a poor archer. From the King's forest."

She looked pensive. "I'd say you were a bit more than that."

"Perhaps." His eyes twinkled merrily. "A *bit* more."

"Are you going to order?" she asked. "They have fresh sea bass."

"Red meat's what I need. Burger. Blood-rare."

The waitress, taking his order, frowned at him. "I'm sorry, mister, but you'll have to hang that thing over there." She pointed to a clothes rack. "We don't allow longbows at the counter."

He complied with the request, returning to wolf down his Carlburger while Laurie nibbled delicately at her fish. He finished long before she did, flipped a tip to the counter from a coin sack at his waist.

"I must away," he told Laurie. And he kissed her hand. Nice gesture. Very typical of him.

The waitress was pleased with the tip: a gold piece from the British Isles. "Some of these bums really stiff you," she said, pocketing the coin. "They come in, order half the menu, end up leaving me a lousy *dime!* Hell, I couldn't make it at this lousy job without decent tips. Couldn't make the rent. I'd have my rosy rear kicked out." She noticed that Laurie flushed at this.

On the street, which was Broadway, outside the U. S. Grant, Laurie thought she might as well take in a flick. They had a neat new cop-killer thing with Clint Eastwood playing half a block down. Violent, but done with lots of style. Eastwood directing himself. She could take a cab back to Coronado after seeing the flick.

It was dark now. Tuesday's shadow had retired for the week.

The movie cost five dollars for one adult. But Laurie didn't mind. She never regretted money spent on films. Never.

Marl was in the lobby, looking sullen, when Laurie came in. He was wearing a frayed black turtleneck sweater, standing by the popcorn machine, with his hair thinning and his waist thick and swollen over his belt. He looked seedy.

"You should reduce," she told him.

"Let 'em use a double for the long shots," he said. "Just shoot my face in close-up."

"Even your face is puffy. You've developed jowls."

"What business is it of yours?"

"I admire your talent. Respect you. I hate to see you waste your natural resources."

"What do *you* know about natural resources?" he growled. "You're just a dumb broad."

"And you are crude," she said tightly.

"Nobody asked you to tell me I should reduce. Nobody."

"It's a plain fact. I'm stating the obvious."

"Did you ever work the docks?" he asked her.

"Hardly." She sniffed.

"Well, lady, crude is what you get twenty-four hours out of twenty-four when you're on the docks. And I been there. Or the police barracks. Ever been in the police barracks?"

"My brother has, but I have not."

"Piss on your brother!"

"Fine." She nodded. "*Be* crude. Be sullen. Be overweight. You'll simply lose your audience."

"My audience can go to hell," he said.

She wanted no more to do with him, and entered the theater. It was intermission. The overheads were on.

How many carpeted theater aisles had she walked down in her life? Thousands. Literally thousands. It was always a heady feeling, walking down the long aisle between rows, with the carpet soft and reassuring beneath her shoes. Toward a seat that promised adventure. It never failed to stir her soul, this magic moment of anticipation. Just before the lights dimmed and the curtains slipped whispering back from the big white screen.

Laurie took a seat on the aisle. No one next to her. Most of the row empty. She always sat on the aisle down close. Most people like being farther back. Close, she could be swept *into* the screen, actually be part of the gleaming, glowing action.

A really large man seated himself next to her. Weathered face under a wide Stetson. Wide jaw. Wide chest. He took off the Stetson and the corners of his eyes were sun-wrinkled. His voice was a rasp.

"I like to watch ol' Clint," he said. "Ol' Clint don't monkey around with a lot of fancy-antsy trick shots and up-your-nostril angles. Just does it straight and mean."

"I agree," she said. "But I call it art. A basic, primary art."

"Well, missy," said the big, wide-chested man, "I been in this game a lotta years, and *art* is a word I kinda like to avoid. Fairies use it a lot. When a man goes after *art* up there on the screen he usually comes up with horse manure." He grunted. "And I know a lot about horse manure."

"I'm sure you do."

"My daddy had me on a bronc 'fore I could walk. Every time I fell off he just hauled me right back aboard. And I got the dents in my head to prove it."

The house lights were dimming slowly to black.

"Picture's beginning," she said. "I never talk during a film."

"Me neither," he said. "I may fart, but I never talk." And his laughter was a low rumble.

Laurie walked out halfway through the picture. This man disturbed her, and she just couldn't concentrate. Also, as I have told you (and you can see for yourself by now), she was losing her mind.

So Laurie left the theater.

Back in her apartment (in Coronado), Judy was there, looking for a slipper. Alan had gone, but Judy didn't know where; she hadn't seen him.

"What color is it?" asked Laurie.

"Red. Bright red. With spangles."

"Where's the *other* one?"

"In my bedroom. I just wore one, and it slipped off."

"What are you doing in this apartment?"

Judy stared at her. "That's obvious. I'm looking for my slipper."

"No, I mean—why did you come *here* to look for it? For what reason?"

"Is this U-210?"

"No, that's one floor below."

"Well, honey, I thought this was U-210 when I came in. Door was open—and all these roach pits look just alike."

"I've never seen a roach anywhere in this complex," said Laurie. "I'm sure you—"

"Doesn't matter. All that matters is my slipper's gone."

"It can't be *gone*. Not if you were wearing it when you arrived."

"Then *you* find it, hotshot!" said Judy. She flopped loosely into the green reclining chair by the window. "You got a helluva view from here."

"Yes, it's nice. Especially at night."

"You can see all the lights shining on the water," said Judy. "Can't see doodly-poop from my window. You must pay plenty for this view. How much you pay?"

"Four-forty per month, including utilities," Laurie said.

Judy jumped to her stockinged feet. "That's twenty *less* than I'm paying! I'm being ripped off!"

"Well, you should complain to the manager. Maybe he'll give you a reduction."

"Nuts," sighed Judy. "I just want my slipper."

Laurie found it in the kitchen under the table. Judy could not, for the life of her, figure out how it had got into the kitchen.

"I didn't even go *in* there. I hate sinks and dishes!"

"I'm glad I was able to find it for you."

"Yeah—you're Little Miss Findit, okay. Little Miss Hunt-and-Findit."

"You sound resentful."

"That's because I hate people who go around finding things other people lose."

"You can leave now," Laurie said flatly. She'd had enough of Judy.

"Can you lay some reds on me?"

"I have no idea what you mean." (And she really *didn't*!)

"Aw, forget it. You wouldn't know a red if one up and *bit* you. Honey, you're something for the books!"

And Judy limped out wearing her spangled slipper.

Laurie shut the door and locked it. Then she took a shower and went to bed.

And slept until Saturday.

I know, I know . . . what happened to Wednesday, Thursday, and Friday, *right*? Well, it's like that with crazy people; they sleep for days at a stretch. The brain's all fogged. Doesn't function. Normally, the brain is like an alarm clock—it wakes you when you sleep too long. But Laurie's clock was haywire; all the cogs and springs were missing.

So she woke up on Saturday.

In a panic.

She knew all about Saturday's shadow, and each Friday night she carefully drew the drapes across the window, making sure it couldn't get in. She never left the place, dawn to dark, on a Saturday. Ate all her meals from the fridge, watched movies on TV and read the papers. If the phone rang, she never answered it. Not that anyone but Ernest ever called her. And he knew enough not to call her on Saturday. (Shadows can slip into a room through an open telephone line.)

But now, here it was Saturday, and the windows were wide open, with the drapes pulled back like skin on a wound and the shadow in the middle.

Of the apartment.

In the middle of *her* apartment.

Not moving. Just lying there, dark and venomous and deadly. It had entered while she slept.

Laurie stared at it in horror. Nobody had to tell her it was Saturday's shadow; she recognized it instantly.

The catch was (Ha!) it was between her and the door. If she could reach the door before it touched her, tore at her, she could get into the hallway and stay there, huddled against the wall, until it left.

There were no windows in the hall. It couldn't follow her there.

Problem: how to reach the door? The shadow wasn't moving, but that didn't mean it *couldn't* move, fast as an owl blinks. It would cut off her retreat, and when its shark-sharp edges touched her skin she'd be slashed . . . and eaten alive.

Which was the really lousy part. You *knew* it was devouring you while it was doing it. Like a snake swallowing a mouse; the mouse always knows what's happening to it.

And Laurie was a mouse. All her life, hiding in the dark, dreaming cinema dreams, she'd been a mouse.

And now she was about to be devoured.

She knew she couldn't stay where she was—because it would come and *get* her if she stayed where she was. The sofa folded out to make a studio bed, and that's where she was.

With the shadow all around her. Black and silent and terrible.

Waiting.

Very slowly . . . very, very slowly, she got up.

It hadn't moved.

Not *yet*.

She wished, desperately, that ol' Humph was here. Or Gary. Or Alan. Or Clark. Or Clint. Or even Big John. They could deal with shadows because they were shadow people. They moved in shadowy power across the screen. *They* could deal with Saturday's shadow. It couldn't hurt *them* . . . kill *them* . . . eat *them* alive. . . .

I'll jump across, she (probably) told herself. It doesn't extend more than four feet in front of me—so I should be able to stand on the bed and *leap* over it, then be out the door before it can—Oh, God! It's *moving*! Widening. Coming toward the bed . . . flowing out to cover the gap between the rug and the door.

Look how *swiftly* it moves! Sliding . . . oiling across the rug . . . rippling like the skin of some dark sea-thing. . . .

Laurie stood up, ready to jump.

There was only a thin strip of unshadowed wood left to land on near the door. If she missed it, the shadow-teeth would sink deep into her flesh and she'd—

"Don't!" Ernest said from the doorway. He had his .38 Police Special in his right hand. "You'll never make it," he told Laurie.

"My God, Ernest—what are you doing with the gun?" Note of genuine hysteria in her voice. Understandable.

"I can save you," Ernest told her. "Only *I* can save you."

And I shot her. Full load.

The bullets banged and slapped her back against the wall, the way Alan's bullets had slapped Palance back into those wooden barrels at the saloon.

I was fast. Fast with a gun.

Laurie flopped down, gouting red from many places. But it didn't hurt. No pain for my sis. I'd seen to that. I'd saved her.

I left her there, angled against the wall (in blood), one arm bent under her, staring at me with round glassy dead eyes, the strap of her nightgown all slipped down, revealing the lovely creamed upper slope of her breasts.

Had *she* seen that in the cab near the grocer's, or had I seen that? Was it Ernest who'd talked to Gary outside the U. S. Grant?

It's very difficult to keep it all cool and precise and logical. Which is vital. Because if everything isn't cool and precise and logical, nothing makes any sense. Not me. Not Laurie. Not Ernest. No part. Any sense.

Not even Saturday's shadow.

Now . . . let's see. Let's see, now. *I'm* not Laurie. Not anymore. Can't be. She's all dead. I guess I was always Ernest—but police work can eat at you like a shadow (Ha!) and people yell at you, and suddenly you want to fire your .38 Police Special at something. You *need* to do this. It's very vital and important to discharge your weapon.

And you can't kill Saturday's shadow. Any fool knows that.

So you kill your sister instead.

To save her.

But now, right now, I'm not Ernest anymore either. I'm just *me*. Whoever or whatever's left inside after Laurie and Mama and Ernest have gone. That's who I am: what's left.

The residual me.

Oh, there's one final thing I should tell you.

Where I am now (Secret!) it can't ever reach me.

All the doors are locked.

And the windows are closed. With drawn curtains.

To keep it out.
You see, I took her away from it.
It really wanted her.
(Ha! Fooled it!)
It hates me. It really *hates* me.
But it can't *do* anything.
To get even.
For taking away Laurie.


   Not if I just
       stay
          and stay and stay
       here
I'm

                safe

where

      it can't

ever
find
me (Mama)
me (Laurie)
me (Ernest)
*me!*

J. F. PEIRCE

# THE DOUBLE DEATH OF NELL QUIGLEY
## OR, TWO VIEWS OF A MURDER

---

*Montague House*
*London, England*
*November 8, 1973*

*Mr. Ellery Queen*
*229 Park Avenue South*
*New York, New York 10003*

Dear Ellery:

Yes, I remember! When you saw me off on the plane to spend my sabbatical year in England, I promised to write "within a fortnight" and send you my address. Yes, I know a *fortnight* is two weeks—not eight months. *Eight months!* Has it really been *that* long? It seems only yesterday.

No, I wasn't skyjacked to Outer Mongolia. Nothing so prosaic! In fact, I arrived in London on schedule (with only a touch of jet lag) and immediately set to work in the British Museum. But before the week was up, a clue that you would appreciate (that in England all crimes must be tried in the city or county where they were committed) sent me posthaste to the borough of Shoreditch, where I've spent the last eight months digging into court records of the Middlesex Records Office for the years 1585 to 1592.

Though I didn't come up with the name I was looking for, what I found doubled my heartbeat. So in apology, since you're both a student and a scholar of all things criminal, I've chosen you to be the first to share my discovery—which should make my name a household word in the literary world.

Following, therefore, is a paraphrase of the court record of a murder committed in 1585. Not only is there a murder, there is also a mystery. And while the murder is solved, I'll leave it to you to discover both the mystery and its solution.

## THE DOUBLE DEATH OF NELL QUIGLEY:
### *or, Two Views of a Murder*

Justice Jennings rapped imperiously on the door of The Theatre, in the Liberty of Holywell, which is part of the Middlesex parish of St. Leonard's, Shoreditch. Almost immediately, the door was opened by Constable Sackbutt, a small, slightly built man with a wisp of white hair on his forehead that came to a point and seemed to mirror his goatee.

The Constable made a quick, nervous bow to the Justice and said: "Good afternoon. It's good of Your Honour to come."

Justice Jennings spoke in a low growl that fitted his bulldoglike appearance. "I came because your message said it was a matter of life or death."

"Aye, it is *that*, Your Honour," the old man said, bobbing his head like a chicken pecking in the dirt. "It is . . . in a manner of speaking."

Justice Jennings' growl deepened. "It should be enough that I give of my time without recompense without having to run hither and yon for no purpose. At least someone pays you to serve in his stead. But enough! Tell me the matter."

Constable Sackbutt pulled at his wisp of a beard. "There's been a murder done, Your Honour," he said.

"Here? At The Theatre?" Justice Jennings said, his growl becoming a bark. "I'll order it closed! *That* will put an end to rowdiness and bawdry!"

"Begging Your Honour's pardon," the Constable said, shaking his head quickly. "It didn't happen here. It were in a tenement near Bishopsgate."

Justice Jennings raised his shaggy eyebrows. "Then why fetch me here?" he demanded.

"If Your Honour will take a seat in the lower gallery, I'll try to explain."

"Very well, but be quick about it."

"Aye—just come this way, Your Honour."

Justice Jennings followed as the old man limped ahead of him, talking back over his shoulder. As the Constable walked, he "thunked" his long staff down hard on the wood flooring, and it was obvious that it served him both for protection and for support.

"As Your Honour knows," he said, "there's been a suspected case of The Plague, and I was on watch near Bishopsgate this afternoon to prevent people from congregating for fear it would spread. I was walking along the highroad when I heard a woman cry, 'Stop, murderer! Stop!' and made haste to see who called and discovered a young woman struggling with a young man just inside an open doorway. I at once charged them to stop, on my authority as a Constable, and, to my surprise, they did.

"The woman, as pert and pretty a young thing as ever I saw, gave her name as Susan Coburn, and she accused the young man of attacking her when she discovered him in the act of strangling a woman named Nell Quigley, who lived there in the house."

The Constable paused to catch his breath, then continued: "The young man, for his part, said that his name was Hamnet Hathaway. He denied the young woman's accusations and said that on arriving at the house he had met Susan Coburn in the act of leaving. Stopping her politely, he said, he asked her to direct him to Nell Quigley's apartment. Whereupon, he said, she attacked him without provocation and cried out, 'Stop, murderer! Stop!' "

Arriving at a vantage point overlooking the platform stage, supported by wooden trestles and surrounded by a dirt pit, the Constable halted. The Tiring Room behind the stage was heavily beamed. The playhouse itself consisted of three galleries and was mainly of timber, with some ironwork for reinforcement.

Justice Jennings stroked his heavy jowls with his stubby fingers. "Who is—or *was*—Nell Quigley?" he asked.

The Constable helped the Justice to a seat before he replied: "May her soul rest in peace, Your Honour, she was a woman no better than she should be. Her business was men, and since I keep a close eye on her kind in the quarter, she plied her trade here at The Theatre and farther south at The Curtain. Her usual method was to strike up an acquaintance with a gentleman at a play—usually one who struck her fancy because of the size of his purse—and then, when the play was over, invite him to accompany her home to sample her wares."

Justice Jennings shook his head angrily, causing his jowls to quiver. "Such bawdry must be stopped!" he shouted. "I'll close both playhouses!"

"Begging Your Honour's pardon," Constable Sackbutt said, pulling at his beard, "though closing the playhouses will no doubt help to stop the spread of the one plague, I doubt it will stop the spread of the other. If Your Honour would keep such women from using their ends for a means, he will have to close their legs, not the playhouses."

Justice Jennings threw up his hands in resignation. "Of course, you are right, Constable. 'Tis true 'tis pity; and pity 'tis 'tis true. Tell me, what kind of woman is this Susan Coburn—the same sort as Nell Quigley?"

"Except for her clothes, Your Honour, I would say no. She dresses the part of a strumpet but speaks and carries herself like a gentlewoman. No, like a lady! I suspect that she's down on her luck, that she's known better days, for she's dainty and refined. Though when she struggled with young Hathaway, she seemed almost a match for him."

Justice Jennings nodded in approbation. "They say that when a woman's life or honour is at stake, her juices flow more freely and she's able to protect herself with a strength she knew not she possessed."

"Aye, 'tis so, Your Honour," the Constable said, bobbing his head quickly.

"This Hamnet Hathaway," Justice Jennings continued, "what kind of man is he?"

"Quite personable, Your Honour, though beginning early to bald. He's a most courteous and soft-spoken young man and most persuasive, which is why we're here."

"Oh? How so?"

"He made a point I could not dispute, Your Honour. He said that when I came upon him struggling with Susan Coburn, he could have slipped from her grasp, knocked me down, and fled, but that instead he stayed, gave his name, and answered my questions most politely. Therefore, in return, he requested that I permit him to perform an experiment."

Justice Jennings frowned. "An experiment?" he said, his voice seeming to come from the depth of his bowels. "What sort of experiment?"

"He asked to be allowed to put on two playlets, interpreting the facts of the murder in two ways. Since I could see no harm in it and since he put it so eloquently, I could not but agree. How did he phrase it? Ah, yes. 'Good Constable,' he said, 'I have heard that guilty creatures, sitting at a play, have by the very cunning of the scene been struck so to the soul that presently they have proclaim'd their malefactions; for murder, though it have no tongue, will speak with most miraculous organ.'"

"'Tis eloquent indeed," Justice Jennings said, his frown deepening. "For your sake, Constable, I hope the young man will make as favourable an impression on me."

"I'm sure that he will, Your Honour. I'm sure that he will," the Constable said quickly. "Ah, here comes Mr. Burbage, the Manager of the playhouse. No doubt he can tell you more about the young man. Permit me to introduce you."

"I know Mr. Burbage well," Justice Jennings said drily. "He has appeared before me on sundry occasions. Have you not, Mr. Burbage?"

"That I have," the Manager said heartily, "and may I say that it's always a great pleasure to see Your Honour."

"That's hard to believe," the Justice said, shaking his head, "but I'll let it pass. What can you tell me about young Hamnet Hathaway?"

"Ham? A bright young man, Your Honour. Mark me, he'll go far. Though he's been in London less than six months, having come, I believe, from Arden, he's made the most of his opportunities. When he first came here, he earned a meager living holding horses at the playhouse door—for those gentlemen who had no servants to perform the service for them. And being conscientious, he was much in demand. Then, one day, while he was holding the horse of a gentleman, he observed that one of my ticket-sellers suffered from the itch and reported it to me."

"The itch?" Justice Jennings repeated. "I'm afraid I don't understand."

Mr. Burbage smiled. "He observed that when the ticket-seller collected the price of admission from a playgoer, he ofttimes scratched his head, letting *my* pence drop into *his* collar, instead of into the lockbox where it belonged."

"I see," Justice Jennings said. "If memory serves, Mr. Burbage, the fellow must have learned the trick from you. I recall that Mr. Brayne, your partner, had you up on charges of doing much the same thing and of cheating your actors as well, by having the Smith make you a secret key to open the common box from which came the actors' shares."

Mr. Burbage laughed heartily. "Your Honour has a long memory indeed—but that's ancient history. As Your Honour well knows, *charges* are one thing and *proof* another."

"Enough!" Justice Jennings said, "What of young Hamnet Hathaway?"

"Well, Your Honour, after that, there being an opening for a ticket-seller, I offered him the job, but he asked to work backstage instead, so I agreed. Since then he's performed a variety of tasks. He's mended costumes, helped to dress the actors, held the promptbook, swelled a crowd scene, played the parts of a ghost and an old woman, and even set his hand to rewriting an old play of Robert Greene's to fit our players.

But the name *Ham* ill-suits him, for he never hogs the stage, as do most actors."

Justice Jennings shook his head as if in disbelief, setting his jowls aquiver. "He sounds like a rare lad indeed," he said. "Tell me, how does he get on with the other players?"

"Quite well—now that they understand him. At first he set their teeth on edge. Mine too, for that matter."

"Oh? How so?"

"With questions, questions, questions. 'Why do you do this?' or 'Why don't you do that?' and so on. We thought him a bloody busybody, begging Your Honour's pardon, till we got the message he was trying to learn and only wanted to help. Since then he's made himself nigh indispensable."

"How judge you his character?"

"Well, he's no Puritan, Your Honour, but then, what player is? He likes his dram when his throat's dry, which is fairly often, and he has a sharp eye for a well-turned leg or a bare bosom."

"Ah!" Justice Jennings exclaimed. "That's more to the point. Tell me, did he know Nell Quigley?"

"Aye—at least, by appearance and reputation. She came to The Theatre often, though you wouldn't have called her a playgoer. She came to see men, not to see plays, but she was a good sort. She was here earlier today. She'd come from The Curtain, where she'd learned the playhouses had been closed for fear of The Plague."

Justice Jennings frowned. "If she knew The Theatre was closed, why, then, did she come here?"

Mr. Burbage laughed heartily. "Out of professional courtesy, you might say. Since she couldn't ply her trade for pay, she came to offer me her services for free, by way of a bit of fence-mending, so to speak. Unfortunately, we were rehearsing a new play, so I couldn't accept. Besides, I live next to the playhouse, and my wife's in and out."

"I see. Was young Hathaway about when you spoke to the strumpet?"

"Aye, Ham and I were talking when she came up. I'd just given him the rest of the day off, since we had no need of him."

"Did he overhear your conversation with the wench?"

"Aye. He waited till she left, then asked me to lend him three shillings."

"And did you?"

"Not bloody likely, begging Your Honour's pardon. It's not that I don't like the lad or that he's not honest, but he could take The Plague and die or become involved in a drunken brawl and be killed. Then where would I be? So instead I suggested he sell his sword to one of the actors who's been wanting to buy it."

"And did he?"

"I don't know, Your Honour, but I can find out."

"Later. Tell me, do you know where he went after he left here?"

Mr. Burbage laughed again. "By his own report, to see our Nell. I told you he had an eye for a well-turned leg and a bare bosom, and Nell was well endowed by her Maker with both."

"Where's Hathaway now?"

"Backstage instructing the players. If Your Honour will excuse me, I'll tell him you're ready."

"Aye, and tell him to hurry."

Mr. Burbage bowed as he left, and Justice Jennings nodded imperceptibly in return, then let his gaze sweep the playhouse. Seeing four women and two men seated in the gallery across the way, he turned to the Constable. "What persons are those?" he asked.

Constable Sackbutt studied the group a moment before he answered. "The young woman seated to herself," he said, "is Susan Coburn. The other women all live in the tenement where Nell Quigley was murdered. After checking to make sure that she was dead and had indeed been strangled, I searched the premises and took statements from the women, all of whom testified to hearing an argument between Nell and a young man, so I brought them along as witnesses. It's in large part on their testimony that Hathaway's playlets are to be based."

"And the men?"

"The Manager's sons, whom Hathaway has set to watch the women—though for what purpose I know not. The one on Your Honour's left is young Richard Burbage, reported to be a fine actor. The other is Cuthbert Burbage."

"Are the women acquainted?"

"Those from the tenement are, and they all knew Nell. None knew Susan Coburn or she them, but she says she knew Nell, having met her at The Curtain. The woman in yellow is Elizabeth Carmack, whose apartment is just above that of Nell Quigley. She gave the clearest testimony. I have it all writ down."

"Good! Let me see it."

Constable Sackbutt bobbed his head in sudden embarrassment. "Young Hathaway has it in his hands, Your Honour—the better to instruct the players, he said."

Justice Jennings growled. "He may have your head in his hands as well!"

"Aye. Ah, here is young Hathaway now."

The accused strode to the front of the stage with an easy, natural grace. He had a slender build, and the oval shape of his head was accentuated by his high forehead, the result of beginning to bald. His hair was long and swept back from his clean-shaven face. His most prominent features were his questioning mouth and his widely spaced, deepset, hooded eyes through which he intently viewed the world and all its creatures.

The actor made a sweeping bow and began, "Honourable Justice, worthy Constable, and esteemed Ladies! We are gathered here to witness a murder in two acts in which poor Nell Quigley will be twice killed—once by me and once by a person whose name is not known. I will leave it to you after witnessing these two acts of murder to judge who is the real murderer. My life is in your hands. We begin with Susan Coburn's version of Nell Quigley's murder."

"Notice, Your Honour, how he moves to the rear of the platform," the Constable said, "and knocks upon the facing of the inner stage, whose curtain slowly opens."

"Thank you for your instruction, Constable," Justice Jennings said drily. "I would be lost without it."

"'Tis nothing, Your Honour. Nothing. Notice how the person playing the part of Nell Quigley moves as if to answer the door and prepares to speak."

NELL QUIGLEY: "Yes? Who are you? What do you want?"

HAMNET HATHAWAY: "I'm one of the players, sweet Nell. I saw you earlier at the playhouse. And since our Manager couldn't come to play with you, I've come to perform in his stead."

NELL QUIGLEY, *laughing*: "What, send a boy to play a man's part? Surely you jest. Ah, I remember you now, Infant. I've seen you play. Why, you're not yet dry behind the ears, and I'm no wet nurse to minister to you. Be gone! I'll have no part of you!"

HAMNET HATHAWAY: "But I'll have part of you, woman, whether you will or no."

"Look, Your Honour!" Constable Sackbutt said, excitedly. "See how he seizes her as if to force his unwanted attentions upon her!"

"I see, Constable. I see."

NELL QUIGLEY, *angrily*: "Take your hands off me, sirrah, or I'll give you a present—a pair of cuffs, one for each of your pretty cheeks! I know your kind and your reputation."

HAMNET HATHAWAY, *angrily*: "You go too far, woman! Here is a present for *you*—a necklace for your lily throat!"

"Look, Your Honour! See how he makes a necklace of his fingers to strangle her. See how she struggles in vain to cry for help."

"I see! *I see!*"

"Look, Your Honour! Now a pretty maid comes to the door and peers in. It's Susan Coburn, I warrant. Now young Hathaway looks up and sees her. Now he drops Nell Quigley's lifeless body and starts toward Susan Coburn, who flees. Now he catches up with her. They struggle!"

SUSAN COBURN, *struggling with Hamnet Hathaway and crying out*: "Stop, murderer! Stop!"

CONSTABLE SACKBUTT, *calling off*: "Hallo ho! Who calls there? What's the matter? Speak, I charge you!"

"By my troth, Your Honour, I warrant that's me."

"Enough, Hamnet Hathaway!" Justice Jennings called, loudly. "We know what transpired thereafter. Show us now your second act of murder."

"As you will, Your Honour," Hamnet Hathaway replied. "But give us a moment, please, to bring Nell Quigley back to life and make a change of costume."

"Very well, but quickly."

"I wish you had not brought the play to such a sudden stop, Your Honour," Constable Sackbutt said, shaking his head sadly. "I would have had you see how bravely I studied the victim's body, how carefully I searched the premises—finding a man's jacket, shirt, and shoes 'neath Nell Quigley's bed. Doubtless some poor devil was with her when his wife came knocking at the door, and he fled through the window without his clothing."

He hesitated a moment, then went on: "If I were young Hathaway," he said, "I would have started my play with *that* scene, as a comic prelude to the tragedy that followed—to give it the greater emphasis. Ah, here's the young man now, ready to continue."

"And now, Honourable Justice, worthy Constable, and esteemed Ladies, we present the second murder of Nell Quigley as *I* envision that it happened."

"Notice, Your Honour, how he leaves the stage and a young lad of sixteen or seventeen summers takes his former role. See how the lad moves to the rear of the stage and knocks."

"Enough, old man! *Enough!*" Justice Jennings protested. "I have eyes. I can see! I have ears. I can hear! Be still and listen."

NELL QUIGLEY: "Yes? Who are you? What do you want?"

YOUNG LAD: "I'm one of the players, sweet Nell. I saw you earlier at the playhouse. And since our Manager couldn't come to play with you, I've come to perform in his stead."

NELL QUIGLEY, *laughing*: "What, send a boy to play a man's part? Surely you jest. Ah, I remember you now, Infant. I've seen you play. Why, you're not yet dry behind the ears, and I'm no wet nurse to minister to you. Be gone! I'll have no part of you!"

YOUNG LAD, *angrily*: "But I'll have part of you, woman, whether you will or no."

NELL QUIGLEY, *angrily*: "Take your hands off me, sirrah, or I'll give you a present—a pair of cuffs, one for each of your pretty cheeks! I know your kind and your reputation."

YOUNG LAD, *angrily*: "You go too far, woman! Here is a present for *you*—a necklace for your lily throat!"

"Look, Your Honour, they struggle, but this time Susan Coburn does not appear at the door. Now the villain drops Nell Quigley's body, as an impatient child might drop a toy. *Now* look what he's doing! He's taking off his jacket, his shirt, his shoes. Now he's putting on one of Nell Quigley's dresses, lacing it up! Now he makes ready to leave. Ah, young Hathaway appears and stops the villain."

HAMNET HATHAWAY: "Begging your pardon, Miss, but can you direct me to Nell Quigley's apartment?"

YOUNG LAD, *seizing Hamnet Hathaway and crying out in a falsetto*: "Stop, murderer! Stop!"

"Look, Your Honour, they struggle."

"Yes, Constable, I see!" Justice Jennings said, throwing up his hands in resignation.

CONSTABLE SACKBUTT, *calling off*: "Hallo ho! Who calls there? What's the—"

"Quick, lads!" Hamnet Hathaway shouted, leaping into the pit. "Susan Coburn's trying to escape! After her, lads, after her!"

"Look, Your Honour! Mr. Burbage's sons are chasing Susan Coburn! Look how awkwardly the poor lady runs! Ah, they've caught her easily. But see how vigorously she struggles! Gracious, what language! And I thought her a lady."

"Good work, Dick, Bert!" Hamnet Hathaway shouted, rushing to assist them. "Bring the wench here—to Justice Jennings."

Struggling and screaming, Susan Coburn was dragged before the Justice, and all three young men were required to restrain her.

"Now, Dick," Hamnet Hathaway said, "if you'll lift the strumpet's dress, we'll see what treasure it conceals."

"Stop, sirrah! Cease! *Desist!*" Constable Sackbutt shouted, rising to his feet and raising his staff as if to strike the actor; but his protests were in vain, for Richard Burbage lifted the young woman's skirt, to reveal a man's hose and knee breeches.

"'Pon my soul!" Constable Sackbutt exclaimed, dropping back upon the bench and letting his staff fall with a thud. "This is passing strange."

Justice Jennings shook his head in disbelief. "Tell me, Hamnet Hathaway, since you seem to know, who *is* this person?"

"I know not his name, Your Honour," the young man replied, "but I suspect he's one of the boy actors who play women's parts at The Curtain."

"And what caused you to suspect him? Obviously you did—since you had men watching him."

"Because he seized me for no reason and cried, 'Stop, murderer! Stop!' I was sure then that he was the murderer, since he wished to direct suspicion to me, no doubt because I'd seen him leaving and could associate him with the crime."

"But why didn't he just step into the street and hurry away?"

"Since I had stopped him and asked for directions to Nell's apartment, he knew that I'd probably discover her body before he could make good his escape—because he couldn't run in Nell's dress and shoes. If Your Honour will look closely, you'll see that her shoes are too small for him. No doubt his feet are killing him, *her* shoes squeezing *his* feet just as *he* squeezed *her* throat. There's a certain justice in it. I'm sure Your Honour appreciates the irony."

"But what caused you to suspect he was a boy and not a woman as he appears to be?"

"A number of things, Your Honour. When he addressed the good Constable, his manners and speech were those of a lady, yet he was dressed like a strumpet. Too, Elizabeth Carmack reported hearing Nell call him 'Infant,' which is the slang term for a boy actor who plays women's parts. But it was the way he was embusked that made me sure of it."

"The way he was *embusked*?" Justice Jennings repeated.

"The dress he's wearing is tightly laced to raise and reveal breasts he does not have. Only a woman well endowed by her Maker with a bounteous bosom would wear such a dress. When the lad decided to disguise himself, there was no way for him to hide his lack of bosom with plumping, or padding, as he would have on the stage."

Justice Jennings shook his head as if in disbelief. "How do you know such things?" he asked.

"From working with costumes and from dressing the actors. We could never use such a dress on stage. And unfortunately for the lad, Nell had no other kind. When the Constable searched her room, I checked her wardrobe."

"I see," Justice Jennings said, then turned to "Susan Coburn."

"What is your name, lad," he asked, "and what say you in your defence?"

"My name is Jeremy Peyton, Your Honour. I play principal women's parts at The Curtain. When I went to see Nell Quigley after overhearing her offer herself to our Manager, Mr. Lanman, she laughed at me—made false charges against me, implied that all boy actors are homosexuals. She was dirt! *Dirt!* She deserved to die!"

Justice Jennings shook his great head sadly. Turning to Constable Sackbutt, he said, "Take him before the Sexton and charge him. Tell the Sexton he's to be bound over till the next session. Then take him to prison. No doubt the other prisoners will welcome the sight of him."

Jeremy Peyton blanched. "Pray send me not to prison dressed like *this*, Your Honour, I beg you!" he pleaded. "Punish me any way you will, kill me now! But don't do *that* to me!"

Justice Jennings hesitated, then nodded in agreement. "Very well," he said. "Probably it will prevent a riot. Constable, ask Mr. Burbage if he'll lend the lad some clothes and spare someone to assist you to take him to prison."

"Yes, Your Honour."

"I have some clothes in the Tiring Room he can have," Richard Burbage said, "and my brother and I will assist the Constable."

"Very well. I'm sure he'll thank you both."

Constable Sackbutt bobbed his head to the Justice, then turned to the Burbages. "Take him along to the Tiring Room, if you will, lads. I'll join you in a moment."

"This way, dearie," Cuthbert Burbage said, winking at the prisoner, and both he and his brother snickered.

"Well," Justice Jennings said, addressing Hamnet Hathaway once the others had left, "you've done a good job of work this day, young man. Have you ever thought of taking up the Law? The courts can use one with your obvious talents."

"Thank you, Your Honour," Hamnet Hathaway replied, "but I've found my calling. Where else could I create a world of my own? And begging Your Honour's pardon, when a man can become a god, why settle for being a poor devil of a lawyer?"

"A devil, perhaps," Justice Jennings said drily, "but not a poor one. However, I agree that you've found your calling. You've a way with words. What was it that you told our well-meaning friend the Constable? 'Murder, though it have no tongue, will speak with most miraculous organ.' "

"Aye, Your Honour," Hamnet Hathaway replied, smiling slyly, "and if it have *no bosom* either."

FINIS

Well, Ellery, I'm sure you've spotted all the clues, added them up and deduced who Hamnet Hathaway is—or *was*.

From 1585 to 1592 are the famed "seven lost years" of his life—from the time he fled from home to avoid prosecution for poaching to the first published reference to him in London, in Greene's A *Groatsworth of Wit bought with a Million of Repentance*.

Since most of what we know of him comes from court records, I searched those of Middlesex and Shoreditch for his name—because The Theatre was located there. And while I didn't discover *his* name, I did discover numerous references to one Hamnet Hathaway of Arden, which I assume to have been his alias. For *Hamnet* was his son's given name, and *Hathaway* and *Arden* were his wife's and his mother's maiden names, respectively. Does it not follow then, as the night the day, that Hamnet Hathaway was none other than the world's greatest playwright—Will Shakespeare?

With warmest personal regards,

*Frank*

P.S. By coincidence, old chap, today—November 8, 1973—is the 350th anniversary of the publication, by Jaggard and Blount, of *Shakespeare's First Folio*.

ISAK ROMUN

# THE ENJOYMENT OF AN ARTIST

---

Our music critic should
have reviewed the Lesirrek concert and handled the interview. He was
only a part-time music critic, however. In the other part of his time he
ran a music store. And that night there was a sale. So my editor, who
remembered that I had a respectable record collection and hoped I
knew my way around a fugue, dropped the assignment on me.

Beyond the excitement of Frédéric Lesirrek's appearance in
Paulsburg, there was to be the excitement of discovery. The second half
of the French pianist's program was to be given over to works by one of
those "lost" composers. This was Etienne Sobel, an individual hidden
so effectively from the glare of history that I had never heard of him,
much less heard anything by him.

The concert promised to be stimulating. As it turned out, it was—

though that was due less to the music played than to the music that
wasn't.


The Paulsburg Academy for the Performing Arts was old without the
dignity of age, like a drunken relative you love but find it hard to
respect. The place had a dreariness not even the most innovative light-
ing could dispel. Its programming was dreary, too. The week before,
Victor Herbert's *Natoma* had been put on by a company the critics
simply labeled terrible. Before that, there was Josef Bayer's ballet *Die
Puppenfee*, a work of such improbable dullness that it is seldom staged
nowadays even in Austria, the composer's homeland.

On the way in, I met Kinseca, the Academy's director, two hundred
pounds of loose flesh encased in a five-five frame and a custom tux that
did nothing to hide the bulges. He bared his big white teeth at me in a
smile with as much warmth as yesterday's oatmeal.

"Going to put us on the front page?" he asked.

"Not the front page; a nice piece in Sunday's entertainment section,
though."

"We can use any help," he said absently, leveling his smile at the
customers streaming through the lobby. "A good house. If every night
were like tonight, the Academy might end up in the black now and
then."

"Get yourself a better program manager."

"*I* do all the programming," he said.

"Get yourself a PR man, then, and more publicity. Anything that
gets you close to the front page."

He put his hand up to his chin and began to pluck at it. A bell rang. I
waved goodbye and left him standing in the now-deserted lobby, hand
still at his chin, a thoughtful look on his face.


Lesirrek was great. He seemed to slide magically and altogether too
swiftly through the first half of the concert. He opened with Bach and
moved effortlessly through Mendelssohn and Mozart to arrive at a
Chopin group brought to a stunning close with the *Ballade in G Minor*.

The lights went up for the intermission, but the audience refused to let Lesirrek off the stage. While the concertgoers applauded, I went backstage to get a leg up on my interview.

I saw Jacques Martinal there. He was a gray, ancient man, unbent by age and with energy in his slender frame. His bright brown eyes were alert, restless. He seemed preoccupied. I reflected that this was perhaps natural among single-client managers of the Martinal stripe—those who are more than managers, combining the role of businessman with those of mother hen and father confessor.

I had heard of Martinal. He wasn't always the fussy aesthete he appeared to be that night. During the war he was in the Resistance, a tough nut who went about his work without pleasure, without passion, without regret. He had destroyed enough German convoys to earn a Croix de Guerre from his grateful nation.

Right now he was too busy watching his charge to give me more than an annoyed nod when I introduced myself. ("Monahan, Paulsburg *Advance-Indicator.*") Lesirrek came offstage then, but looked expectantly back to where he had stood. Martinal went over to the pianist and laid a finger on his arm. They talked. I knew just enough French to get the gist of what they were saying.

"That's enough, Frédéric."

Lesirrek turned a flushed face. "Please, *maman*, just one more." He gently disengaged himself.

"No encores!"

"All right, all right." Lesirrek laughed and went onstage.

"The roar of the crowd," I said. "He's human like the rest of us."

"Mr. Monahan," Martinal hissed, "Frédéric Lesirrek is brilliant in the extreme, devoted to his art to the point of mania. He is capable of being a demon or a saint, but he is quite incapable of ever being 'like the rest of us.'"

If I'd intended answering *that*, I was saved the trouble by the reappearance of Lesirrek, diminishing applause behind him. To me, he looked neither demonic nor saintly.

Introductions were under way, and Lesirrek had asked my first name (I admitted reluctantly to Oscar), when we heard a sound, a muffled sound—*bumph!*—a tired groaning, an explosion of contained dimensions, and onstage the piano collapsed into broken wood, disarrayed keys, and quivering wires.

Several things happened then. Martinal crossed himself. Lesirrek muttered in French and English. Kinseca, who had appeared out of nowhere, ran between the stage and the wings. The audience gasped collectively but, remarkably, kept their seats. I hurried to the nearest telephone.

I was back on a news beat.

It took me moments to pass on the details of the concert and its exploding piano to the rewrite desk. Then I made arrangements for a nightside reporter and photographer to come over to the academy and get the rest of the story. I intended to get my interview with Lesirrek.

As it developed, I didn't. Not as I planned, anyway.

To start with, after answering some questions for the police and negotiating with Kinseca, Martinal had spirited the distraught Lesirrek from the hall. There would be no second half of the concert. No Etienne Sobel. Kinseca was onstage announcing that Monsieur Lesirrek would return in two months' time and all tickets for tonight's concert would be honored for the future one and so on.

When the Academy director came offstage, I got the name of the hotel where the musician and his manager were staying. I went over there.

Martinal opened the door and said, "Yes?" One of his eyebrows formed a question mark lying on its side. I was among the forgotten.

"Monahan, Mr. Martinal. Of the *Advance-Indicator*. The interview?"

"Oh, yes." He stood aside and I entered what appeared to be a sitting room. "Now, Mr. Monahan, all you can say about what happened tonight is that it is the work of some local crank of whose identity the police have an idea."

"I guess that's all I could've said, anyway. Isn't it?"

He took a small impatient breath and said, "Yes."

"Okay, so bring on Lesirrek."

Martinal sat down in a stuffed chair, a pattern of *fleurs-de-lis* in its fabric. "He is, in a manner of speaking, already *on*. He is here in my person."

"In a manner of speaking, that's not exactly what I had in mind."

"That is the only way this interview will work. Frédéric is asleep, sedated." He gestured vaguely toward a door behind which I guessed was a bedroom. "Even without the circumstance of sleep, he would be in no condition to talk to you. He is much too shaken up. And tomorrow we travel."

I must have looked uncertain, for he went on, "Come, Mr. Monahan, we have already been asked the very same questions you will ask and we will give the same answers we have given before."

"'We'? You talk as if he's here."

"That should tell you the quality of the interview will be no different than if he were."

I thought about going back to my editor empty-handed. "All right," I said, "I'll go along."

Martinal smiled, motioned me to a chair. "I have a very nice wine here. I won't burden you with its pedigree. Take my word, it's very nice. A glass?"

I indicated a small one, got my notebook out, and settled into the chair, hoping my first question would be one Martinal had never heard.


After about an hour and three more small glasses of wine, I had all I needed for my article.

"Anything else?" Martinal asked. "Photographs? I have a folder."

"Abe Slaughter, our photographer, caught Mr. Lesirrek at rehearsal earlier."

"I forgot. Well, again, anything else?"

"That explosion. The way you warded off questions about it as soon as I got here makes me think you know more."

"If I could answer questions so my responses would not see print . . ."

"It's called 'off the record,' and I'm agreeable." I put away my notebook to reassure Martinal.

"Very well. Before tonight, there have been letters. Threatening letters."

"Against Lesirrek?"

"Not against his person, as such. Only if he did something."

Now the night's events made some sense. "Play the music of Sobel?"

Martinal nodded.

"How about the police?"

"The police know as much as they have to know."

"Who is Sobel?"

Martinal fell back in his chair, tented his fingers, and looked musingly at the ceiling.

"Etienne Marie Louis Jean-Baptiste Sobel. Born in London, September tenth, 1752. His parents were at odds with some royal personage, it seems, and had fled France. Time and a softening of attitudes took them back in 1763.

"Etienne had shown marked musical abilities in England. His first teacher was his father, a court violinist. But the son favored the keyboard. In France his gifts flowered. In the year of his return, the eleven-year-old Sobel played a duet with the seven-year-old Mozart, who was visiting Paris.

"When Mozart left, young Sobel dominated a substratum of musical Paris for a number of years. He composed easily and continually. His work is good, solidly structured. It is not endowed with that mark of transcendent genius Mozart brought to *his* compositions, but it is unworthy of the neglect it has suffered."

Then, as if puzzled, Martinal exclaimed, "I can't imagine what anyone could have against Sobel or his music."

"Maybe he had enemies whose descendants have long memories."

"Oh, he had enemies enough. The Revolution had caught up with Sobel. His enemies were of the worst kind—and the most dangerous: Robespierre and his fanatical following. Not that Sobel did anything to Robespierre, simply that he was a follower of Danton, Robespierre's political rival. Sobel fell with his idol. Between June twelfth and July twenty-eighth in 1794, the day of Robespierre's downfall, no fewer than 1,825 persons perished on the Paris guillotine. Danton was first. Etienne Sobel followed sometime during that forty-six-day bloodbath."

"How did Lesirrek come across Sobel's music?"

"In a Christian Brothers school not far from Paris. Frédéric's youngest brother, Richard, attends the school. The librarian, Frère Cajetan, had Richard contact Frédéric about a bundle of foolscap manuscripts found in the attic of the old school building. Frédéric and I drove there one weekend, examined the manuscripts, and, *voilà*, Sobel was reborn.

"We scheduled Sobel in several of our concerts, but each time an anonymous threat caused us to substitute at the last moment. For the Paulsburg concert, Frédéric was insistent: *he would play Sobel*. Who could suspect Frédéric to be in danger *here*?"

Martinal raised himself from his chair and went to a sideboard. "Do you know French?" he asked.

"A little, picked up during the war. I could make out what you and Lesirrek said tonight. I can't handle anything harder."

Martinal withdrew four stapled pages from an attaché case and handed them to me. "While awaiting execution, Sobel wrote a kind of testament. You are holding a typewritten transcript of his handwritten original. The testament's main purpose was to provide instructions for the disposition of the manuscripts that Sobel, fearing arrest, had previously entrusted to a colleague. The colleague's name was Lemensonge—probably a *nom de guerre*. Beyond the instructions, there is a good deal of information about Sobel, much of which I've already told you."

"Okay to take this?" I held up the testament.

"Why not? The subject of Sobel was to figure in the interview. But remember, you can't launch off from the testament to speculate on this other business, the business of the threats and the exploding piano. I don't want to encourage a madman to further excess."

"I know. One thing, though. Will Lesirrek play Sobel when he returns?"

"He will not!" Martinal said stiffly. "I have his promise. Sobel will have to await another discoverer."

He paused a moment, then asked, "Do you have everything you need?"

"I think so."

"Good. Then shall we . . ." Martinal picked up the wine bottle, now empty. "I can send down for another, or perhaps you'd rather leave."

I didn't use the testament for my write-up. But I did want to know what it said. I sent it to a translator. A week or so later, it came back. I opened the envelope, saw what was inside, but didn't read it. I put the envelope and its contents aside for later attention.

I didn't look at the testament for a number of weeks. About the time Lesirrek was due back for his makeup concert, I felt I'd better brush up on the events of that night two months before. Because I had covered the original concert, I got the makeup as well.

As a starter, I pulled the papers out of their envelope and read through the translation of the transcript. The testament was divided into three parts: Sobel's early life before returning to France, his success as a musical prodigy, and his part in the Revolution, including his condemnation by the Revolutionary Tribunal.

The first two parts told me generally what Martinal had related.

The third part disclosed that Sobel's dedication to the Revolution had continued until the time of Danton's execution. The testament told how the musician, foreseeing his own end and concerned that his contributions would die with him, had begun collecting his compositions. These he bundled up and entrusted to Lemensonge, who was not under the unwelcome scrutiny of Robespierre's Committee of Public Safety.

Shortly afterward, according to the testament, Sobel was arrested and taken to the Conciergerie, a prison, where he remained, except for his trial, until that final trip to Madame. The account was filled with details of arrangements for smuggling the testament out of the prison, the secrecy of its writing, the bribing of a guard to secure postage for the document when it should be concluded.

I put down the translation and picked up the transcript. Now that I had the contents of the narrative in mind, I wondered whether I could make my way through the French. Though I could make out some words, mostly nouns (garçon, maison, timbre-poste, and prisonnier were a few), the attempt was, on the whole, a waste of time. It had been a long time since World War II.

I gave up, put aside the transcript, and went back to the translation. My first reading had been hurried; now I would study the testament.


I got to the Academy late. The exploding piano had done nothing to scare off business—might even have promoted it. The place was packed, and there was an SRO sign outside the ticket office.

The first half of the program was over, and Lesirrek had launched the second with the motoric *Mouvements Perpetuels* of Francis Poulenc. I didn't go to my seat; some SRO ticket was probably in it anyway. Instead, I went backstage. I wanted to see Jacques Martinal.

He was standing in the same spot he had been in the last time Lesirrek was onstage in Paulsburg. Except this time the little manager seemed more relaxed, as though he were enjoying Poulenc's lithe certainties. I went up behind him and touched his elbow. He turned.

"Mr. Monahan, what brings you back here?"

"I want to talk about Sobel."

"I can tell you nothing beyond what's in the testament."

"Okay, let's change the subject. Have you ever heard Fritz Kreisler's *Pavane in the Style of Couperin?*"

"You haven't really changed the subject at all, have you?" He smiled and wagged his head. "We can talk in Frédéric's dressing room."


Seated in the dressing room, Martinal began, "You must understand Frédéric Lesirrek. His powers go beyond the interpretive. There was a period when he stopped performing."

I consulted my notebook. "He took off three years and devoted himself to composition."

"Specifically, a piano concerto."

"Which was never performed."

"The last pianist-composer was Rachmaninoff, as far as modern concertgoers and conductors are concerned."

"So, to get back at a musical world that had rejected him, he composed music with the intention of attributing it to another, just as

Kreisler did. But Lesirrek outdid Kreisler; your Frédéric not only composed the music but composed Sobel as well.

"It was a joke—*ein musikalischer Spass,* as Mozart would have said: a musical joke; a means of chiding those who would accept Lesirrek the composer in counterfeit but not in actuality. Frédéric's brother planted the compositions and the testament at the school, then arranged somehow for Brother Cajetan to discover them. We were to promote Sobel and, when he showed signs of becoming established, admit the hoax in the same cheerful spirit in which Kreisler admitted his."

I leaned toward Martinal. "That doesn't explain the threatening letters to Lesirrek. Nor does it explain the exploding piano."

"We've circumvented the possibility of violence. Frédéric and I have agreed to decently bury Etienne Sobel."

"There's still a mystery here. Somewhere out there, there's a nut roaming loose. Don't you want to get to the bottom of this thing?"

Martinal shifted in his chair, and when he spoke, I sensed irritation in his voice. "Let the old cat die, Mr. Monahan." Then he asked, "How did you find us out?"

"Sobel—a real, honest-to-God eighteenth-century Sobel—couldn't have written that testament. And if the testament was a fraud, then probably its supposed author was, too. If he wasn't, there was precious little external evidence to suggest his existence. I checked some heavy authorities and none mentions Sobel. I read Niemtschek's biography of Mozart. No mention of Etienne. I came to the conclusion: Sobel doesn't exist except as Lesirrek's invention."

"And mine: I wrote the testament." He laughed softly. "What, specifically, put you on to us?"

"That stamp—*timbre-poste* in French—the stamp Sobel was supposed to have used to pay the testament's postage. It couldn't have existed in 1794. The first French postage stamp dates from 1849."

"Commendable. What else?"

"That's not enough?"

"You missed something. In Great Britain, the Calendar Act for the adoption of the Gregorian calendar was passed in 1750. The day following the second of September in 1752 was to be accounted the fourteenth day of that month."

"Am I dense tonight? So?"

"In 1752 in Great Britain the dates three through thirteen September were not used."

I flipped some pages in my notebook till I found what I wanted. "And Sobel was 'born' in London, according to the testament, on the tenth of September, a date that didn't exist in the England of 1752. Why do I get the idea *you knew there were errors in the testament?*"

"Because I put them there."

"Why?"

"Because we were not out to play God indefinitely. I didn't want the masquerade to go on forever, but felt our voluntary confession would be awkward. Therefore, the testament contained the seeds of our exposure."

"Was this Lesirrek's idea?"

"I composed the testament; Frédéric, the music."

"So, Sobel's music will never be heard," I said, maybe sadly; I like a joke as much as anyone.

"That's not quite the case!"

This was a new voice. The dressing-room door had been quietly opened on my last statement. In its frame stood Kinseca. He didn't look angry, but he wasn't exactly happy either. Beyond him, we heard piano-playing. It was distant, but I recognized it wasn't Poulenc. It wasn't Tchaikovsky either, which was to follow the Poulenc.

"Sobel!" I watched the color in Martinal's face drain away. He rushed out the door headed in the direction of the stage.

I followed.

Martinal halted at his usual station: in the wings, looking out upon the stage. His figure went limp. He held on to a nearby curtain rope. I think if he hadn't, he would have fallen. His eyes, usually bright, arrogant, dominating those upon whom they rested, seemed to flicker and go out.

I listened to the music, gripped by it. Not because of its merit—it sounded like indifferent Mozart or average Stamitz—but because of my secret knowledge. I was listening to what sounded eerily like authentic eighteenth-century music, a true composition in music's classical mold.

As the work neared its end, I moved closer to Martinal and whispered, "His secret is safe with me."

The music stopped and a flow of tempestuous clapping eddied up to and lapped over the stage. Martinal turned his tired eyes upon me and whispered back, "But, Mr. Monahan, is *he* safe with his secret?"

Then Lesirrek was off the stage after his first bows. I asked him, "A statement, Mr. Lesirrek. In your opinion, what is Etienne Sobel's place among composers of his period?"

The pianist stared at me. "Who are you, sir?"

Martinal explained. "Frédéric, you've met Mr. Monahan—briefly. Remember, of the paper here in Paulsburg?"

"And who is Frédéric?"

The pianist didn't wait for an answer. Beyond us the applause was too appealing, too insistent. He returned to the stage.

When he came back, I asked, "Could I have your name, sir?"

"Tonight all Paris knows my name."

And Etienne Sobel went out to take another bow.


Martinal was speaking.

"I'm afraid he wears Sobel as someone wears a mask. A mask he cannot now get off." The manager lapsed into silence.

We were in the hotel suite of the two Frenchmen, the same suite they had occupied months before. The pianist was not there. He was in a private room at St. Scholastica's. Martinal had spent the evening arranging for his client's admission to the hospital, for the later trip home to France, for the cancellation of Lesirrek's remaining American concerts. Now, Martinal, exhausted, his nerves ragged, seemed reluctant to let me go. Swallowed up in an overstuffed brocade chair with a yew-tree design, he talked disconnectedly of Lesirrek and the pianist's career. I responded in the appropriate places, careful not to crowd the old man's unwinding process. Martinal's silence, though, told me that now might be one of those moments when I should say something.

"A mask. That's interesting. Let's see." I put on my portentous look and intoned, "'For the enjoyment of an artist the mask must be to some extent molded on the face. What he makes outside him must correspond to something inside him; he can only make his effects out of the materials of his soul.'"

"That says it, Mr. Monahan."

"I didn't, though. I wish I had. Chesterton wrote those words, probably before I was born."

"Are you still curious about the threats? The demolished piano?"

I shook my head.

He went on. "There were periods of transference before. But not like tonight. I felt—I knew—that if he ever performed Sobel to an appreciative, applauding audience, it would drive him over the edge, into the deep pit of his own imagination. The danger of fathering a fantasy is adopting a child."

"So you'd do anything to discourage Lesirrek. Send him threatening letters. Take a chance on blowing up his piano during intermission. Carefully blowing it up, though—just enough to make it inoperable and not hurt anyone unless that person were close to it—that's why you didn't want Lesirrek to play encores! You could manage the explosion. The Resistance gave you all the expertise you needed."

"I did all those things. For nothing."

"Where do you go from here?"

"I will take Frédéric or Etienne—I'm afraid the latter—back to France. By whatever name, he is my client."

"Just thought of this. How did you explain the letters and the exploding piano to him?"

"I don't follow you."

"He must have suspected you. He knew Sobel wasn't real."

"He didn't."

"Didn't? Did you say *didn't*?"

"He didn't," Martinal repeated.

I thought about that, then said, "He convinced himself early on that Sobel *was* real. Before he convinced himself that *he* was Sobel."

"Yes, that's it."


Etienne Sobel is back in Paris now, in a small, exclusive nursing home. I saw the musician-composer there when I was on a European trip. He is happy. Every day he can be found in his room, spacious for a place of that sort and rather like a candlelit study, playing the piano, putting new music onto notepaper, looking forward to great triumphs.

Frédéric Lesirrek? I don't know what in the world became of him. He disappeared from the face of the earth.

# BETTY BUCHANAN

# GEE WHIZ, MY LOVELY

I'd been hired by a Mr. Smith to find Mrs. Smith. He didn't want her back, but he was anxious to talk over divorce proceedings with her in order to establish another, and undoubtedly younger and prettier, Mrs. Smith. I'd found her staying at the Studio Club in Hollywood, and Smith and I met there in the early evening. I talked her into conferring with him in the library; then I went back to the lobby, slumped on a sofa left over from the comfortable old Mission Style era, and listened to the voices of the guests and visitors with my eyes closed. Suddenly someone said, "You're a private eye, huh?"

I looked up at a very tall, very pretty girl. She was wearing a dark green velvet suit that matched her eyes and voice, and her beautiful face was a blank waiting for an expression to alight on it like a butterfly. "I said, 'You're a private eye, huh?' " she repeated. I nodded. She sat down next to me, and the sensation was a little like having the Statue of Liberty join you in a rowboat. "I heard you talking to those two people."

She nodded a head of red-gold hair toward the library entrance. "I want you to find Harvey for me. That's what private cops do, isn't it? Find people?"

"Look," I said. "I've had a day like a mudslide. Our little friend in there has been moving all over town, and I've been tagging along in a car with no third gear and a slow leak."

"I said I want you to find Harvey," she repeated, and this time I saw a blank, calm lioness look in her eyes. I hesitated, and she dug her nails into my upper arm as she grabbed me and pulled me to my feet as if I were made of stuffed cotton.

"Wait a minute, sister," I began, and then, realizing that people in the lobby were beginning to glance at us with more than passing interest, I added, "Okay, okay, we'll find him, but let's get out of here. You don't want me to blow the Smith job, do you?" She relaxed her grip, and we went out and stood on the low steps in front of the building. "Now, what's the story?" I said, pretending that I really wanted to hear it, but plotting to weave out and get away fast, provided my car started before she snaked me out with that wiry arm.

"It's funny seeing you," she said.

"Ha, ha—it's funny seeing you too," I said. And I meant it.

"I mean you're a private cop. You're funny for a private cop."

"Yeah, sometimes I just sit in the office and have a good laugh about it."

"Do you know about me?" she asked suddenly.

I didn't say, Yes I know about you—you're a gorgeous nut in a town famous for its gorgeous nuts. And you're in Hollywood because it's the end of the line for you, and you want me to help you to believe that it isn't. I didn't say it; there was something sad and fierce and compelling about her. In other words, she scared me.

"Look," she said again, "I only want you to find Harvey."

"Who's Harvey? A dog?" Again I got the fingernails in the arm, which was beginning to feel like pulled taffy.

"Harvey loved me," she said. "You can see I've been away? Sometimes it shows."

"Away?" Yeah, I got it. Away.

"Harvey said it would be best, and that after things were all right we could be like we were before. He was the darlingest-looking fella you ever saw.

"Do the cops know where you are?" I asked.

"Cops? No, the cops don't want me." Her eyes narrowed, and I could see that her dime-sized brain was working. "All I had to do was walk out of the place. They always said it was voluntary. Harvey told them when I went in that it was voluntary. On account of I didn't do anything."

"What didn't you do?"

She got cagey. "You find Harvey and he'll explain it. You hear?" She tweaked my arm to drive home the point.

"Listen, you dopey girl," I said, trying to unlock myself from her, "you haven't even told me his last name. Or yours. Do you remember them?"

"Think I'm dumb or something? Hamilton. Harvey Hamilton. He's a darling guy. Cute as tap shoes." She slapped something into my hand. I looked and found I was holding one hundred dollars in tens. I looked up and she was gone. I went back into the Club and asked about the tall girl in green velvet.

"I don't know," the woman at the switchboard said. "She came in right after you did. She's not a resident."

So I had $100. Maybe I could save it toward a real office instead of the old place in the D. W. Griffith Building on Cahuenga. I decided not to hang around and see how the Smiths made out. After all, I had contracted to find Mrs. Smith, not to talk her into lying down and rolling over.

I went around the corner, got into the old Oldsmobile, and drove up to the office on Cahuenga. The people in the other offices had gone home. I sat down, put my feet up, and wished that George from the Brown Derby would walk in with a bottle of cold champagne on a silver tray. Cold champagne.

I was about to drift off when a noise brought me out of the reverie. Ah, well, it probably would have been California champagne, anyway.

"I said I would like to speak to you." My eyes went back into focus and I saw that a young man was standing in front of my desk. To say he was good-looking would be to say that a combination of Buddy Rogers, Joel McCrea, and Cary Grant in their primes would have been passable. He must have made hundreds of women happy every day—all they had to do was look at him.

"Hey," I said on an impulse, "your name isn't Harvey, by any chance?"

"No, it isn't," he said. "Why?"

"No reason. I was just remembering something I'd rather forget. If you've come about the rent, I've got it right here, but I warn you I'm thinking about a classier place up on the Boulevard."

"Rent? No, I need the help of a private detective."

"Who told you about me?"

"Nobody. I saw your name on the alphabetical listing in the lobby. It sounded familiar, and I thought that was a good omen. But you're not what I expected to see, if I may speak frankly."

"Do. I'm never what people expect to see. Especially me when I look into the mirror in the morning."

"How much would you charge to come to a nightclub with me where I have to meet and do business with some people?"

"What business? What people?"

"A delivery. It's legal, at least on my side. But I'd like certain arrangements to be made beforehand, and I'm not sure that I'm capable of making them. And I sure as hell can't be *seen* making them. Understand?"

"Sure—I go to a strange nightclub to do something I'm not told about with a guy who isn't named Harvey. That about it?" He laughed, but didn't reply. "We meet your buddies and I leave alone. The cops follow me down Sunset to Westwood Boulevard and pull me over while your buddies exit by the front door with the heroin."

"What *are* you talking about?" He laughed again, and said, "My name is Roy Leiniger, and it isn't heroin, it's diamonds." He reached into an inside pocket and then held out his hand. The stones cascaded onto the desk like cold champagne, and the multicolored glints leaped off them like the dancing lights of a summer sea.

"Someday, Roy," I said, "when I'm really rich, I'm going to have my own office on Hollywood Boulevard and I'm going to eat those things for breakfast." He picked up the clasp and held it above the desk, and the diamonds fell into a chain. It was the longest diamond necklace I'd ever seen. "Gee, I wish you were Harvey," I sighed.

"What is this Harvey business?" he said, scooping up the necklace and stuffing it back into his pocket.

"Nothing. It's just something I say every once in a while, like Twenty-three skiddoo or So's your Aunt Emma."

"I see," he said politely.

"I ask for one hundred dollars as retainer and twenty-five dollars a day," I said. "The reason I'm more expensive than the others is that I've got so much to live up to."

He put the money down, and the old desk immediately looked as if it had been refinished.

He explained what he wanted. We were to meet the next night at The Performers Club at the end of the Sunset Strip. I was to join him at a table with two other people and witness his giving the diamonds to them. And—oh, yes—I was to arrange to get a picture of this. Simple. Simple as arranging for the Warner Brothers Golddiggers chorus line to infiltrate the steam room at Twentieth Century–Fox.

I showed up the next night looking fairly presentable. Roy looked like his same old drab combination of Buddy Rogers–Joel McCrea–Cary Grant. "You look fairly presentable," he said condescendingly. Well— The Performers was a classy joint and had been since the days the patrons drank gin out of coffee cups. It was run by a retired movie star who liked things to look a little on the Cecil B. DeMille side.

Inside, the place was like New Year's Eve on the Île de France, minus the paper hats. We sat down at a table near the band and were joined in a few minutes by two slightly overweight men in tight dinner jackets and slightly too-short pants. Roy slapped his breast pocket and the two men turned pale and jumped like drumsticks on a tight drumhead. "Gee," said one, "I thought you were going to reach right into your pocket and bring them out."

"I am," said Roy. "Be prepared." He glanced at me and I gave him a subtle nod. He pulled out a package, and just as it changed hands, the drummer in the band behind us fired off a series of rim shots, the wandering camera girl flashed, the waiter at the next table dropped a tray of glasses, and the owner of The Performers Club pulled up a chair, sat down, and said, "Hiya, Phil." Immediately after all that, the floor show started, with a line of chorus girls in ostrich plumes. Perfect!

Gee whiz! I said to myself, you are one good private eye. You deserve a nice office on the Boulevard. The two men had been startled for a moment, but now they settled back. Roy had a look in his eye that said maybe I could have another $25. Then the two men got up and said goodbye. "What did you say your name was?" one of them asked me.

"I didn't say," I said. "What did you say yours was?"

"The same," he said. They left.

"Whew!" Roy said, "I didn't think you could work it. When can we get a print?"

"Pretty soon. They've got a developing-and-printing room in the back. So do you mind telling me what we just did?" He looked pointedly at mine host, the ex–movie star, who said, "Seeya later, Phil," and left. He meant it, too, because I had to pay for those glasses out of my per diem.

"I'd rather not explain, but I'll tell you this: those diamonds were mine. Before we were married I gave them to my wife-to-be. She's a very rich woman. I was not rich at all, but the diamonds, which I happened to inherit, impressed her very much. I arranged to have them traded for enough credit to make some very wise investments. When I had made a great deal of money, I bought them back. My wife, who had been told they were stolen, was thrilled when they were apparently found by the police and returned. Unfortunately, those men—"

"—the cops—" I said.

"They'll soon be ex-cops. They have just blackmailed them back. Or rather, they think they have. You see, it is essential that my wife believe me to be the man she thinks I am."

"Why the picture?"

"It's always best to have a record of these things. It helps in planning the next move, which is to get them back without publicity and without getting shot at on the steps of The Performers Club. Or anywhere else."

"But where did the diamonds come from to begin with?" I asked.

"You're being paid not to ask that question," he said, sounding as cold as a creditor. "Maybe I'll call you up and let you know when those cops have become ex-cops." He smiled a quick, insincere smile, and he didn't look like Buddy-Joel-Cary anymore. "Let's go get that picture."

We went back to the dressing-room corridor and found a cubbyhole where a girl was bending over a table, with her back to us, looking at some eight-by-ten prints. She was a very tall girl, and she was wearing the chorus ostrich plumes. She turned as we entered.

"Hello, Harvey," she said. "I knew you'd show up sooner or later. Now can I have my diamonds?"

"*Your* diamonds!" I exclaimed.

"The ones I loaned to Harvey, like I kept telling them at the funny farm. Things are okay now, Harvey, huh?"

He looked like a man who had just lost his last nickel in a pay phone. "They're okay," he said.

"You did good, eh, Harve? So where are the diamonds?"

"I'd advise you to get back to your chorus line," he said. "And if you bother me again, I'll have you put away. And this time it'll be for keeps." He turned to go, but he wasn't fast enough. She had reached into her purse which lay open on the table and pulled out a small gun. She squeezed the trigger before he'd got to the door. He fell at our feet and lay still.

"So that's Harvey," I said. "He was some looker."

"Where are the diamonds?" she said. "They're mine. This nice old guy I was married to gave them to me. He died. He fell out of a window in this terrible accident just about the time I met Harvey."

"I'll bet he fell out of that window *after* you met Harvey," I said. "And some cops outside have your diamonds."

"Cops?" she said.

"I decided not to take any chances. I got my cops to come and meet his cops."

"You're some smart private eye. Why were you suspicious of Harvey?"

"I figured out why I was hired. He thought I was stupid. Lots of people take one look at me and decide that. Sometimes I count on it. If there was going to be any shooting later on, I figure I was the one who was going to be found with a gun and two dead empty-handed cops. Something like that. Why else would a guy hire somebody he thought was a dumb, inexperienced private eye? But what are you doing in here?"

"I'm interested in photography," she said. She reached into her purse again and pulled out another $100.

"Thanks," I said. I could see it already—the keen little office on Hollywood Boulevard, maybe in the bank building. With a frosted glass door and black-and-gold letters that spelled out my name: PHILIPPA MARLOWE, Private Investigator.

Gee whiz—Daddy would have been so proud!

# ABOUT THE CONTRIBUTORS

THOMAS ADCOCK is a former newspaperman whose wife and older daughter are both accomplished actresses. He is the author of *Precinct 19* (Doubleday & Company, New York; Éditions presses de la Cité, Paris) and he contributes regularly to *Ellery Queen's Mystery Magazine*. Adcock is currently at work on the first of a series of novels starring Neil Hockaday of the New York Police Department's "SCUM Patrol" (for Street Crimes Unit—Manhattan). The author makes his home on Manhattan's West Side, where he is only five minutes by foot from Broadway.

JON L. BREEN is the author of 3 novels, most recently *Triple Crown* (Walker, 1986), and more than 50 short stories in the mystery field. His 2 volumes of criticism, *What About Murder: A Guide to Books About Mystery and Detective Fiction* (Scarecrow, 1981) and *Novel Verdicts: A Guide to Courtroom Fiction* (Scarecrow, 1984), were Edgar Award winners. With his wife, Rita, he edited the recent anthology *American Murders* (Garland, 1986). He lives in Fountain Valley, California.

BETTY BUCHANAN comes from a theatrical family and is a longtime observer of the Hollywood scene. She was educated at Disney's, George Pal's, MGM, RKO, 20th Century–Fox, and Universal studios, where she worked as a press agent, cartoonist, extra, and in special effects. She also attended the Académie de la Grand Chaumière in Paris. While she was Assistant Editor of *TV Life* and Hollywood Editor of *Daytime TV*, Betty interviewed everyone from Groucho to Tom Selleck. She's the author of 2 novels, several short stories, and innumerable free-lance articles for *Photoplay*, *Billboard*, *The Village Voice*, and other publications. She is currently contributing a memoir to English film historian Kevin Brownlow's study of Buster Keaton.

STANLEY ELLIN (1916–1986), a past president of the Mystery Writers of America, was born in Brooklyn, New York, and lived much of his life there, marrying his wife, Jeanne, in 1937. His first published short story, "The Specialty of the House," was greeted with immediate acclaim upon its publication in *Ellery Queen's Mystery Magazine* in 1948, and was recently voted the all-time favorite among mystery and suspense stories. He was a three-time Edgar winner, for short stories in 1954 and 1956 and for his novel *The Eighth Circle* in 1958. He received the Grand Prix de Littérature Policière for his novel *Mirror, Mirror on the Wall* in 1975, and was honored with the MWA Grand Master Award in 1981. The story reprinted here, "The Moment of Decision," won first prize in the 1955 contest sponsored by *Ellery Queen's Mystery Magazine*.

RON GOULART sold his first short story in 1952, and his first mystery short story in 1963. Between those two dates, he graduated from college and put in several stretches as an advertising copywriter in San Francisco and Hollywood. He'd toyed with show business earlier, doing stand-up comedy and various kinds of acting while in high school and college. In the late 1960s, he settled down in New England to concentrate on writing. After a recent mystery-panel appearance, though, a gentleman approached him with the suggestion that he ought to be appearing in the Catskills.

JOYCE HARRINGTON was born on the East Coast, grew up on the West Coast, and as a result is a laid-back Type A person. An early love of theater convinced her she had a tragic soul, but after an extensive dalliance with both theater and tragedy, irony saved the day and writing set in. But seriously, folks, Joyce's first story, "The Purple Shroud" (*Ellery Queen's Mystery Magazine*, September, 1972), won a Mystery Writers of America Edgar, and ever since she's been trying to figure out what to do for an encore. Two novels and a bunch of short stories later, she's still trying. Her latest novel, *Dreemz of the Night*, was published by St. Martin's Press in the spring of 1987. The story in this book, "Death of a Princess," grew out of the two years she lived in Parkersburg, West Virginia, and was active in the local community theater.

EDWARD D. HOCH is a past president of the Mystery Writers of America and the author of more than 700 short stories, mainly in the mystery field. His 28 published books include *The Shattered Raven* and 3 other novels and, as editor, the annual *Year's Best Mystery & Suspense Stories* published by Walker. In 1968, he won the Edgar Award for his short story "The Oblong Room." He and his wife, Patricia, live in Rochester, New York,